CW00346195

Blackwood

Or a novel that isn't really about Bridge

by

Claire Dowley

First published by Trowland Creek Publishing House 2022,
Norfolk, UK

Reprint 2023

ISBN: 978-1-9163975-0-7

DEDICATION

Sue Booth my dear friend and neighbour for 27 odd years.

CONTENTS

1   One No Trump

2   Two Clubs

3   Two Hearts

4   Three Hearts

5   Four No Trumps

6   Five Hearts

7   Five No Trumps

8   Six Diamonds

9   Seven Hearts

10 Bid and Made

1. ONE NO TRUMP

Stephanie's partner was laying down his cards. Her *one no trump* call had encouraged Peter's *two club* response. A perfect Stayman convention. She had four heart cards in her hand, and with a vague understanding of the convention, had called *two hearts*. She neither heard the opposition's *double*, nor factored in that Peter's response might have been weakish preferring to imagine that he had called *three hearts*. She therefore went to four. Peter had been a little surprised but could do nothing. He returned to his recurrent thought that this was just another poorly bid hand by some fairly ordinary Bridge players. Adrienne led the four of spades and he was, yet again, dummy. He laid out his three spades to the king, four clubs to the ace, two diamonds and four hearts to the jack. A perfectly misheard Stayman convention meant that yet another cock-up was about to play out.

Stephanie looked at the cards on the table, furrowed her eyebrows, sighed, took a swig of wine and then remembered to thank him. She thought – odd bid,

1

bit high – and knew she was scuppered. As she sipped her wine, a £7 Lidl special, she remembered that she had forgotten to put in her hearing aids. She would go to the study and get them when she next filled up her wine and wondered how she was going to remind herself to do that; no point setting an alarm, she might not hear it. She thanked her partner again, took a sip of hope, sighed, drummed her fingers unconsciously on the green velvet Bridge cloth, dipped a biscuit in the slightly hot guacamole and sighed again. Plans had to be made. She had no idea how she was going to make ten tricks when she could only see eight. Her mind tried to construct the finesse, the cross trumping, the short suiting, but navigating the cards into game was proving elusive. One who preferred to cackle with joy from a win rather than drown in pinot from a loss, Stephanie tended to take a long time thinking out her strategy.

Out of the corner of her eye, she sensed an oddly shimmering orange glow reflecting off the darkened water in the marina below her window. In her mind rose the wavering images of vaguely exotic yachts nosing jetties. Sitting at the Bridge table, her romantic sensitivity envisaged them caressing the water, gently bobbing up and down in the soothing rhythms of the still night. How often had she sat alone in her apartment, overlooking the marina, caressing her own bottle of Lidl chardy wondering about where her life had gone and where it was about to go. This particular evening she sighed and sipped again, leaving all maritime thoughts unregistered.

The other Bridge players had started to talk about things other than the cards and their gentle murmur also passed unheard as she continued to think about how she would cover that irritating Jack of

Spades who seemed to be winking knowingly at her from the soft green velvet.

"What's she like?"

"Anorexic," a giggle arose as the speaker gulped and gurgled her glass of Morrison's sav blanc.

"Harsh."

"Accurate."

Another chink of a wine glass against a front tooth.

"Heavy on the make-up. Bit gothic."

"C'mon, just 'cos she's a woman. You wouldn't bitch like that if it was a man."

"Actually, I call her an anorexic anaemic goth. Can you have blonde goths?"

Stephanie was still pondering which card to play over the jack. As dummy, Peter was merely dabbling his toes into a conversation which was far more interesting for the other three, "Must have been some blonde Germans back in the day."

"Foundation like concrete, bottle blonde, thin as a rake. Loves the attention."

"A blonde goth with thick red lipstick, white, white skin and a smile like Wallace."

"... and Grommet?"

A nod, and universal giggling.

"That's the one."

"What do you mean that we are in goths? We're in hearts." Stephanie smiled at her own funny joke.

She really was as deaf as a post and the wine was starting to play with reason. Continuing to drum her fingers into the tablecloth and with a deep sigh, she eventually covered the winking jack with the two of spades, and at last the hand was underway.

Descriptions of the new Headmistress would have to be put on hold as this group of vaguely ageing teachers played their weekly game of Bridge and exchanged the all too important gossip of their school and the local town. Rounds of cards were played, tricks gathered and the game progressed against the chatter.

Every now and then there would be a hiatus.

"Stephanie you need to play."

"What?"

"Stephanie you need to play."

Sitting at ninety degrees to Stephanie and speaking with an inflated voice, Alice could sometimes get fairly frustrated by Stephanie's audiological challenges and was usually the member of the group who tried to keep the games going.

"What? Is it my turn? Did I win that one?"

"Yes!" Everyone around the table echoed in unison.

"With the Ace of Diamonds. In your hand."

And unusually quickly and with a flurry of cards, Stephanie won the next trick with the Ace of Clubs in her hand, "Sorry, sorry, was just having to change my plan."

"Of mice and men..." Alice muttered under her breath and then quickly wondered why she'd bothered and just added, "and wanking."

"What?" The echo reverberated around the table.

"Oh nothing, nothing, just got something in the back of my mind and it came out."

"Wanking?"

"No, no, I shouldn't have said it."

"Well you have now."

"Let it go."

"You've got to be kidding... you can't just say that and expect us to shut up."

"Confidential, confidential. Honest. It'll come out."

They all looked slightly miffed at Alice, as though they had been left out of a secret that was shared by one. But Alice was resolute.

Sitting out this hand, Robert prised himself, just a little painfully, out of his chair as the play seemed to be quickening and asked if anyone wanted their wine glass recharged. Another unison "Yes" didn't seem to disturb the play as they all, in some sort of Pavlovian fashion, raised their glasses, drained them and offered them for a top up. Robert scurried around between fridge and table with the skills he'd acquired while waiting on tables in a rather upmarket restaurant in a rather upmarket part of St Louis where he had studied Arts at university in what seemed many, many moons ago.

Stephanie rumbled and tumbled her fingers on the velvet and then swept up the trick with such aplomb that one would have thought that she'd made a Grand Slam. To aid her thinking, she fiddled with the recently acquired trick, shaping it into a perfect rectangle before placing it exactly square on top of the previous tricks. Every now and again, she would deliberately tap the column of tricks to count how many she had. This time, the taps reached eight but she had to get ten and there were only two more tricks to go and she had run out of trumps – she wondered if she had misheard the bid and remembered that she had forgotten to count the diamonds. She discarded the club and hoped for the best. Luck, or uncanny subconscious was on her side and Alice dropped the winning diamond, meaning that Stephanie had it in the bag. It really was a pretty ordinary group of Bridge players.

The contract was won, a cackle emitted, much praise was given and all round swigs were taken from replenished glasses while smiles were given to the cheese platter and hummus dip. Alice collected the cards with an interpretative swoop, shuffled and placed the pack on her left while Peter cut the other pack to Adrienne who started to deal.

That orange glow in the corner of Stephanie's eye flickered a little more in her consciousness but the camembert, warmed by the heat in the apartment was creeping over the plate to her left and was irresistibly distracting.

Adrienne dropped a card and all heads ducked under the table to retrieve it. Once found, it was strategically placed randomly back in the deck and the dealing continued.

"How was her opening speech?"

"Didn't go." You could bet your house on Alice avoiding any kind of formal occasion, especially one that might mean having to listen to some graduate from some place like Lowestoft Tech waxing not so lyrical about the merits of knowing one's students.

"Has yet to show substance," Stephanie was generally more diplomatic.

"Cutesy?" Alice always critical. "Not sure whether she can or can't think. She certainly doesn't."

"Oh come on, you're all so bloody arrogant. Judgemental." Adrienne would always be the one to find good in anyone even if there was none. And the general consensus in this case was that there was none.

"Wait and watch, that's what I reckon. Wait and

watch."

"Oh bugger," Adrienne was looking at the dealt hands. "Misdeal. Everyone count their cards."

A scurry and counting ended up with Alice having twelve and Peter having fourteen, so Alice chose one blindly from his hand.

"Such a bitch," Adrienne grinned at Robert who had been silently watching from afar while dipping into the cheese and wines.

"Who's the bitch?"

"You," Adrienne laughed at Alice who shrugged. She was a teacher – she'd had worse.

There was a muffled knock on the front door and heads turned to see a rather younger woman make a vaguely grand gesture as she almost skipped towards the table armed with more wine and cheese.

"Sorry ladies and gents, so late, but I'm here."

"It's past ten."

"Yeah, got stuck with a student explaining our biology prac."

"And she's here now. Do you want to hop in?"

"Nah, I'm just here for a drink. You carry on."

"Well we're talking about you know who."

"Ah," the ever most politically correct Karin rarely entered into gossip. "The one that takes the same walking route every day. Out of the school grounds, up the High Street, round through the park, down and around the marina and then in at the side gates. Just passed her actually."

"That's the one."

"Nice walk of a morning."

"She does it in the evening."

"Well, I've seen her in the morning, around the marina end of the walk."

"That'll keep the weight off. Twice a day."

Robert had finished filling up wine glasses and asked about the cake. It was the evening of their communal birthday. Years previously Peter had worked out that their average birthday was May 27th and this year he claimed their average age was 53. A surprise indeed as most were clearly almost in their dotage, but it is a figure reduced considerably by Karin who was only 45.

This group of current but mainly erstwhile teachers had convened almost every Thursday for nigh on ten years. Over the years their relationships had deepened; their understanding of Bridge had not.

And this particular evening, that starts our narrative, found them collected at Stephanie's flat which was one of six in a block that had been converted from a large, rambling Victorian house on the edge of the school grounds. The flats were cosy and really only suitable for single teachers. Too often, the school would put a bright-eyed young married couple in one of them saying that it was short-term. For a few months, this 'wet-behind-the-ears' couple would drool over the million pound views across the marina and into the sea beyond, comforted by the proximity of squillion pound yachts and the owners that must go with them. But then they tended to gain confidence, bought a puppy, got pregnant and realised that other teachers had far grander houses somewhere else on the campus. A period of bleating, blaming and general begging ensued before they were moved to more spacious but perhaps not so chic accommodation cushioned by the school's boarding houses and classrooms. Stephanie had had many, many short-term neighbours and was known to comment that if there was an infertile couple anywhere

– better move in – would work wonders.

Teachers' houses in a boarding school provide a cornucopia of levels of political intrigues and general machinations. Single teachers tended to avoid the Term Two fights which plagued the staff room. Given that the deal was that all teachers lived for free in prime real estate in return for working in one of the boarding houses, the levels of inequity in said prime real estate was a running sore. Stephanie was content with her cosy flat overlooking the marina and all the workings therein but then Stephanie was single and avoided much of the on-campus gossip.

For the most part, half of our little rag-tag Bridge group were generally playing Bridge or golf or looking after grandchildren and travelling. They had retired from the political minefields that haunt both vaulted and unvaulted corridors and quadrangles of secondary education. They had all worked at the school and between them could offer nearly ninety-five years of service in the classroom, in the boarding house and on the sporting fields. They were those old-style, loyal teachers who had greatly cared for both their students, their subjects and their school.

And it is this school that is central to our story. It is one of those bluestone affairs which at the beginning of the 21st century is clinging desperately to the cliff of respectability high above a rather splendid rendition of a 1920s marina. While bearing a royal prefix, the marina had once been chic but in the latter half of last century had transitioned into shabby chic and was perhaps now more shabby than chic. The royal yacht club, rather like the adjacent school, was tightening its loosening grip on respectability with every receding year.

Stephanie was one of those teachers whose toes teetered in both the romantic illusions of a better past and the raw realities of a too crude present. Alone with her chardy, surveying the water, she often could almost hear the echoes of those past sailors whose colonial leanings suggested travels in the east and discussions of the west; they belonged to a past that was hankered after by a few but left unimagined by many.

Similarly, the school's walls echoed of those nineteenth century benighted traditions which were now termed bullying, humiliation and terror; to put it plainly - abuse. A school where boys were buggered in the name of Empire and girls accepted in the sixth form in the 70s. A school that had once taught The Greats and not much more except how to maintain a veneer of respectability over the internal trauma of the tortured mind. New money from that imagined east and the ease of entry into polytechnics turned into universities meant that the importance of A Levels in Business Management, Legal Studies and Psychology held far more sway than good old History at Oxford. Oxbridge was the unimagined allure, but the new money of the vaguely educated middle classes reflected in the school leadership and a growing cohort of teachers had shifted the focus, and students were now pointed in the direction of vocations rather than solid academia. The world had changed. This oxymoronic existence almost bled through osmosis between the school and the yacht club and their histories had been intricately interwoven over the two centuries. Indeed, the old school tie and crest on the blazer pocket – *Navigant Tecum Sapientia* – were remarkably similar to those on the tie and blazer of the royal yacht club. One could almost imagine that the same designer in town was commissioned for both in the same week and produced one but charged for two.

"I was visiting my aunt, in Eaton Square, last week when her friend, the Duke of Sutherland, dropped in. He and I were in next door beds in Remove. Haven't seen him for years. He has a salmon beat on the Tweed, so we're going there for a week in August." Peter often spouted the most random of comments, but it did, at least, give Stephanie a little more time to cotton on that she needed to bid.

"Do you like killing salmon?"

"Don't know, haven't done it yet."

"The ghilly does it for you."

"It's not about the killing, is it? Well that's what I thought. It's about the battle of getting it to take the fly."

"Dunno – not my type of thing."

There was a bit more shrugging, a bit of dipping in the guacamole gorge and scrapes at the remains of the smoked salmon dip. All took a sip of wine while they waited until someone said, "Stephanie! You need to bid."

"What? Is someone talking to me?"

"Yes, you need to bid," Alice ensured that Stephanie was looking straight at her when she moved her mouth in a slightly exaggerated way.

Stephanie drummed the table.

"Gosh, they're sticky. We must get some new ones. Anyone travelling business soon?"

"What's your bid?"

"It's all the cheese and crisps we eat that makes them so sticky."

"Oh, what the heck. Let's go *one no trump*."

Robert could be heard rattling in the minute kitchen as he fumbled around for candles for the cake. He had decided it was best not to ask Stephanie for directions as that would slow the game up even more and so he fished about in the bin liner and cling film drawer looking for the much needed candles. The evenings were now long and by ten o'clock it was dark enough to light the candles and sing an egregious 'Happy Birthday' to each other. It was one of those auspicious evenings when the day had felt almost hot and had faded into a long warm elongated dusk and the skies had given up on their grey veneer as the old blue was allowed to peep from behind the higher clouds. For no particular reason Robert felt something akin to pride and new beginnings as he lit the candles, turned out the lights and lifted the cake aloft in readiness. The candles cast a fiery promise of something more as transient shadows made flickering jerks against the cream painted walls.

But that orange glow we've heard of before now shot to the front and centre of Robert's focus. The candles on the cake paled against the flames in the marina.

Generally phlegmatic at heart, Robert almost dropped the cake, its plate and gingerly fluttering candles on to the table and pretty well threw himself in the direction of the window. Stephanie was about to say something but following Robert's arc and gaze stopped, her mouth agape. Her lips flapped silently, but the others, whose backs were essentially against the window and as yet ignorant of the scene, waited for her to play a card.

A yacht appeared to be alight, a decent sized white yacht, perhaps forty feet in length with one of those blue, go smoother stripes, running around just below the gunnels. Flames were lapping out of the cabin and through the open portholes. More flames were starting to explore the outside of the cabin, venturing through the hatch and touching the blue canvas canopy over the cockpit.

Robert stood transfixed. All thought of the candles' waning wax dripping into the icing went up in smoke. Stephanie was about to move but couldn't. Alice and Adrienne stared at the cards in their hands. Karin and Peter stared at the cards on the table.

The blue canopy disintegrated into the cockpit and the space where it had once been was engulfed by flames and smoke. Either the acrid smell or the increasing noise of the spitting and crackling alerted other boaties on neighbouring yachts. Hours earlier many of these had retired below to imbibe, ingest and enjoy the soothing caress of the incoming evening tide as it lapped and lipped its way against the amalgam of timber jetties and stone walls. These boaties were perhaps jolted, rather rudely, out of their semi-comatosed existence and were now hopping around, some rising out of their hatches whilst pulling on tops with one or two having to pull up bottoms. Others were already fully clad and running for the fire extinguishers dotted hopefully along the jetties. All were clutching a mobile, either because they always did or because they were dialling 999. Two were taking photos, and one a selfie.

"Oh shit!" Robert opened the window, perhaps to hear or smell better, perhaps just to feel a little closer to the action. There was no wind but the cooler evening air coupled with a little of the growing pollution invaded the senses of the other card players suggesting that all was not as usual. Stephanie had stopped gaping and gawking and turned to squawking from the perch of her chair. Karin saw the orange glow and joined Robert, and the others heard the tumult through the now opened window and at their own rates of realisation started to take in the scene.

The flames emerging from the cabin were increasing in energy with every passing second. They seemed almost excited as they soared and roared towards the boom and wrapped themselves warmly around the mainsail and then crept towards and up the mast. The blue canvas cover of the mainsail was the first to follow the disintegration of the canopy as it melted and floated away from the boom. The flames gathered, feeding on the destruction, stretching higher and higher and into the upper reaches of the halyards, embracing the salt encrusted sheets. Below the fireworks around the mast, flames crept out of the portholes and along the deck in an insidious invidious cancerous invasion. The mainsail dripped back into the cabin and added to the disease. The yacht seemed to have come alive as it wriggled and squirmed in its last throes before it would completely submit to the flames and the smoke. Big blue letters which formed part of the encircling blue stripe claiming *She's the One* dripped into each other before they melted completely off the hull and flowed into the dark current of water around her stern.

All stared at the action, speechless, motionless and for a moment wineless. Now that the window was open, they could hear the crackle of destruction and the voices of mild panic and controlled direction.

A pyjama-clad bearded man scrambled towards an ancient fire extinguisher encouraged by a wife sporting fairly anachronistic mauve fluffy slippers. A bald chap in just his yellow smiley-face boxers yelled something useful but unheard from an opposite jetty and then decided to leg it around to help. Old Tom clambered from his craft onto the jetty, wobbled towards the heat, felt the heat, turned and retreated to his craft and below deck, never to be seen 'til morning. A gaggle of women gathered a safe distance away, near the entry gate, and offered advice and critiques and someone asked, at least five times, if anyone had dialled 999. At least six times a response was given in the affirmative.

Robert remembered the candles on the cake, looked around and saw that the candles had safely drowned in the cream topping and happy in the knowledge that fire was not going to come from behind, he turned back to look at the rather more exciting activity in front of him.

The smiley-face boxers man had unhooked another fire extinguisher and was running along the boards of the jetty while trying to read the instructions. Faded words and an ungainly design made running and reading difficult. He stopped, turned to his mobile and googled 'fire extinguisher use'. He and the pyjama-clad man with the wife with the mauve slippers, grappled and haggled with the red tin and eventually a whoosh and a sloosh produced a stream of foam which spurted into the night air, first hitting the mauve slippers before it could be turned towards the cockpit of the fading *She's the One.* No sooner had the spurt hit the side of the hull than it gave out an almighty burp and dwindled to a mere trickle of white liquid falling at the feet of the two men. Frankly, it was all too little all too late. The now defunct fire extinguisher was all of two feet high and the flames were nigh on twelve feet and blooming.

In the distance, the sound of a fire engine, its siren poking its way through the medieval cobblestone streets towards the not so ancient marina and soon to be erstwhile yacht, could be vaguely discerned. There was something comforting about the sound, something that suggested someone else was in control, that salvation was nigh, particularly when most had realised the limitations of the fire control measures at the marina could offer merely transitory hope. For a brief moment there was calm. Those in the marina watched the flames creeping along the deck, along the cockpit and towards the diesel tank.

Slightly above the action, a sense of resignation engulfed those in Stephanie's apartment as they listened to the approaching sirens invading the stillness of the May night air. From their seats in the dress circle they watched, marginally and probably momentarily dumbfounded, the unravelling scene of the melting yacht where fibreglass gently mixed with wood and canvas, lulled by the dulcet tones of the fire engine.

Alice blinked and as she opened her eyes, she saw the explosion just before she heard the 'boom' reverberate. The flames had reached the diesel tank. Time seemed to stand still as all turned towards the scene of smithereens of ex-yacht descending really quite elegantly into the dark, still water. The explosion had been clear and momentary. The aftermath would be tangled and drawn out.

Our lot watched those on the jetty, who, in unison, dropped to the boards, far too late if there had been any shrapnel, covering their ears and heads as best they could as they plummeted. Explosion over and thinking that they were safe, the prostrate sailors on the jetty started to rise in slow and deliberate movements gingerly watching the shredded remains of canvas and salt-encrusted jib sheets flutter gently onto the rather heavier detritus of masts, hatch doors, mangled fibreglass and life-belts. It is difficult to comment on which was the more impressive - the sound of the explosion or the rather beautiful shower of a detonated multi-million pound yacht. Either way, both had outrun the arrival of the fire engines which were now tearing around the final corner of the cobblestone street leading down to what had been an old fishing port now transformed into shabby marina equipped with exploding yachts.

    Crowds from nearby houses started to flow onto the road and there was a feeling that the second act was about to begin. Two of those in the gathering crowd were the school's security guards, Gary and Frank, whose work had, this evening, taken a rather more imaginative turn than usual. Moments earlier they had been sitting in their office, sipping sugary tea and eating sugary doughnuts. Their normal routine followed a discussion of which football team would be or had been relegated and which fans had been banned from matches. They should have been watching the numerous screens of the numerous security cameras around the campus. Partly, this was to ensure that the campus was secure, but mainly, they rather felt, it was to check on the movements and misdemeanors of students and staff. What Gary and Frank didn't know about after hours nefarious deeds just was not worth knowing.

    The addition at the school of security cameras a couple of years earlier had created much more interest for our two burgeoning security guards. After all, it was all good sedentary viewing, the contraction of their walking load correlating exactly with the widening of their girths. Every now and again one or the other would grunt, reach out into the box of doughnuts, add another teaspoon of sugar to his tea and make some erudite comment about this football team or that which was promptly refuted by the other through a mouthful of Battenburg cake. The odd comment on page three was made and a muffled agreement generally ensued, followed by a quick cursory flick from screen to screen. Sometimes comment was made on a particular late night visit from one staff house to another but usually they weren't that interested. This was the normal serene routine of a Thursday nightshift at this most prestigious of elite schools perched on the southern coast. The explosion, therefore, certainly made them sit up.

Awakened from their vaguely comatose semi-stupor, and glancing at each other, they simultaneously heaved themselves out of their office chairs, armed each of themselves with a very heavy torch and a walkie-talkie and wandered, unmoved towards the marina. It was not immediately clear to them where the explosion had come from but as they tumbled out of the office, a suspicious orange glow in the night sky over the marina might just intimate that a commotion of sorts could be there. Purposefully and gently, they navigated their way through the growing crowd but like most, were stopped at the gate as they did not have a swipe card to allow them onto the jetties. All that Gary and Frank could do was watch and talk into their walkie-talkies to some imaginary guard that they had strategically left back in the office.

It is difficult to say who arrived first - the journalists or the fire brigade. Either way, both were keen, fired up and ready to shoot. By the time they arrived, someone had managed to retrieve a swipe card from those on the inside but by then there was really little left of *She's the One* who was sinking serenely into the watery grave and settling comfortably into the murky depths. All that remained was the burnt end of her painter belligerently attached to the mooring ring on the jetty.

Robert went around filling up glasses and by now no-one really minded which wine they were drinking so long as it offered a modicum of solace. Adrienne squeaked. Stephanie didn't hear Adrienne but suggested that she had thought that she had heard an explosion but it didn't seem as loud as the scene outside warranted; she therefore resorted to just saying, "Oh my God, Oh my God, Oh my God." Alice ate. Peter started to tell a drawn out tale about an old school chum whose boat had blown up in Buenos Aires. Something to do with Colombia apparently. Karin sat on the edge of the sofa, drank wine without blinking and thought of skulls.

Much activity resulted in nothing much until eventually the fire brigade managed to drag a long black rubber pipe up the jetty and towards the dwindling flames. Rather half-heartedly they spurted water at tiny floating flames which were now starting to resemble those floating prayer emblems that one lets go in places like Varanassi. But that's not a terribly good aside - just trying to paint the picture. One or two spot fires on nearby yachts had been started by falling debris and these were dealt with summarily, and so by the time the police arrived in a flurry of lights and action, there was generally nothing to panic at all. The photographer from *The Mercury* hopped around, excitedly snapping at anything and everything except the scuppered yacht. The police leapt out of patrol cars, leaving the lights flashing and, as excited as the photographer, barked redundant orders about everything being in control. Remember these police and journalists, and even the fire brigade, rather like our security guards, tend to find much excitement in rescuing a cat up a tree. An exploding yacht was not really on their radar of expectations. The boaties on the jetty wandered back to their own yachts to watch the antics at a politic distance and the crowds feigned disinterest while continuing to watch the remains of the scene.

The Bridge group did feel a little removed from the action. It was very important for them not to miss a trick. Who else in the staff room tomorrow would be able to recount the scene from go to woe? Who else would be able to elaborate, articulate and exaggerate? After all, they had just witnessed a rather magnificent explosion of a rather magnificent yacht in the rather shabby royal yacht club. The event had, indeed, livened up a normal Bridge night even though usually there was little serious, staid or ordered when rubbers were played with much wine, cheese, dips and gossip. Conventions were created and discarded. Hands were played and cards mysteriously lost. Bids were made that defied reason and by the end of most evenings six empty wine bottles lay by the side of the bin waiting to be put in the re-cycling and all felt like mighty fine Bridge players who could hold their own in the upper-echelons of Andrew Robson's students.

While each player was wondering how they would recount this evening's occurrence to those near, dear and far, there seemed to be a tad of a pause in the scene below and Adrienne suggested that perhaps they should attack the cake. Molten wax was fished out of slightly liquid cream and slices navigated their way to individual plates where they would play havoc with even the mildly lactose intolerant. While the candles had disappeared, the group did try to pipe out a rather discordant "Happy Birthday" to themselves but somehow what had, in past years, been a source of much hilarity, this year faded into a feeling of limp mediocrity.

They attacked the peach upside down cake made by Stephanie, one of her favourite recipes passed down through the maternal line that presaged from farming stock in East Lancashire. The cake seemed to have capsized onto the platter and was engulfed by waves of whipped cream and extra golden peach syrup. Plates were laden with the flotsam and murmurs of its taste and texture were politely and mostly sincerely passed on. Alice did not have a sweet tooth and so she lied.

The smell of burning, melting fibreglass, rubber and wood infused the apartment and the acridity mixed with the cream and peach to coagulate in the back of the throat and Alice felt the stinging sensation of sugary syrup on her tonsils and smiled politely as she swallowed.

Below them, the tide of crowd was ebbing and those within the compound, with shuffling feet and hanging heads, leaked back to their own boats. One or two stalwarts, perhaps from further afield, stayed a while longer, perhaps hoping for more drama, or resolution. But they had to settle for the repetitive interviews of the journalist who could find out nothing more than it had been a Beneteau 38 named *She's the*

One. Nobody on the outside appeared to know who the owner was, and those on the inside, who might have known, had taken their secret back to their sleepy berths.

More cake was consumed and this was washed down with more Sav Blanc. Their minds had forgotten the card game and the *three no trump* bid had vaporised as quickly as the Beneteau 38.

And while they were pondering the rather anti-climatic drama and deciding that no more Bridge could be played that evening, on cue, and from the wings appeared the shiny new gothic Headmistress.

She did not appear to have had time to administer her normal plumage. Gone were her power dressing grey or black suits and gone was the white, white foundation and red, red lipstick and here were her tracksuit pants and puffer gilet from Joules which did little to enhance the worn, drawn and distinctly dull 10pm face. Presumably she had received a call from our friendly security guards and had felt the need to heave herself out from beneath the duvet and to prance down to the marina where she could make a dramatic entrance. She would have to report to the Board in the morning. In reality, her tiny, diminutive figure was barely perceptible even among the dwindling crowd and no-one would have really noticed her moving towards the gate of the jetty as though she had a swipe card and an entitlement to enter. At the last moment, she appeared to check herself, pulled back her hand, shuffled her feet, stopped and peered in wonder through the netting.

Minutes later, an equally short man with hair that looked rather like that wire-wool that we use to scrub pots and pans or block up mouseholes, bounced and bounded up to her side. His body movements seemed electrically charged with a sort of ecstasy that mimicked the drug and reeked of insincerity but were responsive to her slightest movement. She brushed him aside as she would have done to an annoying mosquito but unperturbed and clearly on some sort of manic high, he started talking to Frank, poking at his mobile and then holding it to his ear; he was, of course, in total control. All was happening here.

Mid conversation, a tall, lanky fellow with a shaved head, a contemporary ruse to disguise the onset of baldness, also tried to position himself on the right hand side of the square mouthed goth. His head, rather small atop a long skinny neck, inclined towards her and he, too, feigned some sort of controlling attention. He too was waved away in some demi-regal manner and he melted back into the school grounds with little ceremony while she attended to a message on her mobile.

The cameo appearance of the Headmistress and her deputies ended up as a bit of an anti-climax and the thought of playing more hands of Bridge became a possibility; after all, it was only 10.30 and there was always more wine to drink. Murmurs of "Shall we play?" rippled through the apartment but they were all still entranced by the movements of the firemen below who were shouting orders about how to pack up all the hoses while chatting randomly to the police. It seemed that the excitement of the night, the week, the year, perhaps even longer had been and gone.

The goth followed her deputies back through the school gates, sporting that pale-lipped, tooth-ridden insincere square smile and she therefore missed the screeching arrival of the Land Rover, the spewing of its

23

driver onto the pavement, the rushing of the man through the gates and down the jetty and the chthonic howl that reverberated across the darkened depths.

But the journalist remained for the scoop and the front page of the next day's *Mercury* would have a rather grand picture of a spanking new Beneteau 38, which had been grabbed off some Google search, combined with a picture of some smouldering flotsam alongside the headline, *My Wife's On That Boat.*

2. TWO CLUBS

As the now pretty pissed Bridge group heard that howl, all thought of another hand dissipated. The scene below took on a different guise. What had been a rather amusing rendition of the destruction of millions of pounds of yacht belonging to someone who probably had more millions of pounds stashed away in some tax haven paradise island, transformed into a rather grisly death scene. Even, one might just venture to call, a cremation. The firemen abandoned their neatly rolled hoses, the gossip with the police stopped and most eyes fixated on the direction of the rising commotion. Many ran, some strolled, towards the man now continuing his howls beside the empty cage where his wife had, only minutes before, been floating. The journalist trotted alongside; now he had a story. Policemen were on the walkie-talkies, firemen their mobiles, the journalist beckoned to his photographer and the drifting crowd stemmed its ebbing current, turned tide and tsunami-like returned to watch the show.

The howling man, pacing and stamping, pulled

at an imaginary hat and stepped out circles around the
end of the empty cage before looking into the murky
depths, perhaps with some misplaced hope that his
wife might phoenix-like, rise from the soggy ashes of
the smouldering flotsam. But the unbroken surface of
the water remained resolute, certainly in no mood to
entertain such fantastical thoughts, and its calm veneer
masked the chaos below.

A police woman ran to the man's side. Another
offered a supportive arm, another gave quite a hefty
pat to his shoulders. The jetty swarmed with a sea of
uniforms and horror. The man had fallen on his
haunches, been raised and had fallen again. His howls
seemed to reverberate in the souls of those watching
and Alice could feel that lump of despair form in the
lower part of her throat. At one point he lay on his
stomach and hung his head over the jetty as if by
getting closer to the water, the boat carrying his wife
might magically and miraculously be raised and life
would be re-wound by an hour or so. But nothing. That
boat was sunk.

Alice and the others could hear another siren,
tracing a similar route to the fire engines and police
cars. Alice had often wondered about the sounds of an
ambulance siren. She always felt that it was a sign of
hope. There was a sense of urgency as the lights and
the siren suggested that the patient inside was indeed
alive. Instead, the sight of a silent lightless ambulance
felt like doom. What indeed is the point of flashing
lights if inside the light has gone out. Alice rather
thought that the sound of this siren seemed at best
hopeful and maybe just a little inappropriate.

"Is there any more wine?" Robert felt that
more was needed at this point. Peter thought about a

brandy, Adrienne a toke, Stephanie a port and Karin imagined a soggy smouldering skull trapped between a berth and a hatch.

Alice said nothing, looking dark but thinking nothing and Adrienne squeaked something about it all being too much.

Stephanie scraped around in a cupboard and found a couple more bottles of chardy which were opened, poured and vaguely tasted with slightly suddenly retrousse noses.

"Tad vinegary."

"Been in there for years."

"Better than nothing."

"Too pissed to tell."

Robert proffered the remains of the guacamole dip.

"Not much hope."

"None at all."

"Burnt and drowned."

"Rough end."

"Which was first?"

"Oh don't."

"Well she couldn't have burned if she'd got wet."

"If?"

"S'ppose not."

"That explosion would boil and burn her."

"She's not a witch."

"Not even a mermaid."

Robert went to fetch the remains of the cheese platter and put it on the side table next to the window. They were going to need sustenance for this next act of the drama.

"This could be an all nighter."

"I suppose they're going to have to raise the wreck this evening and get the body out?"

"Do they know for certain that she's in there?"

The insistence of the ambulance siren continued to suggest that the body could possibly still have a pulse and the voices on the jetty clearly carried through the still night air and up to the eyrie.

Despite the husband's howls, the police did not necessarily believe that the woman was on board and asked some of those pertinent questions such as, "Sir, why do you think that your wife was on the boat?" and "When did you last see your wife, Sir?" kind of reminiscent of that painting where the Roundheads are asking the young prince about his father. "Have you tried to call your wife, Sir?"

At this point, the man took out his phone, had a desperate look at the screen and pinned in a password. It didn't work. Perhaps he had mispressed. He tried again. Nothing. Looking desperately at the policeman he tried again. Nothing. No messages. He pinned in some more numbers. Listened. Nothing.

"You've got to raise my boat. Why aren't you doing something? She might be alive down there." A scramble, a thought, "An air pocket, or something."

"Sir, please try to answer our questions. We have informed the correct authorities about raising the vessel but we need your co-operation." His calm sense of authority rumbled through the air. " We need to be certain that your wife was on the boat when it caught alight. We need to understand why she did not get off the boat when it was clearly in trouble."

"How the hell would I know? I just know she told me she'd be sleeping on the boat tonight."

"Okay Sir, thank you. Still no new messages?"

The man gave a withered, beaten look and focused back on the space where the boat had been.

The ambulance arrived. Paramedics ran down the jetty and uniforms joined the uniforms. There was really very little that could be done. All flaming floating flotsam had sunk. There was much calm in the marina and probably much calm in the melted submerged cabin just ten feet below them on the marina bed. But body or no body, it was generally agreed that someone would have to dive into said cabin to determine the whereabouts, or not, of the man's wife and one can only imagine the thoughts of the two sleepy police divers who were woken at about 10:30 PM to come and search for a body that may or may not be there.

The man had stopped howling and was now fixated on his phone. It looked as though call after call kept going through to an emotionless voicemail informing him that the phone was out of range or turned off. It was the last desperate attempt to hold onto the life they had up until this evening, one last semblance of their married life, a moment before that abrupt explosion. Others were making phone calls to their very much alive spouses and letting them know that this could turn into quite a long evening. For Frank and Gary, our committed security guards, the thought of tea and pink iced doughnuts returned and a quick discussion saw them decide to return to their office, perhaps to come back a little later to see how the act had progressed.

Scraping the last remnants of the cream wave from his plates Peter looked at his watch as he tried to remember what time he was due on the first tee the following morning; usually it was ten but a funny, niggling feeling suggested it might be ten past ten.

Alice was wondering if she needed to prepare anything for her A level set or whether she needed to revise what she had taught in the last lesson because she had the distinct feeling that the concept had been lost on most of the class and Stephanie was getting anxious about whether she could get her kitchen cleared up before having to face her Form 5 French class where the subjunctive was proving difficult. Robert suggested that there was another spurt of chardy for those who wanted and Adrienne looked at the wreck of the capsized peach cake and helped herself to the last crumbs. Karin licked out the last of the guacamole dip and Alice ate a carrot stick.

"What's happening now?"

"Not much."

"A lot of milling around and the chap that looks like the husband doing a lot of head scratching, ear pulling and looking in the water."

"What's the point of the ambulance?"

"Protocol?"

"Political correctness?"

"Oh god, too much of that around."

"To be precise, social correctness; don't want the press to create a scandal."

"That'd be a hope."

"I suppose you have to look for a body."

"Awkward if they didn't look and then she was found tomorrow morning cold, wet and dead." Alice was always coldly direct.

"She could be warm, dry and alive?"

"In the arms of another."

"Awkward, again."

"Just saying."

"Yeah, gotta search now, just in case."

"She could turn up later."

"In the arms of another."

"Not sure if that is good or bad."

"Well, good for her..."

"You'd think she'd have her mobile on."

"Have you never had an affaire? You don't want to be disturbed mid coitus, so to speak."

"Let's hope..."

"...the sex is good." They all laughed at their own ridiculous, or not so, fantasy.

"Who knows?"

"Perhaps her battery is dead."

Adrienne started to clear up Stephanie's kitchen. She generally needed order and cleanliness. Alice finished off the cheese and her wine. Karin stared at the scene from her perch on the arm of the sofa. No one wanted to move; after all, from the theatrical point of view, the scene had been set, the complication was clear for all to see and now there must be a resolution. A final act needed to be played out, the climax, the culmination, dare one say a catharsis had to be reached. Perhaps the wife would nonchalantly wander back with beau in tow. Perhaps there would be a phone call saying that she was in the Bahamas. Perhaps she would just meander back from the petrol station with a pint of milk and another packet of Vogue Blue cigarettes.

Golf tee-off times, rotten students and that perennial looming doom of report writing faded into the background. No one wanted to leave this makeshift theatre until the final curtain call had clearly been taken. Those in the dress circle did not know that they were waiting for the police divers but there was a general consensus that now that all the white wine had been drunk, a cheeky little pinot didn't look all that bad

31

after all. Peter pulled the cork, poured and they sipped, sat and watched.

An hour later and another two bottles opened, you would have thought that our audience would have been more than a tad tipsy but the coolish night air coming through the open window, together with the thought of a cold damp corpse only yards away from the warm cosy apartment, held a magnetic sobering gravitas. Alice knew that this was far more interesting than trying to suggest to twenty fourteen year olds that revision was important. Karin had given up the thought of marking some lower six Biology tests before the following afternoon's lessons. Adrienne was wondering whether she would be too tired to attend campanology practice the next morning and Peter was just going with the flow, knowing that he would have another story to add to his menagerie of generally irrelevant tales of daring and adventure. But nothing seemed to happen. The curtain for the final act seemed stuck, a glitch in the action which, mixed with alcohol, meant that logical cognition and general expectation of action were interrupted.

Stephanie started to clear up a little more manically and Robert, picking up the hint, announced that he was calling it a day, bid everyone goodnight and disappeared, fairly unceremoniously out of the door. Alice and Karin took this as a cue and also decided to migrate towards their own houses on the other side of the campus. They would miss the next act and wove their way through the campus, under the windows of dormitories where junior students were sleeping in blissful ignorance. The very idea that their teachers could be wobbling drunkenly homewards was just not on their radar. Through slightly ajar windows of more senior students who could be heard gently tapping on keyboards, the sure signs of studying or gaming. At one point, Karen tripped and fell in a ditch. Alice tried to help her out but in doing so fell down on top of her. They giggled quietly, hoping that they had been neither seen nor heard. In the melee, they were vaguely aware that the Headmistress was still gliding around the campus on her midnight walk. She floated past the pile of bodies in the ditch and seemed not to notice, focused on the matter in front of her. By quarter past midnight both were in their beds snoring, vaguely wondering in their dreams whether a security camera or two had watched their ditch grapple.

Peter had remained a little longer in Stephanie's flat but with no action or wine eventuating, decided to cycle home. His wobbles over the cobbles of this sleepy hollow of a town left only Stephanie and Adrienne to watch the final act of the night. An act that had begun with the passing of that gothic ghost who seemed to sail around the marina on her midnight walk, so ethereal, almost imperceptible, but their murky minds were muddled by the wine and so this memory was lost in the subsequent action.

The police divers arrived in an unmarked van and parked between an ambulance and a fire engine. In a half-asleep kind of way, they opened the back of the van and almost like automatons unloaded wet suits, oxygen tanks, ropes, flippers, torches, more ropes and a long black plastic bag with a long black zipper and more ropes. In the half-light of the streetlights, both the women undressed to swimming costumes and pulled on wet suits. A solitary policeman came along and seemed to be briefing the women on the situation. Lots of nodding while pulling and zipping and heaving of heavy equipment through the gate of the marina but absolutely no one else came to help. In no hurry, the women lugged and flip-flopped the equipment to the empty space where *She's the One* had been moored and was now lying, sunk, a few feet below where she had floated but hours before. They took a bit of a look. There was more nodding of heads and the odd knowing hand gesture and the women donned their tanks, masks and flippers, held onto a few ropes and underwater torches and did a bit more nodding. Any sense of urgency was confined to the husband who had resorted to wringing his hands, staring and shuffling around in a circle.

Stephanie and Adrienne continued to conjecture that perhaps he already knew that she was dead, or perhaps he knew that she wasn't there because she was having an affaire. Perhaps he knew a truth in his own heart. Adrienne, who was staying in the apartment that night, decided to take the moment when the divers disappeared into the dark water to brush her teeth and get into her pyjamas. She had already made herself a hot water bottle as the May night air was fairly chilly and it was nigh impossible to close the window in case a snippet of conversation was picked up and could be used to add to the burgeoning story that was to be told around the town and the Common Room the next day. Stephanie had retrieved her hearing aids during the tuneless singing of *Happy Birthday* and now had them turned to high as she continued to watch the lights from the marina reflecting in the gentle movement of the ripples on the surface of the water above the divers.

All was quiet as the entire ensemble, including those in the apartment on the school campus, watched

34

the murky yellow lights of the torches flicker and twitter downwards. There was really nothing to say or do but watch. It was one of those moments that seems interminable, as though time stays still or moves to a half beat. Those moments when you're not quite sure when you took your last breath and you end up gasping, just in case it was a very long time ago. After all, you don't want to die too. Adrienne sat on Karin's abandoned perch. Stephanie gulped. The husband on the jetty continued to circle amid gasps. The charged silence lingered over the beams of flickering torches flitting just beneath the surface.

Perhaps it was ten minutes but it felt like two hours. Perhaps everyone knew the result but needed that concrete confirmation. No one spoke. But the two women left over from the barely-played-Bridge group knew before they saw. That howl, which seemed to reverberate from the depths of the Styx repeated itself and was the dead giveaway.

He must have seen the shadowy outline of his wife's body cradled in the arms of a kind-hearted Charon before it reached the surface. Everything from beneath confirmed the thoughts above. A whimper preceded the surfacing but all was too obvious as the diver appeared with the damp, limp body. The head rolled back and an arm dangled and dripped its fingers on the surface of the water, as though they were trying to keep in touch with what was not.

The silent still moment was exchanged for movement. A posse of emergency workers hung over the edge of the jetty. The same police woman stood beside the husband gently holding onto his arm. Perhaps she thought he would jump, perhaps she thought he would collapse. He watched and moaned.

Around him, the energy that had been lacking before the reappearance of the diver had shifted. Ropes were unravelled and fastened in an attempt to heave the body, and it was quite a heavy body, onto the jetty. A few gentle commands, a few moments of urgent requests and the team really quite effortlessly hauled the really quite cumbersome lifeless body upwards and onto the jetty. Her hair was the last part of her to leave the water. A chunky piece of gold bling was entangled in the tresses and together they seemed to weep back from the drooping head as if to say that all was better down there.

A mellow hush was the only appropriate response from those who watched the retrieval. Little else could dignify the scene. Hope evaporated. Here was the body, a rather portly body of what had clearly been a well dressed woman having just been raised through ten feet of water and laid, as delicately as possible, on a jetty that was becoming increasingly damp with the descending dew – definitely dead.

Now the paramedics took over and the purpose of the long, black, zippered bag became apparent as the husband's howls had turned to choked sobs hacking through the night air and fading into nowhere. The paramedics respectfully played out the act in the script. That training manual kicked in and the emergency services reverted to those unthinking processes which meant that they could go home safe in the knowledge that they had done a great job as they had followed everything by the book. The husband watched his wife's body as it was loaded into the ambulance where it would, presumably, be taken to some cold grey soulless mortuary. Somewhere in his imagination he must have been thinking in terms of slabs, knives, postmortems, ashes, burnt skin and a stomach full of Louis Roederer. Or maybe, he thought of guilt, loneliness and questions. Perhaps he just thought of nothing. That empty moment that does not even proceed to "What now?"

The firemen wrapped up their hoses. The divers returned their gear to their van and the police returned to their walkie talkies with the vague hope that the next call might return them to their normal world of pissing drunks and stolen bikes. Our two security guards had not returned to the scene and so it was the husband who was left alone to close the gate of the marina. As he walked towards his Land Rover, which was parked slightly closer to one kerb than the other, the light of his mobile screen flickered. He looked at the message and clambered into the car.

Adrienne and Stephanie decided to call it a night. It had been a big day.

****

And it had been a big day for Patricia too. What had started out as a normal, run-of-the-mill Thursday turned turtle and things became unusually startling. Something was in the air. Trouble was afoot. Teachers could smell it. Students could touch it.

Maybe things started at morning tea break but perhaps that was just because that was when Patricia heard about it. Things had been going wrong for a long time before. Rumours and gossip were rife and this was such a good story that it travelled faster further and became even more distorted and warped than it really was. From its inception, the tale had gathered legs and tentacles that had crept into ever secret crannies, crevices and corners in the fabric of the institution. Students had known about it for a long time, and what they did not know, they made up. By the time it reached the ears of Patricia, the facts had been eaten by wildfire and the flames had burnt the ears of all.

That morning Patricia left her office just before the not so dulcet sound of the bell signalling the end of period 2. She wanted to get to the morning tea early. The school was quiet. The odd student was wandering around out of class either to go to the loo or perhaps a music lesson. A cleaner was squeezing out the last of a mop, having cleaned the maths corridor after a student had thrown up coagulated porridge before being sent to the San. As she walked through the main quad, the smell of shepherd's pie being cooked in the school kitchens mixed with the smell of spew and Dettol.

The main quadrangle was one of those that adorned so many of these quasi-exceptional schools of questionable exceptional substance. Its very fabric that cradled students in a nefarious sense of community, care and entitlement, promised a future of power and wealth. The offices hugging its edges offered academic and pastoral programmes that featured front and centre in the glossy marketing photos on posters, prospectuses and other paraphernalia. The hard copy prospectus had been replaced by the soft website which sported images of stiff erect clocktowers, cricket pavilions, the odd girl playing netball and reams of students dressed in West End-quality costumes who had been choreographed within an inch of a Hollywood call up. Prospective parents pandered over the propaganda, dreaming of their progeny's undoubted success. Libraries, science classes, English and History were a thing of the past in this school of the twenty first century sitting on eighteenth century stones.

Normally, Patricia would bypass the Common Room, a room that physically mimicked the shabby chic yacht club. Worn out leather sofas and threadbare velvet chairs stood drably on a patchy red carpet where the solid richness of the colour felt dangerously close to an antiquated brothel. Morning tea was a hideous occasion, a quasi-society drinks party without the alcohol or pretentious canapes, a political moment in some of the teachers' lives where they could be seen and sampled as they hobnobbed with their betters in an attempt to climb another rung of that horrific ladder. For others, it was a moment to dive onto the morning tea sideboard and stack their plates full of sandwiches, cakes and grapes, but for the rest, it was moment to be bored brainless by the ladder-climbers, the gluttons, the gossips, the self-promoters, the grateful and the almost dead. They would have to listen to the ladder-climbers waxing lyrical about how great was their, and less often a student's successes. Or there were those who thought that the best way forward was to hold black babies in Africa and post the mandatory photo to FaceBook, LinkedIn and Instagram whilst ensuring that this philanthropic experience was not only included in that old chestnut, the CV, but boasted about in the Common Room and promoted by their agents to the next school in their career progression. These were the people who talked about lesson plans, enquiry-based learning, learning intentions and almost knew what pedagogy meant, but they had little idea of a Socratic question or even a sense of abstract humour. Their educational speak was bandied about with abandon but never ventured further than the Common Room.

Often Patricia just wished that failure was

celebrated – not out of her usual scepticism – but just because she felt that failure is often good, an excellent way to learn. She found it exhausting having to listen to how great everyone else was and how they were all striving to improve. Morning tea seemed to accentuate this feeling, and so more often than not, she would pass by the door of the Common Room and make a cup of coffee in her office.

But today was odd. She looked at the spread of food on the sideboard and helped herself to three rather dried up sandwiches which had been left over from a Board meeting two evenings before. Salmon and some sort of mayonnaise, the usual ham and tomato and that old favourite, honey. She poured herself a cup of coffee which was sure to have adopted the taste of the aluminium urn that it had been sitting in for the past hour or so and found herself a precious seat before the rest of the staff would pour through the door, hugging and puffing about the issues they had encountered in period two.

She was weary. A thirty-two year career in teaching had rubbed off on her and not much could surprise her now. The last eleven of those years had seen her running a girls' boarding house where she had been on call every hour of every day and every night for every whim and whisk of one or other of the forty teenage girls and their mothers. She had seen the introduction and subsequent damage that electronic media can achieve. She had cared for countless anoxerics, cutters, overdosers and phoneys. She had negotiated one suicide and two deaths in a car crash. She had suffered the greasy looks, complaints of unfairness, incompetence and favouritism. She had circumnavigated hair colouring, tattoos and piercings in places where one just doesn't want to know. Some years, straight hair was in and curly pubes were out. Brazilians, bleaching and holidays in the Bahamas went in and out of fashion. Mothers were advising labia removal to infantalise their darlings and then all of a sudden, they weren't; by then, for some, it was too late. Their daughters were doing drugs, using glow-in-the-dark condoms and needing the morning-after pill. They were shellacking, bronzing and bitching. Patricia had been lied to and lied about. She had been yelled at, sworn at and derided. She had listened to endless stories of despair, existential angst of loss and grief, and that was just from the mothers. She had shared the joy of success, the community of food and the just downright stomach-hurting, cheek-aching laughter that comes with running an adolescent girls' boarding house. It was tiring and rewarding, and she'd had enough. This was her last year.

She would be sad to leave the rambling old building that had once been four cavernous redbrick Victorian houses. Originally they had been built as holiday residences for those grand people from London in the nineteenth century.

Architecturally, it was now a mix of old tradition which hinted at respectability, and new glass and aluminium which suggested raciness and modernity. Excellent for the Marketing Department. In essence, it was a maze of corridors and staircases with loads of hidey holes for drinking, smoking and sex.

Patricia saw her job as one that navigated the course through advice, acceptance and just plain ignoring the antics of teenage girls. After all, girls will be girls. So long as the morning-after pill was available, so long as the smoking was done near a window, or preferably outside behind the dustbin shed, and so long as drinking was done after she had put them to bed, she did not think there was a problem. When they were all tucked up and the alarms were set, what could go wrong? Lights out and doors locked and alarmed were her cues to go home to Henry who would have rolled a joint, the contents of which had been grown between the tomato plants in his greenhouse, and together they would sigh with relief that another day had been successfully negotiated and there was another day's salary in the retirement coffers.

But that morning her assistant had approached her with a problem.

Alice had been on duty in the boarding house the evening before and had been vaguely inveigled by a couple of students. Vaguely, because one is never sure with some girls. They had had a confidential chat and Alice had gone home needing to tell Patricia as soon as possible. A phone call after duty was not the thing; after all, everyone knew Patricia would be stoned. Alice did know that in this highly litigious moment in educational history the sooner one can pass a problem up the ladder, the better. Best to rid oneself of the issue and duck the barbs. After all, don't we know that anything a student or its mother does is the responsibility of the teacher. Always best to shift that possibly nefarious responsibility up. And so, Alice taught the first two lessons and was very quick to leg it over to the Common Room where she hoped she would find her Housemistress cradling a hot tea and a plate full of mid-morning snacks.

"Got a bit of an issue." In her usual, direct manner, with little introduction or nicety, Alice stood before Patricia.

Patricia thought along the line of friendship fights, jealous mothers, cheating, smoking, failure to clean a fridge in the kitchenette, or even failure to use the used tampon bin in the correct manner. Any number of the usual suspects were floating through her mind before the cruncher hit.

"Jessica is masturbating in the dormitory." Alice said it as it was, waited for it to sink in and added, "The whole school knows about it." Another pause. "Talk of the town so t'speak."

"What the fuck?"

"Sort of. Fucking herself so t'speak." Another pause. "A lot."

"What the fuck?"

"She's wanking a lot."

"Fuck."

"Um." Another pause. "Come across this before?"

"Na."

"Um."

Both teachers looked at each other. Their training, or not, on how to teach the river systems of South East Asia, *Othello* or surds to teenagers, did not really equip them to deal with public masturbation in a girls' dormitory. Neither had done nor been given any research on the topic. There was a very accurate rumour that one of the boys' boarding houses had an ejaculation board where boys would publicly ejaculate and then measure the distance gained. The boy who managed to spurt the furthest was a hero until he was outspurted. But boys will be boys. Girls didn't tend to do this so publicly.

"Right."

"How do you know?"

"Simone came to tell me."

"The Year 11 girl? Think she's been in the house for a couple of years?"

"Came to us from Marlborough. Nice kid. Works hard."

"Thought it was Oundle."

"Rugby? Oh one of the biggies."

"Got her. Not a player."

"She came with Rosie. I think for moral support. Simone said she thought she'd bring the House Captain because then we would believe her." Another pause. "I told her we trusted all students."

"Of course we do. Of course we do. Right thing to say." Patricia's mind was full of untrained, uncontrollable thoughts, many more than she wanted. "So?"

"Well, Simone says that Jessica has been masturbating really quite openly for most of the term and the rest of the dorm is now getting a bit sick of it all."

"I bet they are. I bet they are." Patricia took a bite of most of a honey sandwich.

"Now, Jessica - which one is she?"

"The Welsh girl..." Alice was going to go on.

"How long has she been with us?"

"Came at the beginning of this term."

"Got her, got her." Patricia screwed up her face and her forehead puckered under her greying fringe.

This was something she was actually going to have to address. If a student had come with another student and that other student was the House Captain, it was very difficult to sweep this one under the carpet. Coupled with this, she rather felt it was probably true that the whole school knew about it and probably had known for quite a long while. It was only a matter of time before her superiors, that nebulous body known as Administration, or The School, found out. She had found herself in uninviting waters. She had to act. She did not want to.

"So what shall we do?"

"Perhaps you and I should chat with Simone again. Perhaps, if she feels uncomfortable, she can bring along Rosie too. I'll take notes. That's the most important thing, to protect you and me. You do the questioning."

Clearly, Alice had had all night to think about the road forward. She was slightly younger than Patricia and knew the imperative as opposed to the importance of process and policy. It was imperative that any perceived undermining of school policy was a mere intangible shadow against the vast evidence of following protocol. At all points, everything had to be convincingly obfuscating and convoluted into the circular to ensure that everyone was covered.

"When do you want to do this? Can you come over during prep this evening?"

Alice visibly writhed. This would be when she would be playing Bridge. She'd prefer not, but also one had to play that political game to ensure that if you were not going up the ladder, at least you stayed on the same rung. It was never good to suggest that you had interests outside the establishment.

"Got a lot of marking tonight. I've gotta get it done as I promised to give it back to the kids tomorrow."

Patricia read 'Bridge night'. Everyone knew about Bridge night.

"How about straight after class? I've got tennis,

but I'm sure I can fudge something and get someone to cover me."

Patricia coached, or rather oversaw the coaching of the fifths summer tennis team which trained after class. It was a motley group of sixteen and seventeen year old girls none of whom had any intention of breaking into a gentle glow let alone a sweat. The dangers of doing so were insurmountable: a broken fingernail, smudged mascara, a boy watching. Much of any game and most of training was taken up in discussing whether the zip on their skirts should be worn down the side of their hips or over their bottoms. The girls would sporadically adopt provocative poses, hips out, chins up, tits aloft, to test the benefits or otherwise of the zip position. Other girls would watch, comment, adopt or experiment. Matches consisted of a few volleys, a rough search for a stray ball, the odd stretch and sticky buns after the first set as they talked about plans for the weekend whilst the opposition plotted game plans for the second set to ensure the match was in the bag.

Patricia planned to organise another teacher to cover this most important training session in the girls' educative process so she could focus her energies on wanking. Alice and she agreed on the time and spent the rest of the day pondering. Patricia wondered whether she should tell anyone higher up the chain now or wait until after the meeting. She wondered what the students would say. Indeed, what would the parents think? God, how embarrassing. She was not looking forward to what would be some tricky conversations. Should she seek advice from another housemistress? After all, one did not want to show frailty or weakness and one always had to give the impression that one was running a boarding house where humanity, harmony and dignity fell at the forefront of all that happened. Perhaps it was best to remain silent. Internal statements rather than questions. Silently, the words 'fucking wanking', screamed in her throat, her heart and her head.

At four o'clock, the two girls arrived at Patricia's office where she and Alice were already ensconced. The office was warm and friendly with a cosy sofa and a few armchairs scattered around, all upholstered in the House colour of a rather dirty mustard, more Dijon than English. Simone looked more nervous than her House Captain, Rosie, who exuded the confidence that comes from being popular and the excitement that this was really something to gossip about in the most adult of ways. Alice, pen poised over an already dated and 'Masturbation Incident' entitled pad, was wondering where to note the students' names. Patricia made the customary greeting, thanking them for their responsibility in coming forward to help the community and harmony of the House, the usual, 'put you at your ease' type of approach. The two girls sat back in their mustard chairs and crossed their legs in the most elegant and sophisticated manner, Simone following Rosie's lead by about a second and a half.

Simone was a good looking, doe-eyed girl with auburn hair and that permanent suntan that hinted of constant holidays in sublime locations such as the better side of Majorca or Crete. Rosie was a much more pallid blonde and her skin would have turned red, blistered and dropped off with the slightest hint of sun. More Celt than Mediterranean.

"Okay, Simone, can you just fill me in on the conversation you had with Ms Howard last night? I understand you are concerned about the welfare of Jessica?"

"Yes." Simone nervously clutched one hand and rubbed her crossed knee at the same time.

Rosie put out her hand in a reassuring and not at all condescending way on Simone's lower arm.

"I was trying to tell Ms Howard that the other girls are getting very uncomfortable."

Rosie gently caressed Simone who slightly squirmed.

"Don't get me wrong, I like Jessica, and I feel terrible saying this, but, well, it's just that…" She shifted her bottom on the chair. "Just everyone, everyone, I mean everyone is talking about it, and it's just not right."

The caressing ever so slightly intensified.

Her eyes could not have opened any wider and their brown brilliance stared with all the innocence a knowing fifteen year-old could muster. But the teachers knew this was not a player.

"It's okay Simone, you're doing the right thing," Alice was scribbling and offering encouragement.

"Now then, Simone, we do really have to be more specific." Patricia was more formal. "And I know it is difficult. But can you tell me what she is doing?"

More shifting, coughing and eye-widening. "Well. You know. Sort of. She's doing things she shouldn't in public. Not in the dormitory, she shouldn't."

The tension was building, they could go nowhere if things did not come to a climax.

"I think you need to tell them what she's doing," Rosie chipped in, wanting to get to the rub of the matter. No leading questions, no putting words into mouths. "Just get straight to the point."

"She's masturbating." Simone spurted it out, and there it was, for all to see, on the table before them.

All seemed relieved and breathed a barely perceptible sigh of satisfaction. The moment of squeamish awkwardness passed and now all that had to be done was to find a route through to resolution.

"Right, how long has this been going on?"

"Since she came. All term really."

Jessica was a relatively new student who had started at the school after the Easter holidays. The arrival of a student from another very similar boarding school mid-year was always just slightly suspicious. They always came with a 'clean slate', a fresh start.

"Um."

"When does she do this?"

"All the time." Simone's hands were again becoming animated and the pitch of her voice was rising.

"What do you mean? All the time?"

"Well, lots of times in the day and always after lights out. We tell her to shut up. But she just starts sort of rustling." A pause. "And moaning. She tells us that she's not doing anything. But we tell her we can hear her."

Alice sort of grunted a sound which could just have been a muffled cough disguised as an appreciative gesture as she continued to record notes in a most professional manner. Patricia tried not to catch her eye, just in case.

Once Simone got going there was really little to stop her. "She does it under the covers and sometimes she doesn't even bother to get under the covers. She's got a whole lot of underwear that she puts on and she watches porn on her phone and does it."

"Underwear?"

"Yes, black, lacy, with holes where there aren't usually."

"Oh right." Alice scribbled.

"Does she have anything to assist her?"

The two girls looked oddly at each other and then at the teachers, catching Alice give Patricia a 'What the fuck?' look. Everyone shifted their bottoms. Patricia had articulated her thoughts. Curious, but perhaps not entirely necessary. She checked herself, re-arranged her bottom and quickly asked another question, "How do you know its porn?"

"She showed us one time," and then realising how she had incriminated herself, Simone quickly covered her mouth with her hands. "I'm in trouble now, aren't I?"

Alice was quick to come to her rescue, " No, no, I'm sure you didn't mean to look."

Patricia guided the conversation, "So tell us again. How often does she do this?"

"Three or four times a day."

"Three or four times a day!" Neither of the teachers could restrain from echoing.

"And each time she does it, she does it six or seven times."

"Six or seven times?" Alice started to get the giggles, partly from amazement and partly from absurdity and perhaps a little because she was impressed. She tried to control her body from the shakes created by her internal giggle.

Simone's need to share the situation turned to concern and her voice fell an octave as she adopted the gravitas necessary for the occasion. "She must be doing herself some damage."

Alice's mouth visibly twitched as she barely suppressed a spontaneous smirk and a titter came out more of a snort which she disguised by grabbing a nearby tissue out of a box. She could sense Patricia was gently shaking. But decorum and process must continue.

Rosie wanted to be part of the action. "And you see, the problem really is, that the rest of the school knows about it. They are talking and laughing at her."

"Rightio, okay, well thank you. You have both done absolutely the right thing and we will take it from here. We are so sorry that you have had to go through this and we will be taking steps from here on."

Both girls smiled meekly and mildly and felt most virtuous as they stood up to go.

Simone felt impelled to say, "I feel really bad telling you but..."

And Rosie butted in, "Remember what we all said? You're doing it for the rest of the girls. It's okay." And she took her by the arm in a mother hen kind of way as she guided her out of the office.

The two teachers smiled weakly, nodding their approval but unable to speak for impending laughter, Patricia eventually summoning the composure to utter, "We know, we understand," and "You've absolutely done the right thing."

The door shut and they could hear the girls running away down the corridor. As they turned to look at each other, the laughing started slowly and then rolled into a full throttle of high hysteria. On the surface this would seem as if they were no better than the teenage girls they cared for, but really it reflected a deep unease and uncertainty and just downright awkwardness. Underneath the hilarity were the nagging thoughts of how to approach the parents, the mother, the girl Jessica and the school. As they spurted out amid the laughter the odd phrase that one or other of the girls had uttered, they knew that things needed to be taken seriously. But really. What would her mother say? Actually, more hilariously, what would her father say? And at the root of it all was Jessica's welfare and how to maintain her dignity when all around knew.

Jessica was from one of those second marriages. Those ones where, on first meeting, one is rather tempted to view the mother as another daughter of the husband rather than an object of conjugal satisfaction with trophy qualities. Of course, Jessica was a looker; her mother was a stunner.

Patricia and Alice decided that they had had enough stimulation for one day and resolved to talk again. Alice was pleased to be able to get to her Bridge evening on time and Patricia decided to leave the House in the capable hands of a tutor and go home early and have a joint with Henry.

****

Patricia's thoughts of catching an early joint with Henry did not quite pan out accordingly. The matron had made a birthday cake for one of the girls and so there needed to be a celebration. Emma had a dental appointment but couldn't work out how to get there. Joy had lost her passport and needed it to get to Paris for the weekend. Sarah again went missing only to be found mysteriously on her own near the tennis courts. There was a fight in a Year 11 dorm as someone

52

had lost a Coco Chanel top and blamed another for it. The tutor was caught up giving Maths tutorials which meant that Patricia needed to supervise prep time. In the end, a normal night, and Patricia did not slip out of the House and through her side door until after nine.

Within seconds she was putting on the kettle in her kitchen. Henry was reading some tome on the history of the Slovenians towards the end of the eighteenth century but had left something neatly rolled beside the ashtray next to the kettle. The routine was fairly standard. Kettle on, joint lit, telly on and the day was done. This evening was unsurprisingly the same. By nine thirty, Henry had closed his book, removed his glasses, tapped them on the arm of the chair and pondered into the middle distance. Patricia had relaxed and was very much in control of her thoughts about what the day had served up to her and she was of the clear opinion that everything could wait 'til morning.

And so, the ritual of a couple going to bed, which is presumably different for all, unfolded. Teeth and pyjamas for one while the other let Doris and Daisy, the sausage dogs, out for their final wee. Henry was more than fond of the dogs and never reprimanded the dominant Doris for rushing the door and almost tripping him on the step. He took them for a walk almost every day around the marina and down the coastal path, along the low cliff above the beach – one of those cliffs that could have been the death of Gloucester, but only in his own imagination. Daisy would always follow Henry at a polite distance, while Doris would forge ahead, confident of her place. The walks were perhaps as much for his solace as their exercise.

He had retired from his position as the school librarian five years earlier and, much older than his wife, was enjoying maintaining the framework and heating in the greenhouse while his wife ensured that there was enough money coming in for them both to be soon enjoying retirement. Sometimes he would be called upon to help out in the Library; sometimes he would help, sometimes not. More often when he was there, he would do his own research on the rise of democracy in Eastern Europe rather than help the students.

Their only son was all grown up and living in New Zealand, apparently running an orangery, but it was somehow thought that not many oranges grow in New Zealand, it being too far south and all that. He was certainly doing frightfully well and in no need of his parents' help. Patricia and Henry had therefore invested in one of those apartments in a 'nice' part of Spain and were hellbent on paying it off. Their plans were clear, they had a future. Life was good.

The dogs came in when Henry called and curled up quickly on their beds in the boot room. Henry wandered towards pyjamas and teeth and then crawled slowly into bed; his almost portly frame that needed that walk, never moved quickly. He turned out the light and would be well asleep before Patricia who would always return to the sitting room to watch re-runs of *Escape to the Country*, ventured to think about bed. More often than not, she would fall asleep in her chair. It wasn't that she disliked her husband - quite the reverse - it was just that routines do require quite a bit of effort to break.

And so it was, an hour or so later, perhaps at the same time that those at the marina were thinking about fishing a body out of a sunken boat beneath the marina, that the crash from the bedroom awoke Patricia with a jolting start. For a moment, the sound became part of her nightmare in which a huge noise had come from the class next door and when she rushed in to investigate, she found a class full of teenage girls, dressed in black lacy underwear being titillated by a giant dildo which was floating above their desks. Some girls were clamouring on the desks striving to touch and stroke their desire; others were arousing themselves under desks as the teacher with her back turned to the class was writing on the whiteboard whilst describing blow hole formations in the Sub-Sahara. Suddenly the dildo exploded, and Patricia jolted.

The first inkling that suggested that she was neither in the Sub-Sahara nor the classroom was the sudden urge to cough. This was a physical rather than an imaginative realisation that she was sitting in her chair in her home and the noise had come from the bedroom. Perhaps she smelt before she saw. There was a thick acrid pungency hanging in the air and then the dust floated flagrantly out of the bedroom door and it seemed charged with irritation as it tickled her throat.

"Oh fuurk." She heaved herself out of the chair.

Firstly it was an 'oh fuurk' that suggested mild irritation for being awoken from a titillating dream but as she covered her mouth and nose with her hand and then the front of her pyjama top, the 'oh fuurk' adopted a discombobulating urgency.

"Oh fuurk," she coughed, and then, "What the fuurk?"

She stumbled through the dust towards the bedroom door. The door was jammed, and she could only force it a few inches, enough to peer around but not to get through. She hit it, she banged it and eventually she threw her entire frame at it until it moved just enough for her to squeeze her body into the gap. But she could get no further into the room as there, on the bed through the shimmering, swaying dust, in some mangled and distorted manner, lay most of the ceiling, and there in front of her, lay a large portion of the rest of the ceiling. Patricia choked and grabbed the doorframe. For a transitory moment, time stopped while the dust wavered and the edges of the ceiling moved. She froze. She tried to make sense in her slightly dope-addled mind of the transition between floating dildos and the scene before her. Ideas moved from wanking to ceiling reasonably smoothly and it was at the end of that movement that the dreadful realization came to her that her husband, dear Henry, was beneath the mangled mess.

"Oh fuck! Fuck. Oh my god! Fuck!"

She scrambled through the moving dust and started to lift pieces of mangled plaster and blistering paint while calling out.

"Henry, wake up. Henry. The bloody ceiling has fallen on you." She fossicked some more. "I fucking told Maintenance two years ago that it looked dodgy. Crack in the corner. Henry, wake up. Wake up Henry."

The sense of urgency intensified. Effects of the dope were nullified by the dust. Perhaps he'd drunk more than he normally did and was completely out to it. Then she'd have to explain everything to him in the morning. Could be awkward, she thought and then wondered why. She had to make sure he was alive at least. How to see if he was breathing? Actually, where was he? A hand dripped over the side of the mattress. She couldn't get to him. She couldn't lift the plaster. It felt like supporting beams had fallen too.

"Henry, Henry." The pitch in her voice raised to that of a cockatoo squawking threats to other cockatoos in some remote Australian bushland.

There was no response to her screech.

"Oh fuck, fuck." Now she was breathless and rushed back to the kitchen, picking up the internal phone. She dialled 541, at the same time uttering the number under her breath, "541, 541, 541, come on, come on, pick up, pick up, come on, pick up will you?"

And so those security guards, whom we've come to know reasonably well, had a second untoward job that evening and this is perhaps the reason as to why they had not stayed at the marina for the entirety of that job. We had unkindly presumed that they had returned to more sticky, sugary, pink doughnuts, but in fact they had responded to a call on the walkie-talkie that Patricia and Henry's bedroom ceiling had just plummeted, beams and all, onto their bed.

Neither Gary nor Frank had been particularly keen to leave the drama at the marina. After all, it was almost a once in a career thing. Florentines from the kitchens, leftovers from another important meeting, had arrived at their office, and even these paled into insignificance compared to an exploding yacht. So, the insistence of a forwarded call to Gary's mobile was more than irritating.

"Main'nance, g'evenin," Gary growled.

"Fuck it, fuck it, get here now! I think he's dead. The fuckin' ceiling." The breathlessness rather than the insistence of aggressive imperatives was the first thing that struck Gary. It suggested, to him, a modicum of panic.

"Who's this?"

"Patricia, Patricia, at Campion House, Head of House Residence."

Why her boarding house was called after a

catholic saint is anyone's guess and a permanent conundrum for the Anglican boarding school.

"Get here now! The ceiling! The ceiling! Dead. Fuck."

The tone had a good go at rankling the generally implacable Gary but he was not one to react to a woman in panic.

"Where are you exactly?"

"At home. Please, please. I can't move it. He's under there."

"Yes, yes, we just have to get our paperwork correct for the morning inspection."

Frank had opened up the running clipboard as Gary heard the next 'Please' whispered through the phone, a plea, a hope and he replied, "Yes, yes, just writing it down and we'll be on our way."

And so for the second time that evening, our two security guards got a rather unexpected call and they were completely torn from their normal routine and thrust into another scene of mayhem and destruction. It all felt a bit like they weren't paid enough and their training hadn't really covered these sorts of incidences.

They waddled their adipose bodies, at a reasonable pace, towards Patricia's house. Their torches dangled off one hip and their rarely used walkie-talkies held tightly to the other. All seemed quiet as they passed the generally satisfied calm of the boarding houses. Students were tucked up safely in their dorms and most staff were beavering quietly at marking and lesson preparation.

The contrast, on arrival, at Patricia's house was stark. A vague cloud of dust seemed to be seeping out of previously unknown orifices and cracks and the sound of strangled coughing from both human and dogs cut through the still night air. Much of the former ceiling had changed its shape into wafting dust and was floating elegantly out of the house while the rest of it was firmly rested on top of Henry.

Patricia was waiting for them and rushed out to hurry them towards the pile of rubble. While she had been able to squeeze around the door into a gap to survey the scene in the bedroom, the slightly more generously endowed guards found it harder to manoeuvre and had to get their shoulders behind the door to force it into the room. A cheap, flimsy door did not give too much resistance and soon it became part of the detritus on the bed. It was difficult to move and difficult to breathe.

Gary told Frank to call 999. Even at this point, he knew that they could be into something that was just a tad out of their league. All their movements, their grunting, their heaving, their crashing had not managed to stir Henry. Patricia, still holding onto the thought that he had had too much to drink, was weeping in the background between caterwauling uncontrolled screams and trying to get the dogs into the garden where they could breathe.

Gary was the first to behold the carnage. A large piece of plaster covered the bed and three toes poked out from beneath one end while a hand draped rather elegantly, if but a bit dramatically, over the side, dripping from beneath a floral pink duvet cover. But that was about the sum of what could be seen of Henry.

Without speaking, the guards gingerly started to lift the plaster. As they puffed and huffed, the plaster seemed to melt in their hands and the process took rather longer than was kind. There was little to no movement from Henry below. Actually, let's be honest, but we have to let Patricia down slowly, there was none.

In the distance, and for the second time that evening, could be heard the insistent whine of the ambulance, fire engine and police sirens. This time they could come through the main gates of the school and did not have to weave themselves through the cobbled lanes of the medieval part of the town.

The firemen were the first on the scene and had the same feigned air of urgency as they tried to assess the situation. Questions asked of Patricia were quickly deflected to questions to the security guards and within moments they were into the bedroom and dealing efficiently with what they beheld, just as their training had taught them to deal with a large piece of ceiling plaster atop a body on a bed.

"Dusty?"

"Bit."

"Breathing apparatus?"

"Asbestos?"

"More than likely."

"Looks older even than asbestos."

"Best be safe."

"Yep."

Patricia continued to hop about shouting things like, "Quick," and, "Get on with it," or "He's dead, isn't he?" and, "I know he's dead."

The ambulance arrived while the firemen were digging out their oxygen tanks and donning masks that looked like they were going into Chernobyl. Everything was a process and everyone followed the protocol.

"A male under the rubble."

"State?"

"Haven't reached him yet."

"We'll secure the area. Not sure what's more to come down from above."

"We'll come in behind you."

"Rightio."

"What's taking you so long?" Patricia's impatience was making her feel sick. The rising panic formed a knot in her ribcage and was ready to explode into her throat.

"Please be calm. We need to ensure our members are safe."

"What about my husband?" Her pleas were lost in the dust.

One paramedic held onto Patricia's arm and guided her into the kitchen. The offer of a cup of tea felt a little bit of an understatement but thoroughly English. It was a distraction between the bumping and bashing as the hazmat clad firemen made their way towards the bed and the now presumed erstwhile Henry.

And erstwhile he was. A rather large pointy piece of plaster had managed to pierce the artery in his neck. A direct hit so to speak which, thankfully, meant that he would have known nothing. There would have been no opportunity to move even if he could have accelerated his slow crawl. Perhaps he had heard the initial crack as the ceiling started its rapid descent but that really would have been the sum of it. The paramedics took one look, felt hopelessly for a heartbeat and then went to collect a body bag. The lump in Patricia's throat turned into an empty chasm of pressure.

"Who can we contact for you?" A gently asked question arose from the mists of the settling dust and rising emotion. "Is there anyone close by?" The paramedic was trying to soothe.

"Yes. No. I don't know. What time is it?"

"I can call someone for you."

"Jane, Jane. Call Jane."

"Who's Jane?"

"A friend of mine. Lives on campus."

"Okay. Can you give me her number?"

And so we leave the scene at this point.

Perhaps there was a sense of symbiotic reflection as the woman's watery corpse was borne into the ambulance in her body bag at almost the same time as Henry's pierced cadaver was carried into another ambulance in his body bag, both within a couple of hundred yards of each other. And while they were cold, stiff and horribly alone, the vast majority of those living on campus, students and teachers alike, were snuggled in their warm, cosy beds. Most.

But we leave a distraught husband and wife, neither connected but perhaps joined in this story. Jane came to fetch Patricia and the dogs and no one knew where the husband of the sodden wife ended up that night.

3. TWO HEARTS

By morning tea, on the day after these two slightly unseemly deaths, the vast majority of the staff had heard about one, other or both, and the bright shiny new Headmistress obviously needed to take the limelight and make the most serious of announcements. Standing in front of the staff, most of whom were scoffing into mounds of jam sandwiches on the sideboard in the Common Room, she looked as though she may be off to the beach for the afternoon. Wearing a long-flowing black dress that accentuated her bosom at the top and hid her lack of hips at the bottom she had tied back her bottle blonde hair and applied a brilliant white foundation thus accentuating her gothic features. A purply-red lipstick topped off the look and an elderly English teacher who was currently teaching Bram Stoker to one of his senior classes did take a second look.

Despite being at the school for a mere nano-second of its illustrious history, actually two terms in total, she had already taken it upon herself to adopt the position of naming it "her school", a habit that riled the old and tickled the young. Her speeches tended to be ones driven by the first person singular, full of vague analogies and supported by Youtube clips on PowerPoint presentations driven by a roving mic and two fingers pondering a thoughtful chin. Her wandering suspicious eyes sparkled wide with mydriatic vivacity this particular morning and one could almost imagine Tinkerbell's sister waving a wand as she sprinkled fairy dust over the scene. Somehow this headmistress managed simultaneously to expand and contract the tension in her delivery as she cleverly created a heightened sense of intimate drama. Indeed she never missed a beat as her speech almost became a proclamation of some, let's be honest, some fairly disturbing news.

"My heart is thumping as I have to deliver this news to you. Many of you already know about the very painful news that I have to tell you today. I never thought, six months ago, when I signed my contract and took up this wonderful and prestigious position as Headmistress of this wonderful school, that I would be standing here, in front of you, as your Headmistress and have to deliver such traumatic news. As I said, my heart is thumping."

Her right hand was clutched around her mobile phone, from which she was reading her speech and her left hand ventured a controlled flurry to the place on her chest under which a heart might be. She squarely smiled, and those perhaps straight shiny white teeth gleamed from just behind the purply-red lippy.

"I am so sad to tell you that Patricia Kendall's husband, Henry, died last night as a result of a horrible ..." She stopped and moved her hand purposefully but ever so slightly to feel that vaguely thumping heart. A speck of lipstick had ventured backwards from lip to front tooth, " ... a truly, horrible accident."

She gave a vague forced slight choke, but managed, oh ever so bravely, to carry on, obviously oblivious to the actual emotion of the room where discreet intakes of breath, hands on others' shoulders, downcast eyes and the odd lowering of iphone or newspaper was occurring.

"I have, as you might expect, been working closely with the police and we expect their presence on the campus today."

Her composure polarized, moving from the southern realms of emotion to the northern plains of icy reason.

"Many of you may also have heard of the accident at the marina overnight where a sleeping woman drowned when her yacht caught alight." A roving eye sparkled with iridescent energy and unblinkingly tested the room. "While this is not our business, it is unfortunate, and we expect much police and media activity today. As always, I ask you to tell the media politely, if they approach you, that you are not able to talk to them. Please could you direct them to," a slight pause, "Our Director of Media Relations ..." a slight cough and the back of her left hand was daintily raised to her mouth, as she turned to the grey wiry-haired Deputy, "I'm sorry Paul, what is our Director of Media Relations called?"

"Gareth Rich."

"That's right," giggling, "so you need to direct any questions to Gareth." That beaming smile and a sweep of a bit of dyed blonde hair back behind an ear, "Now have you got any questions that I can answer? Of course, as you can imagine, I am fighting back the tears as Pat is such a close colleague of mine and I know that she means so much to one or two of you."

There was, as we can imagine, a rather stunned silence in the Common Room, partly as a result of the news and partly because of the nature of its delivery.

Stephanie, of our Bridge club fame, did pipe up, "Is there any news of the matter in the marina last night? It's just that a few of us did see quite a lot of it all."

"No. None." The Headmistress's response was short, curt, cut-throat.

Another stunned silence. Thoughts were settling in about Patricia and Henry and the cut-y'dead response to Stephanie's reasonable questions was rattling.

"Be aware that police will be on campus today and you need to deal with student concerns appropriately. Alice will be stepping up as Acting Head of House while Pat is on Bereavement Leave."

And that really was that. The smile never faltered as she walked towards the coffee machine and made herself a filtered coffee. She looked at the array of sandwiches and cakes on the sideboard but perhaps thought that these might go too quickly to her hips and instead went to find the Head of Girls' Games to talk about whether the pupils were going to be allowed to take a Mars Bar to the away match on Saturday or whether this sent a bad message about sugar.

The Head of the Common Room asked for attention for further announcements. Details of Henry's funeral would be circulated. The roster for the upcoming sports day was going online in the afternoon and all staff responsible for timing races could collect their stopwatches from the Sports Office by 4pm. Volunteers for the cake stall could contact the Community Relations department and the coffee van would be arriving as normal. Someone decided that this was a good time to ask for expressions of interest in running the charity fun run that would take place towards the end of the term and another asked if a particular item of uniform was allowed to be worn in the Dining Hall, but no one really gave a damn until someone announced that the staff bar would open as usual that evening.

****

One of the delights of working at this illustrious school perched on the southern shores of a faded empire was the requirement to perform Dining Hall duty at least once a week. The evening following the contretemps at the marina and Patricia's place, saw Alice dragging her heels towards her weekly Dining Hall duty. She had already covered for Patricia at breakfast and now she had to face the hordes of apparently half-starved, ravenous adolescents for the second time that day.

The school's Dining Hall was one of those quasi-Oxbridge halls that hinted of substance beneath its oak-beamed vaulted ceilings. Oak panelling on the walls sported oil painting after oil painting of past Headmasters who sat, stately and sedately, gowned and robed in academic colours, looking down with some comic disdain at the swill beneath. And what an antiquated anathema that was.

Row upon row of long wooden tables and accompanying benches stood stickily atop a heavily waxed wooden floor. Twice daily this floor was polished but, be it as it may, there was always the residual gunk of a previous meal stuck, congealing and vaguely smelling to the floorboards. The general ickiness of the floor was more often than not supported by half wiped tables which, too, smelt of yesterday's fatty deposits of lamb chops or glutenous leftovers of rice pudding. That was on top. Underneath the tables, if you cared to look, or more precisely, feel, there would be hundreds upon hundreds of dried-up chewing gum, stuck in place by the future leaders of the faded empire before they inhaled their bangers and mash followed by fruit jelly and custard. Peas and rice were the worst meals to supervise; students didn't seem to be able to keep these two items on their plates, and by the end of the meal, tables and floors were strewn with a white and green mush coagulating with the wax that could only vaguely be mitigated by antiseptic floor and table cleaners.

A truly gargantuan oil painting hung at one end of the hall depicting some battle or other where knights accoutred with St George crosses were, presumably, overcoming the vast hordes of Moors, or whatever heathens, in the quest for salvation and sophistication. Its present idiosyncrasy had not gone unnoticed by Carmichael Minor who had, during a food fight a couple of years previously, sent an orange flying through the air, hitting and piercing the painting just where an infidel was pictured entering a citadel. The hole was still there for all to see and no one seemed quite to know who in this day and age would do the repair work. The black chasm between the infidel and hope of salvation remained.

On either side of this momentous oil, the

educational doyens of past centuries looked down their noses as the students snuffled in the bain-maries and salad coolers of the present century, piling their plates with food they may not eat sitting at the oaken tables of a past time.

Alice watched the seemingly endless morass of sweaty, smelly teenage bodies file through; most buzzed with excitement, some adopted the pose of adolescent ennui, others watched while Alice thought that with just an infinitesimally slight stretch of the imagination, she was watching the grunting sniffling of pigs at a trough. She wandered around the hall, alert for potential food fights, chatting with the odd student about an essay and joking with others about whether there was any leeway for a homework deadline.

The most important thing was to avoid the high table. This wasn't, as you would expect, because the Headmistress ate at the high table. In fact, our gothic ghost had yet to grace the high table for an evening meal. But because, in the evening, many of the staff would bring their families to eat in the Dining Hall, and their place was the high table. There was nothing worse, Alice rather felt, than being surrounded by married staff and their gaggles of apparently gorgeous toddlers and young children who had to be indulged and praised. If one managed to avoid the young then one was invariably caught by the tediousness of having to listen to one or other wife who would pour out the trials and tribulations of being married to someone who had seemed highly compatible a few years earlier but a complete mismatch by the time their husband had been working at the school for a year. The trick, on Dining Hall duty, was to remain busy with the students, avoid the high table, supervise the clean up and get out to the

Owen Room as soon as possible.

The Owen Room (another name of a dastardly catholic saint) was a dining room for single staff members, a place where they could debrief and share a bottle of wine within the confines of bizarrely comforting conservative walls.

A room that attempted to mimic one of those London gentlemen's clubs of the nineteenth century offered a solace so needed at the end of the day to single staff members. A mahogany dining table controlled the space and was surrounded by similarly dark, heavy mahogany sideboards adorned with silver chalices and ornaments, probably plate. Guilt-edged oil paintings reminiscent of some Grecian attainment, which needed an encyclopaedic knowledge of Greek mythology to interpret, hung heavily over the sideboards. One sideboard was stacked with the evening's fare and staff could help themselves to the same food that was served in the Dining Hall but served on Royal Worcester china plates and eaten with silver cutlery on a starched white tablecloth accompanied by starched white napkins and crystal glasses.

At one end of the room was a smallish green baize door which echoed of the butlers and maids of days gone by, but now opened onto a largish cupboard which accommodated staff's individual wine collections. An honesty system meant that all staff contributed to this cellar and so they all enjoyed wines that they may not have chosen for themselves and much conversation ensued about the origins, body and bouquet. Fun times were enjoyed reminiscing on who had bought what and when, providing a veneer of ancient shabby respectability extant amongst the riff-raff of ego, ambition and shiny action. Many an evening there had been spent arguing the merits of Plato and Aristotle, Euclid and Newton, Shakespeare or Jonson. But that was essentially a bygone era, an era when teachers were interested in such concerns.

More recently, there were times when these older single teachers found themselves in alien and unchosen territory when a newer younger more eager single staff member ventured into an exciting discussion of data, assessment, spreadsheets, career ladders and computers, but almost as soon as such vulgarities were mentioned, someone would sup and sip a bit and change the conversation back to such erudite matters as pregnancy images in *Macbeth* or Kant's categorical imperatives or even, god forbid, their understanding of how a student was working through a thought. The younger teacher would bury their face in their pudding, look thoughtless before making a paltry excuse for a quick exit.

As Alice approached the room, she wondered who would be inside. She rather suspected that more of the young would be there and the conversations were more likely to be about the jargon of nothingness: frameworks, study designs, lesson intentions, marketing campaigns and a young teacher's newfound skill on how to greet students as they came into the classroom. The intensity of the tedium gagged in her throat and she was hoping to get in and out of there as soon as she could and just take a laden plate back to her own microwave to avoid the soulless obsequious sycophants.

The busyness of the day and being on duty in the Dining Hall meant that she dragged herself towards a meal a tad later than she normally would. In a sense, she was pleased that she would miss the bright new marketing campaign discussion. The last thing she wanted to listen to was someone's drivel intended to put them on the map of educational excellence.

She had had to put in extra hours due to the unexpected and slightly gruesome demise of Patricia's husband. The House matron had her knickers in a knot, complaining of the lower sixth kitchenette and how, yet again, it had been left in a filthy state, and so an announcement was made that it would be shut down for the three days. The girls had scowled, howled and thought that they were being treated mightily unfairly but then realising that they were dealing with Alice, they shut up. Fiona Jones had lost her sports skirt yet again, she admitted that it was, yet again, unmarked, but if anyone found it – it looked exactly like everyone else's – then could she have it back. Kylie Smith's mother had been on the phone, yet again, complaining that Kylie didn't have any friends and wanted to know what the school was going to do about it. Alice felt like saying that she could start by trying not to complain about everything but actually said that she would make sure that darling Kylie had someone to go to meals with each day in the Dining Hall. There had been a long conversation with TicTac's mother, who only spoke in broken English, about when she could catch a train to London for an orthodontist's appointment. Anna and Jemima had been caught smoking, yet again, behind the dustbin shed – really, didn't they have the imagination to find somewhere more interesting to inhale? And, even more really, why did they have to get caught? It really wasn't that difficult to not get caught. Alice was wondering how to teach them to be more discreet.

But all this was run-of-the-mill compared to the hordes of police that were seen just outside the perimeter of the fence as the investigation started into the death of the wife on the yacht and the swarm of police on the inside of the fence who were investigating the death of a man pinned to his bed by a plaster ceiling.

And so, Alice anticipated a tiresome week. Longer evenings in the boarding house were on the cards, a slight hangover from the night before, an early morning phone call asking her to take over from Patricia and the news that Henry had been killed all compounded her mood. The issue of the publicly masturbating student was not going to go away anytime soon, and many other colleagues now wanted to know the nitty-gritty details of such extraordinary rumpy-pumpy. She needed a bit of quiet time in the Owen Room after her Dining Hall duty, and so when she entered and saw Piers, her heart sank.

Taking up his usual position as self-appointed head of the mahogany table and enveloped, if not cossetted, by the mock Chippendale armed dining chair, Piers was all on his own. The other single staff members had found lots of other things that needed to be done: reports to write, parents to call, cricket teams to be posted, runs to be run and weights to be lifted. Remnants of wine glasses and pudding bowls were strewn on the sideboard ready for the kitchen staff to clear. Piers sat stately and purposefully at the end, a position he had adopted, during term time, for the last sixty-two years. He sported his usual tweed jacket with brown-patched elbows, brown brogues, a Marks and Sparks checked shirt and an ever so slightly too jolly tie. It was a type of uniform that suggested that he might have some ill-defined and baseless substance. His usual spot found him ensconced on red velvet and dark timber, he was part of the furniture, a portly figure with a now pockmarked face under a pretty bald pate but still attempting to hold sway due to his vast knowledge and connections to so many past and present students. He was apparently, someone said, the last of the Hapsburgs. His own lineage could, so he says, be traced back to Albert III with the long hair.

He had arrived at the school as Piers Varkensboer, oddly over the years this name had slowly transmogrified. A sneaky "von" had been added, and by the moment of this narrative, he was known as Piers von Varkensboer Zharingens, a name that amused some, confused others and irritated the rest.

Essentially, he had been an ordinary history teacher and perhaps later than was healthy, he was transferred into Archives. His encyclopaedic knowledge of lineages of self and students since 1642 meant he was the ideal candidate for the job and he now saw his calling to examine all school files and to write a book on all students and staff. There was more than a sniff of sanctimonious patronisation in his attitude towards others as he lauded his seemingly infinite understanding of the machinations and correlating associations buried deep in the school's psyche and its people. Bemused awe of new staff members generally and quickly turned to contrived avoidance of what was essentially worthless for their careers. The more seasoned teachers often goaded but quickly tired of the continuous name-dropping, lineage claiming and connection-making and too often surreptitiously and heartlessly mocked and ridiculed the poor man.

Only the previous week, the Ag teacher, Phil, a smelly, disorganised fellow, who kept a pig on the backseat of his car and rarely undressed to have a shower believing that two washes could be done at once, had had enough of Pier's name-dropping and general snobbery. Bernard, the Physics teacher, another single lonely teacher, who had similarly rooted himself to the school and whose reputation had been built on one single report that he had written thirty years earlier - *Johnny and I have both failed. At least I tried* - was minding his own business whilst focussing on his relationship with a vaguely floating pork chop.

Phil had leant across the mahogany table, wine glass in hand, while ensuring that Piers was within earshot and asked Bernard, "Do you know who I ran into last week?"

Bernard, sensing a set-up was on the cards, pushed the rather large and squidgy pork chop under the withered and slightly metallic tasting red cabbage, and resorted to sniffing and swirling his generous glass of burgundy.

Both men propped a bit, just to check that Piers' ear was opening and waggling. They needn't have bothered; of course, Piers would be listening.

"Toby Fuller-Sheite."

"Who?"

"Toby Fuller-Sheite."

Two other, rather younger shiny, newer teachers eating in the Owen Room that evening saw the wink between Phil and Bernard and smiled.

Piers was busying himself, face down trying to negotiate the congealing fate of his own pork chop.

"You remember, the Fuller-Sheites?"

"Oh yes," an exaggerated furrowed brow from Bernard accentuated the veracity of the memory. "There were a couple of boys and a girl weren't there?"

One of the other two teachers decided to join in

the perhaps not so harmless fun.

"Yeah, what Houses were they in?"

"Um, I think there were a few more than three. Weren't there some cousins? Lots of Fuller-Sheites."

Piers burrowed his head further into the oozing pork, desperately trying to locate the Fuller-Sheites in the vast natural database of past pupils residing in his brain. But nothing popped up, no amount of searching could rustle up a connection; megabites and gigabites aside, this database was not playing ball. Something was disconnected.

"Who, who, who are you talking about?" his quivering voice asked, quietly disguising simmering smouldering aggressive undertones lurking beneath.

"The Fuller-Sheites."

"I, I, I … can't quite place them."

"No, Piers, we're just trying to remember what Houses they were in. Can you remember Piers?"

Piers shook his head in a manner that almost begged for mercy.

"Yes, I remember now, something about their grandmother being a Sheite from somewhere like Bavaria, from a long line of Sheites."

Someone coughed loudly.

"No, no, no … I, I, I …. can't quite place them. But I'm sure that I'd remember if they were from Prussia."

"I'm sure she was. How odd, Piers, that you can't remember them. What else can we say to jog your memory?"

By this time everyone else around the table could remember the Fuller-Sheites only too well.

"The eldest boy was a brilliant cricketer. A beautiful bowler, full of spin. Certainly a Blue and I think, if my memory serves me well, he played a few games for somewhere like Northamptonshire."

"That's right and didn't one of the girls... they were twins those girls..."

"Oh yes twins."

"... end up at Balliol."

"Brasenose, I think."

"Ah yes, you're right."

"Parents were so nice. He was some sort of ambassador, or diplomat, or something in Bermuda."

"Or was it Bahrain?"

By now Piers was tearing at his French beans having pushed his potato lyonnaise from one side of the plate to t'other.

"I don't think you're right. I don't remember them. I would remember them if they went up to Oxford."

He had gone through all the files in his head and had noted those that still lay unopened in boxes in his study and nothing had come to mind.

"Oh Piers. You must. They were part of the fabric of the place ten or fifteen years ago. And the children must've overlapped for at least ten years."

Piers just wanted to leave. He wanted to get back to his flat and go through the files. He wanted to read about the Fuller-Sheites. Find out why he couldn't remember them. Show that he had ongoing contact with such a prestigious family. He wanted to be sure that he had sent them birthday cards and that they were on his Christmas mailout list. He couldn't stand this humiliation. He needed to get back to those files that he was keeping on long loan from the Archives. After all, he was the Head Archivist at 84 years old. But the other teachers just were not going to let him go and they goaded and goaded until he relented.

Scratching that bald pate and screwing up those ruddy, pock-marked cheeks, he said in a slightly higher than normal tone, drawing out those long vowel sounds, "Ayyyyyyy do remember now," and taking a sip of his wine, "Ayyyyy do remember. It's cooooooming baaaaack to me. Now Toby, you said?"

Intense agreement around the table, and not a knife or fork moved.

"Toooobeeee, now heee and Ayyyyyy had aaa veeeery close relaaaationship regarrrrrding the vaaaaluue of Wittgenstein's *Tractatus*. He went on to read philoooooooosooofeee at Lincoln."

"Worcester."

"Thaaat's right, fooorgive me. Wooooster."

"That's all right Piers, at least we've set your memory straight. It was just impossible to believe that you could have forgotten them all. Soooo kind and gentle a family."

"Oh, oh, oh, yes. My memory, it's still good but perhaps not quite as good as it was last year." Another vague mumble into a wine glass. "A fine family, a fine family," and growing with confidence, "and I think my sister's nephew is married to one of the twins." A poke at the pork chop to the other side of the plate, where it mixed with the sloppy apply sauce, "Ay, Ay, Ay must consult my files."

The rest of the staff remained upright, polite and suitably smug as Piers served himself some bread and butter pudding, topping it with ladles of whipped cream and some familiar apple puree. They made stabs at more small talk around such matters as boarding duty and sports rosters while kicking each other under the table.

Phil made the comment that he could never read Pier's writing and Piers definitively told him that this was because his was an educated hand, adding that he really needed to be getting back home as he needed to brush up on his Wittgenstein and that famous poker. He heaved himself out of the grips of the faux Chippendale and shuffled homewards, leaving his plates and glass to the efficiency of the kitchen staff.

As the door closed, the remaining teachers broke out in turmoil, rolling around their chairs, filling up glasses, saying "Cheers" to each other with the odd high five. The man, who was a myth of his own making, had been done again. But that was a secret for the bowels of this school.

On the outside, on the deeply woven veneer, here was a man who was a magnificent teacher, a brilliant mentor, related to the royal families of Europe and highly educated. How many people knew his Cambridge degree was just the teaching diploma and that he came from a long line of pig farmers who had clung to a few acres of pasture in North Norfolk and the farthest he had been from England was Sark? His myth was revered by the old boys and girls and particularly their mothers, all of who found great comfort in the feeling that they may just be close to greatness, happy to revel in the imagination and be a part of the glory. Perhaps willingly duped. Outrageous snobbery and downright lies were forgiven by eccentricity. Most importantly of all, the new Headmistress was completely enamoured by his very presence. Those with a classical education and the odd unstated backgrounds knew better, saying nothing, only smirking when the odd tang of that distinct Norfolk accent graced the odd word when he was under pressure.

Either way, he was a marketer's dream as his sheer mention seemed to be able to generate vast quantities of dough for the school's latest fundraiser (at present a new rabbit enclosure for the Science lab).

And so, Alice's heart really did fall when she found Pier's wrapped, but deserted, in the faux Chippendale. It would mean that she would have to talk about people, she would have to listen to the names and the connections, and she would have to drop her voice and slowdown her speech as though everything had a resonance of meaning far beyond its intention. She couldn't be bothered. Instead of sitting down with a glass of wine and debriefing with her colleagues, as was the point of the Owen Room, she opened the bain-marie, helped herself to a rather flattened piece of leathery lasagne and piled on some lettuce, rocket and cucumber as she politely asked about Pier's day.

She wished she hadn't.

"Well of course, I did have the Vane-Humphries for lunch. Dear old June wasn't able to go to the Queen's Garden Party last year and was so down in the dumps that I suggested that she came to lunch with me in my flat. I sent down to the kitchens for lunch and they brought up sausages. Really, sausages! Do they not know who this person is? So very inappropriate. They must know who June Vane-Humphries is. So, I spent the afternoon, after she had gone, writing to this new Headmistress to say that this really isn't good enough. Guests of this calibre should not be fed the same food as the students and staff..."

Alice didn't hear the rest, or rather, she didn't listen to the petty diatribe. She grunted approval, nodded and smiled at moments she thought she should while collecting a pear from the fruit bowl. The rhubarb crumble looked jolly good but to take some would mean having to listen longer to the drivel.

"I do hope that this new Headmistress responds favourably to your concerns. I suppose, in the end, we're lucky to be fed at all. And really, I'm all for someone who buys the food, cooks it and then washes up the dishes."

It sounded limp, but it was all that she could muster. With this she was able to sneak out, leaving him to wallow in his feelings that things just weren't the same as when he had started at the school sixty-two years earlier.

She took her supper through the campus to her own flat which was on the opposite side of the school to the marina. Her accommodation was closer to a particularly attractive coastal path that acted, at times, as a sea defence but was mainly a reinforced elongated mound that tumbled its way alongside sand dunes and marsh towards an enchanted pine wood.

Her flat was part of a group of buildings that housed mainly married staff. She chose not to mix with most of them. They were essentially at a different time of life to her: thirty to forty years olds, with 2.3 children, a dog, a mortgage on a dogbox in London and a degree in Education. Many of them thought they were on 'good deals' and for them they probably were. Gone were the days where teachers committed to the school for years, became, for better or worse, part of the fabric and taught generations of families. Here was a generation where vaulting ambition, entitlement and transitory relationships were key. They knew everything about how to teach, they could talk in terms of KPIs and 2ICs, plan a lesson to within an inch of its life where every four minutes was precisely mapped, prepare scenarios for interviews and conjure up all their attributes beginning with 'C'. If they ever wrote anything it was in terms of convoluted obfuscation whose circular content, beginning with 'C', ended up where it had started. Alice could rely on them to help out with spreadsheets, Google docs and tables in Word. They committed to the school for two or three years, paid off a bit more of the mortgage and during their second year were looking for their next position. By the time they had secured their next move and it was discovered that they weren't quite as shiny as they had purported, it no longer mattered and they had been promoted to their level of incompetence.

In stark contrast, the students' well-being and thinking was central to the more seasoned teachers. This old order concentrated on bouncing off the students, responding to their questions, letting a lesson find its own way through to a natural conclusion. But this needed experience, an absolute confidence of the requirements of each examining board and a well-worn confidence that could look, to the shiny young ones, like cynicism. Their subject knowledge, their student empathy and their desire to help others were easily married with the passion for their subject and their desire to stay firmly rooted in the classroom. Career ladders, notoriety, cringing creepers were anathema. They were solidly grounded to the longevity of the school.

Two schools of educational thought resided in Alice's block of flats. Karin, of our Bridge club fame, also had a flat in the same complex, and she and Alice were part of the very unfashionable old order, an order where the student came first.

On the way home, Alice passed the walking Headmistress.

Floating, shiny black wide eyes fixed unblinkingly ahead, piercing the air through the cracking foundation and that purply-lipstick, she seemed barely able to utter a "Good evening," let alone, "What a lovely evening for a walk."

She appeared, to Alice, fairly intent on a task, focused on something hovering in front of her, and small talk to small fry was certainly not on her agenda. After all, where would this have got her on her career ladder? And a stellar career it had been thus far.

Graduating young as a Bachelor of Education from Great Yarmouth University, apparently attaining the dizzying heights of a First from this institution, had flung her into her first state school back in her hometown of Bury. Somewhere up there, in the depths of former prime mining country, this erstwhile Buryite had found a southern accent and ambition. Buoyed along by another female colleague who had suggested that she had immense potential, she ventured onto the high seas in pursuit of career and money in Education.

She applied for, and was appointed to, her first Head of Department position at the ripe old age of 27, her considerable experience recognised by a school struggling to find staff. She headed this Physical Education Department with the acting skills of a graduate from the London School of Music and Dramatic Arts, the clutching at the breast, the wave of the hair, the make-up, the square smile and gleaming teeth that all came and went in an instant, the language of hyperbole.

This was just the beginning of a meteoric career. The next ten years saw her bob from school to school, all within yards of the water, and the possibilities of advancement beckoned just over the horizon between sea and clouds. As Head of Department she had embellished her CV with tales of prowess in winning knife-edge netball games and underdog hockey tournaments. Moving to her next job saw her CV burgeon with stories of how she inspired students to achieve quite remarkable resilience through a programme entitled *Creativity for All* which mysteriously aligned with her myriad of work for lesser known charities, The Society for the Protection of the Essex Hedgehog and Voices for Liverwort Propagation, and thus she was enabled to move incandescently coldly up that tantalising career ladder. Here was a human beyond humans.

By 29, she had a job back near her old stomping ground on the coast of Yorkshire as a Headmistress of a very, very small girl's school which catered for, and that's probably a bit of an exaggeration, the very middle-class daughters of mining meritocracy, a day school of perhaps 200 with a smattering of boarders, from Derbyshire, Lancashire and the far-flung corners of Northumberland. The school hugged that rugged coast so hard to ensure that it was secure on its hill above the grey rocky beach and sufficiently close to a grey, stone harbour where North Sea fishermen would sort their haul before heading off into one of the four pubs on the harbour walls. A sprinkling of visiting yachts would sometimes float through the harbour walls hoping to restock before taking off around Scotland for the summer or heading south for the channel, even perhaps the Med, for winter. It was a dark northern town where vampires could abound and gravestones in the graveyards dated back to the sixteenth century.

As head of this school, and very much her first headship, she discovered the loneliness of rising to such dizzying heights. Gone was the ability to mix in the Common Rooms and share excitements and disappointments with fellow staff members. Not that she had any disappointments; after all, hers was a stellar career. Here she was alone and would often take a brisk walk along the coast path and into the town, sitting on the grey, stone wall to watch the comings and goings in the harbour. She felt that she was communing and this was a good thing to do. Here she was not in the deep end as she had yet to get into the swimming pool. Her northern accent sometimes returned when she least expected it despite those horribly expensive elocution lessons in London. Convinced that the accent mattered, this annoyed her, and she practised her articulation in the mirror while putting on that lippy.

Two years at this tiny school served its purpose and was perhaps the most she could push the veneer of verisimilitude before the bubble popped and so she presented a ballooning CV to her agent. Feats of introducing such innovative initiatives as that old chestnut inquiry-based learning and Japanese were sold on to her next position; a headship on the west coast of Wales. This monolith of a school which inhabited what felt like the remnants of a medieval fort, was, in fact, a Victorian reproduction as only the Victorians could do. It was a cold cavernous grey stone monstrosity and it was a long way from London which meant that its clientele tended to come from abroad, a co-educational melange of 350 Germans, Russians, Chinese and the odd Thai and one Korean. The parents of the students were generally searching, in Wales, for the key to unlock how to do business in the English style. A reproduction fortified castle or a castellated fort marketed on the website seemed to hint that this was the real deal. The school teetered on the top of a cliff, almost threatening to slide down and float westwards towards Dublin; towards another promise.

Below her office, this former head of a small girls' boarding school in East Yorkshire, could see, in the sheltered cove beneath, a small fleet of fishing boats which had barely changed since the building of the faux fort, a rag tag fleet that boasted rust and nets, swivels and drivers and was in sore need of a good paint job. Alongside this arguably idyllic form of years gone by would sometimes glide a swanky yacht which seemed to have either found itself lost or was wanting to be lost in the solitude of outer Wales. A peaceful setting where strangers were noticed and everyone knew everyone's business.

The two-year rule didn't hold quite as fast out in the boondocks on the west coast and our illustrious Headmistress managed to maintain an air of competence for three years. Perhaps because many of the clientele only had smatterings of the vernacular, perhaps because they believed that this was how the English generally carried themselves or probably because they all lived so far away, few questions were asked. The students were happy and really that was all that mattered. The generally Welsh workforce was just pleased to have a job close to home and staff turnover was minimal.

But ambition is rarely happy just to bubble under the surface and after three years she had raked up that CV and added a bit more about the introduction of a programme with the dubious and presumably educationally self-evident title of *Wellbeing for All.*

Single-handedly, her CV claimed, she had created the idea that everyone was entitled to feel well, and had thus devoted her life to this mission, indeed, this calling of spreading wellbeing throughout the world. She had encouraged staff to attend lectures and workshops ad infinitum about the benefit of psychological health, created schemes of work for students to address their wellbeing and had, all on her own, miraculously and quite strategically, saved the lot of 'em.

As this mission approached its natural conclusion, she weighed anchor and sailed forth to another school of equally dubious notoriety and foundations on the south-east coast of England. She appeared to be weaving her way across the kingdom rather as Mark describes Jesus weaving his way to and fro across the Sea of Galilee.

On the south-east coast, she managed another three years where she continued to wax lyrical about the benefits of considering one's own wellbeing. The ego was central. Gratitude was fine. Savouring was all. There was an odd mention of doing things for others. Anyone who questioned was demoted, sacked or given such a bad teaching load that they chose to leave.

After two years she already had her name with an agent in Melton Mowbray, a mob who had invested much in making slim-pickings on CVs look like momentous achievements – a workshop where students ate chocolate squares and tried to hold them in their mouths for as long as possible became a dissertation on how to savour things in one's life as a means to flourishing.

It was all about the tricky mindset. You know the one: the oxymoronic 'growth mindset' or the tautological 'fixed mindset'. Of course, everyone knows you have to have a growth mindset to flourish in this world. And she sure did know this. She was going to grow her career and within months, the Melton Mowbray agent had found a job, constructed the CV, given her a bit of coaching and got her to a second interview and then an offer of headship at this exceptional school on the south coast. She returned to the elocution school and tweaked her accent but did not adopt the Barack Obama style of delivery that so many other Heads were mimicking, preferring her own first person singular, anecdotal mode to impress.

By the time this paean of education was the ripe old age of 38 she was heading to one of the finest schools in the empire. She knew it. She was going somewhere. And that evening, when Alice passed her during her evening walk, she was certainly going somewhere.

Alice clutched her plate of congealing lasagne and had one of those feelings of slight embarrassment – you know the time when you walk into a lamppost – a slight awkwardness and a hope that nobody had seen their interaction: her cheerful "Good evening" roundly snubbed by her Headmistress. She got home to her cold flat, put some coins into the heater, put the plate in the microwave for a minute, poured herself a glass of pinot and sat in front of *Would I Lie to You?* with her supper on her lap. She breathed a sigh of relief.

The beauty of the loneliness. Two glasses later, and none the wiser of the psychology of a liar, she was quietly dozing on the sofa with not much of the lasagne touched when she became aware of the dulcet sounds of sirens. Rationally, she thought she was dreaming, reliving the events of the evening before. Her imagination was rife with sirens, those at the marina and then thoughts of those at Patricia and Henry's house. But as the noise became increasingly insistent, she lifted herself out of her semi-conscious slumber, felt for the remote to turn down the volume and moved towards the window. The siren was neither in her head nor coming from the telly.

It was coming from the lane leading to the Owen Room.

4. THREE HEARTS

Word got around that evening. By thirteen minutes past ten, few staff members living at school, and many that didn't, did not know that Piers had been found face down in his bowl of rhubarb crumble and custard. Posing, a bit like a question mark, at the end of the mahogany table, he had clearly been hit rather hard on the back of the head by one of the silver-plated candlesticks. The imprint of the blow could just be made out as the blood seeped from the remnant of his bald pate.

There had been some discussion earlier in the evening within the bowels of the kitchen as to who would work the early breakfast shift the next morning. A discussion had turned into an argument that gathered legs and the most seasoned kitchenhand, the one who always cleaned the Owen Room, stormed off, leaving a young naive and bewildered trainee dishwasher elevated to the dizzying heights of Owen Room Cleaner. This had meant that the task for this evening in our story was performed perhaps half an hour later than normal. Our young recruit had taken instructions from her manager, pushed the rattly old aluminium trolley through the doorway, bumping both doorjambs firmly and had started to clear up the detritus of the staff's dinner.

At first, she had thought that the old man propped in that old-fashioned chair might have just gone to sleep. After all, that's what an 84 year old man is inclined to do after a good wedge of lasagne, a solid helping of rhubarb and custard, a generous dollop of whipped cream and half a bottle of a heavy Australian Shiraz. She had rattled around stacking plates, glasses, knives and forks for some time but to no avail. He did not seem to be stirring and our cleaner remembered her own deceased grandpa who always started to snore, having dropped off at the end of a particularly wholesome north country meal. But she could hear not a squeak from that throat nor nose.

She called out "Sir" gently, a couple of times and tried to pull the heavily starched white napkin from under his resting hand. She called again and eventually did what one should not do in a modern workplace - she nudged his arm to wake him. At this point his head rolled out of the bowl onto the table and proceeded to unweight the body, firstly slumping between chair and table and then dropping with a thud onto the red carpet. It wasn't until this point that she saw the seeping red raw wound oozing blood from the back of his head. And so, it was also, at this point, that she ran screaming back into the bowels of the kitchens to find her manager. This, at least, is what she remembered to tell the police an hour later and this was the last time that she ever worked in a kitchen.

Gary and Frank put down the packet of custard

creams when the call came through from the kitchen manager. Heaving themselves out of their routine, they waddled and wiggled across to the Owen Room, saw the scene, had become accustomed to death and rang the police. Let's not go through another set of police and paramedic antics but suffice it to say, that within an hour and a half, one more burgeoning body bag was hauled into the ambulance, a different set of paramedics, a different set of police, but the same set of school security guards who felt that the sky was about to fall on their heads, they were so under the pump.

The room was cordoned off with those plastic tapes which sort of remind one of bunting and party-time and the airways were soon ringing hot as word got around that things were getting ever so slightly out of control.

****

The distraught Headmistress did not wait until the morning break the next day to talk to the staff. An email sent around summoned all to the Common Room before classes started. Sometime in the interim, between the revelation of Piers' murder and her fronting the staff, yet again, this doyenne of educational excellence must have wondered what she had inherited. Three deaths in two days must have felt a little overwhelming. There was probably little in her degree in Physical Education for Teaching that would have laid the foundations for this scenario. Did she feel that she needed to put on a brave face? Did she feel that she could show fragility, shock even? Perhaps she saw this as an opportunity. The most cynical could easily see that there was much to be made from the decease of a myth. His demise would, if handled correctly, put many more bums on seats and shekels in the coffers.

Many sitting in the Common Room before class that morning wondered where she would position herself as, yet again, this protégé of ambition and model of education found herself at the centre of her own announcement and her kinship with a kindred spirit.

"Thank you all for coming," a rove of the room, an extra layer of foundation with a blood-red lipstick. That wayward bottle-blonde, almost white, lock fell back over half of her left eye and that enormous rectangular smile against the one stubbornly seeping tear and the hand on the heart provided an idiosyncratic moment that could be difficult to forget. "I can feel my heart thumping in my chest..."

One bright spark quietly whispered to those around him, "Perhaps she should see a doctor.

"Wouldn't want that ambulance back again."

"Take two," murmured another.

"Even déjà vu."

"Always good to have a rehearsal before the main performance," whispered one more.

That hand again wavered, slowly but purposefully, just taking in the moment, from mobile to breast, "...I am afraid to say that I have more disturbing news." The wide bright unblinking roving eye surveyed the room, staring through a dramatic pause, waiting for those in the room to process, moving through to the adoption of the persona of a grieving soul; perhaps she had done method acting at that elocution school. The bottom lip quivered as the eyes, now sufficiently and nicely welling, almost had a Bertha in the attic moment.

"It is so disturbing because of my very close relationship with Piers. He was a man whom I'd gotten very close to. I admired his considerable intellect and I cannot imagine my life without having known him on such an intellectually intimate level."

There were murmurings around the room. Slight shufflings, some thought that she'd better get on and say what had happened, most already knew, and really few were at all moved or perturbed by the news.

"And so, it is with great sadness," she referred to her phone, "that I have to inform you that Piers," another pause, an intake of breath, a tiny seep below the bottom left eyelid, "was found dead in the Owen Room just after supper last night."

There was no intake of breath, no tears; no one felt the need to lean over to their neighbour for that human touch on the forearm or shoulder. Some looked at their watches wondering whether they would be late for class, others continued to swipe right and others swilled around the last of the tea leaves in their cups pondering their futures.

"There will, of course, be a lot of police around again today. As many of you have already found out at breakfast, the crime scene has been cordoned off and we ask all staff to eat in the Dining Room for the foreseeable future."

For a brief moment she lost that feigned horror and sorrow in her efficiency, and quickly remembering her need for sanctimonious saccharinity she chameleonlike tilted herself back into the first person singular.

"I will, of course, be talking with the press, the Old Boys' and Girls' Association, and the police."

She stopped, and somehow her tone changed, perhaps, almost imperceptibly becoming a little higher.

"The police have already asked for anyone who saw anything around the Owen Room in the early hours of yesterday evening to come forward. I will also be talking with the Marketing Department about funeral arrangements. I will keep you informed as we proceed." The stunned silence in the room was not generated by the news but more by the cold, dispassionate tone of its delivery, a tone that no amount of acting could camouflage.

It was again Stephanie who raised her hand, "Can I just ask, or perhaps can I make a comment?"

The Headmistress nodded.

"I think word had already got around, and most of us knew that he had died. Are you suggesting, when you said 'crime scene', that he was murdered?"

"Yes. Hit on the back of the head with a candlestick."

With that she was gone.

And with that, the staff rose from their chairs, now a little more unsettled than they had anticipated. There was a clear difference between the natural death of a rather harmless, albeit boring, 84 year old snob and the murder of a tedious, money-making myth. In that brief moment, the staff knew that their world had changed. A world of process and function had replaced a world of community and humanity. Some felt awkward about leaving others and going to class. They wanted time to share their feelings where that rug of certainty had been very ceremoniously pulled from beneath them but duty of care had to be maintained, classes needed to be attended.

Amidst the melee of chatter and gossip, the

Bridge group managed to gather to touch base with each other to ensure that they were all on for a game that evening. After all, three deaths in two days, there was much to talk about. Someone in their group must know something. Around the cards on the table would be much thought of purpose and passion.

****

Bridge that evening was at Kerin's house. Clever planning in a previous era meant that her flat was attached to a boys' boarding house. Living in such close proximity made her constantly aware of the vagaries and fripperies involved in the activities of teenage boys living together in very close quarters. Her sitting room had a connecting door to their common room and her whole house was fitted with their bells and alarms. It meant that smoking in her house was more difficult and the odd fag had to be taken behind a small brick wall in the garden which was the only nook or cranny where the smoker could remain out of sight, but maybe not smell, of the boys.

And so, it was in this cranny that we find Alice and Adrienne this evening. They had arrived early for Bridge, armed with the normal wine and cheese platter, and a couple of joints. Adrienne's husband grew the stuff in a small but highly efficient greenhouse in the garden at their home a couple of villages down the coast. It was good light stuff and he mixed it with a soft flowery essence which tasted refreshing as the smoke hit the sides and back of the tongue and inveigled its way to some sacred place between the eyes. Retired and resigned, Adrienne was in no danger of flaunting school rules and Alice had given her last fuck about six months earlier and was looking for opportunities elsewhere. They hadn't seen each other for a couple of days and the interim events posed much to ponder.

"So, what's the goss?" Adrienne drew in a big breath and looked at the end of the joint in admiration. "Ed's made a good one here," she nodded her appreciation with a bit of a wave of the hand to direct the smoke away from the closest window of a boy's study. The theory was that even if the boys did smell anything, they wouldn't know what it was because they were all on synthetic stuff now. This crop was good old-fashioned top grade organic.

"Who knows?" Alice took over the toke. "So many theories."

"Three in a week."

"Three in a couple of days."

"Could be a coincidence."

"Could be," Alice held her lungs and then sighed, gently, "Yeah that's good stuff. Say thanks to Ed. Just what I need. Softly relaxing."

"Poor Patricia. She okay?"

"Doubt it. Who'd know? She's just disappeared."

"Who'd kill Henry?"

"Well, no one really did. Ceiling just fell in."

"Coincidence."

"Too right." Alice thought awhile. "Are you suggesting that someone was in the ceiling and at the right moment gave it one hell of a thump so that it fell down and killed him?"

"Or a coincidence?" Adrienne shrugged, "Three."

"Three deaths."

"There'd be better ways of killing someone than

getting a fucking great lump of plaster to fall on him. That's not exactly a certainty."

"S'pose not."

"Not like a candlestick to the back of the head, or a fucking great fire."

"S'pose not."

"D'you think Henry knew something?"

"More like Piers did."

"What would Henry know?"

"I'm just saying that it's odd that three go in two days, and all within two hundred yards of each other."

"Yeah, I know, I know. I get what you are saying. I think most people are more focused on poor Patricia. And frankly, I've had to take over the running of the House and that could be more long term than I want. Who wants to be continually sober in this place for chrissakes?"

"Oh, come on. A bit of humanity."

"Yeah, right." Alice took the toke. "A bit morose moaning too much? Yeah, I get it. I don't really mean it, we're all just a bit discombobulated. Anyhow, I go back to my point. How on earth would someone orchestrate the falling of a ceiling just at the right time to kill someone?"

They could hear voices inside. Peter and Robert had arrived with Stephanie not far behind them. The sounds of chinking glasses and crisps being tipped into bowls filtered through to their cranny and they could hear a parallel conversation.

"All three."

"Three ... things come in threes."

"Anyone know anyone who's spoken to the police?"

"Alice."

"Alice!" the other three chimed together.

"Why?"

"They think she was the last person to see Piers alive."

"You're kidding."

"Nope."

"For real?"

"Was she?"

Lots of serious nodding.

"Well, what did she say?"

"What does she know?"

"Did she see anything?"

"Anyone?"

"Alice!" Karin called into the little courtyard. Partly to summon them to start playing but mainly to hear as much goss as possible.

Adrienne and Alice stubbed out the joint and left it on a small ledge to which they knew they would return when it was their turn to sit out. Feeling clearly calmingly light-headed, they joined the group.

Karin had set out the glasses and bowls with scientific precision, after all she was a Biology teacher. Her house was a cornucopia of paraphernalia from her travels. The crisps were already in a bowl from Jaipur, the cheese on a Florentine platter and Adrienne's perennial guacamole dip, with arguably too little chilli, shone from an Indonesian cup. Wooden objets d'art, colourful ceramic bowls, pictures of interpretations of mountains, rivers and sunsets adorned the walls and Lonely Planet guides were stacked upon themselves on a bookshelf.

Twenty years earlier Karin had made a pact with herself to visit as many countries as her age. She had, by 35, easily exceeded this goal and was heading for doubling, if not tripling the figure. Now at aged 45, this meant 135 countries, and it was getting harder and harder to find suitable countries for a single, female traveller. Too dangerous, too remote, too religious or just plainly too dull. Could Goa be considered a country? Would the Andaman Islands count? Was Cyprus one country or two? Did she really want to go to Uzbekistan? But as we know things come in threes and so the aim remained, and this Easter she was off to Latvia, Estonia and Lithuania. On her travels she spent much of the time either photographing or eating - preferably both - snapping plates of food and posting them on Instagram to the envy of some and confusion of others. Karin was typical of the single teachers at the school, substituting a relationship with a significant other for a relationship with trains, planes and automobiles. It meant that she seemed to be constantly packing or unpacking, knew the train timetable to the airport by heart and had worked out the exact amount of alcohol needed to sleep in a long-haul economy class seat.

Over the twenty odd years that she had been at the school, she had learnt how to fly under the radar. In a precise, ordered and unassuming manner she just got on with her job and managed to stay out of the way of the litany of half-baked administrators and managers who came in with those shiny new ideas to turn the place on its head, and who were looking for jobs within eighteen months of their arrival. Somehow, she managed to stay on the right side of many of these young up and coming educators who knew best and whose career trajectories travelled in a mercurial fashion across the nebulous miasma of exceptional education. They invented programmes on strategic pillars whose substance floated somewhere in that space of befuddling marketing and eduspeak, its dust settling nowhere as they moved on up the ladder across PowerPoint pages full of floating triangles and twirling cones filled with keywords usually beginning with "C". They were clearly moving to better spaces, improving outcomes all along and bemoaning how education could have possibly been effective before their arrival.

Karin was politic and smiled sweetly at these charlatans and cavaliers of education whose careers rested on the ability to sell vacuous programmes to schools using the language of glossy websites. She would smile, nod and retreat into her classroom, closing the door firmly behind her and get on with the business of teaching: asking students to think and question. She taught them what they needed to know. She was a watcher, a clandestine doer. She was a survivor.

Alice and Adrienne joined the group around the table and poured themselves just a little more of the cheap and cheerful Lidl wine. Peter was the most interested to find out about Piers' demise, perhaps because he was now the most emotionally invested in the place. As an old boy of the school, he had been taught, albeit badly, by Piers, and he had a certain kind of fondness for the old boy. Somehow the affection felt by the old boys had that mythical quality that just wasn't shared by the rest of the staff. Peter could remember that deference, the low, slow voice that delivered not much in a tone that suggested everything, that slowing of the expression that intimated some sort of sanctity in every syllable, so that the whole sentence felt like it perhaps belonged in heaven. Staff cringed at the sanctimonious intent, students worshipped the air that carried the myth, mothers moaned their admiration and headmasters milked it for every penny they could. Unsurprisingly, Peter, despite the years, still held fast to his teenage conception of the man.

"So how was Piers when you saw him?" Peter asked Alice, "Did you have to talk to the police? Who else was around?"

Alice tried to respond but the questions kept firing.

"How long after you saw him was he killed?"
"Did you talk to him?"
"When did you see him exactly?"

The litany of questions perhaps reflected the emotion, perhaps reflected a type of factual mind.

Alice chose one to answer, "Yeah."
"What?"

With a shrug of the shoulders, "I just told them it was a general, run-of-the-mill evening." Waving a bit of guacamole on a biscuit, "I mean there he was in his usual place, at the end of the table, eating. I think it was apple and custard that evening for pudding. Not particularly chatty but I didn't want to chat. Took my meal and left. Nothing not normal really."

Alice was naturally reclusive and rarely was in need of a chat; in fact, quite the opposite of Karin. She had come to teaching in a rather circuitry fashion and indeed had fallen into it as a sort of last resort. She had, after all done all the right things for her station in life having been sent to a girls' boarding school in the Home Counties from her home in the depths of Norfolk at the age of eleven. The school prided itself on teaching the girls how to sew, to cook and to use the future tense in French. Piano lessons and deportment were part of the curriculum and hockey sticks sometimes got a workout.

Alice had sewn a pair of lime green pyjamas for her younger brother who had kindly taken them to his boarding school and spent the rest of the term in underpants when they fell apart on the second night. Her displeasure with the irritating nuns saw her put salt in a cake for their pudding and by the time she had told one nun that she didn't believe in God with a capital "G", her parents rather felt there seemed little point in her staying at the school beyond seventeen. They removed her before she was expelled and sent her to a secretarial college in Kensington High Street.

London was an extension of the school milieu and Alice had donned the de rigeur twinset and pearls and created an account at Peter Jones. Within three months of moving to London and living with a rather dour single aunt, she had chummed up with two other girls and moved into a flat with them in Pimlico. Together they ranged London while trying to stay awake during the grotesque shorthand and typing classes that seemed interminable.

At the end of the year she found a job at a theatrical agency and spent a couple of years arranging contracts for significant productions in the West End. Her job did tend to be a bit of a blight in her diary and she spent weekends at house parties, in the summer sailing and playing golf and in the winter shooting and beagling. There were the couple of skiing holidays to Verbier or Zermatt and of course the fortnight on a Greek island.

It was on one of the Verbier jaunts that Alice met Charles, a jolly jovial chap with a weird shaped cock. Within days he had bedded her; within weeks he had proposed. His parents' rundown manor house in Hertfordshire, his job as an account exec. in a trendy advertising agency, and his apparently bottomless pockets were really quite an attraction. Alice thought for a while; after all there was one drawback. But in the end, the pluses outweighed the minuses.

Two children later and still only twenty-six, Alice thought she was quite content in their Holland Park abode with quite an acceptable social life. But things changed one afternoon in Zermatt when Charles was trampled by a wayward horse that had broken free from its carriage. No romantic skiing accident end for him just a few hoof marks on the head and a flight in a box back to Gatwick. As she was leaving a policewoman returned to her Charles' wallet which had been on him at the time.

It wasn't until after the funeral, after the wake, after all the small talk about how awful it all was, that Alice found the wallet under a pile of clothes and she opened it. For a moment she was a little confused; after all, she was on the pill, why would her husband be carrying a couple of condoms for weird-shaped cocks in his wallet? Lots of unformed thoughts from the past few years fell into place and if she wasn't that sad before she opened the wallet then she was much less so after and she felt almost buoyant as she skipped towards the solicitors to find out how much she would have to play with from his will.

Nothing. His generosity had been just that. Founded on nothing. He had spent more than he had. The house would have to go. There were no shares and the rundown manor in Hertfordshire still belonged to his parents.

A rethink found Alice returning to her parents' house in Norfolk, this time trailing two children under five. A gin and tonic before roast beef and Yorkshire pudding saw a family conversation steer towards the future. As the red wine in the bottle diminished, a plan arose. Alice wanted, as a mature student, to study English at university and become an English teacher. Her mother wondered why and shook her head over the lemon meringue pie, hoping that perhaps another suitor would magically appear from the gun cabinet, and that she really wouldn't have to look after her grandchildren. Her father thought that it would be fun and that he could teach them to shoot, sail, fish, play golf. The children slept and she enrolled in the University of East Anglia.

Spending a few years in local schools to cut her teeth and for her mother to help with the children was about as far as she could go and as soon as the children were ready for secondary education, she took a job in this shabby chic school which is the subject of our tale.

It was a constant wonder to Alice as to why teaching was so difficult for so many. So many meetings to discuss ideas that had been discussed for thousands of years. The staff room bored her. The classroom excited her. The older she had become the less patience she had with those teachers who advanced their careers through the weasel words of eduspeak, those who talked in terms of aggregated and moderated marks on spreadsheets, of comparable units of shared work on platforms, of worksheets and modules, of evidence-based data. This concrete evidence that a teacher was doing something was of little relevance compared to the very abstract ability of getting a student to think. She ducked and dived between new fangled ideas such as enquiry-based learning that had come full circle three times in her career. Each time she found it more and more difficult to look surprised when another shiny new teacher felt the need to enlighten her by telling her that the best way to get a student to think was by asking questions. Alice was indeed, one of those silent, perhaps sullen teachers in the staffroom. It was, she felt, safer to remain silent and she saw herself as a sceptic not a cynic but most of the teachers she despised would not know the difference.

"Was anyone else around?"

"Not that I saw. As I said, I just grabbed a bowl of food to take home to the dog."

"I thought it was rhubarb and cream last night."

"Was it? Whatever."

"Did the police ask much?"

"Not much really. I just told them that I'd gone into the Owen Room and basically walked out straightaway as I didn't want to listen to him. I'd done Dining Hall duty, and was just pigged off 'cos it was pea and rice night, so the stuff was everywhere. Really didn't want to listen to his shit. And then too much work going on in the House now, what with Patricia away and dealing with girls who have suddenly revealed how close they were with Henry." Another dip in the guacamole, "I never get that about women. All these issues."

"What? Issues?"

"Oh, you know."

Alice felt like she needed to redirect the conversation and she was less inclined to be careful this particular evening; after all, she knew that however motley this group was, they were all pals and they would firstly forgive and secondly not gossip. But she also knew that this was not the time to tell them about the afternoon that she had just had. The afternoon where she had had to talk to the masturbator and the masturbator's mother about a way forward. Her plan had been to put the masturbator in a room on her own with the explanation to the students, and their mothers, that she was such a heavy snorer and was disturbing the sleep of others in the dormitory. Snorer not masturbator was the plan.

Without Patricia there, and with another much younger tutor taking notes, she had been more than normally anxious about talking to a parent. The thoroughly modern tutor had come armed with a laptop and had proceeded to open a document, title it *Masturbation* and then insert a table headed date, incident, further action. Alice had spied the notes in the corner of her eye and her imagination ran wild. A slight smirk on her face covered the laughter in her mind but the sense of ridiculous and underlying humour was lost on the very serious tutor who was more focused on using this incident in her CV. Here was a real life scenario that she could use in her next interview.

They had called the wanking girl into the office and while the tutor took notes, Alice had spoken, choosing her words particularly carefully.

"Now Jessica, thank you for coming and chatting with us." The tap tapping of the tutor's scurrying note taking polluted the background.

"I'm wondering whether you are aware of why we might have asked you to come and have a chat with us?"

Jessica sat, very crossed-legged, with her fingers slotted just between her two thighs. Alice's head was cocked as thoughts charged between one ear and t'other. Jessica looked somewhat quizzically at both adults, tilted her head, furrowed her eyebrows, pursed her lips and purposefully and slowly shook her head. Time seemed to be slowing.

Alice continued, "Well, we've been hearing a few concerns from a few of your peers who are worried for you."

"Uh!" Her eyebrows raised towards her heavily straightened bang.

"I'm fine."

"Um." This was going to be tricky. "It's to do with your actions in the dormitory."

Those fingers between the thighs shifted and wriggled ever so slightly and eyes stared straight at Alice's. Alice wondered whether it was just better to ask her outright and then they would essentially be at the finishing line or whether to keep skirting around the issue with some sort of sense of Victorian decorum.

She kept skirting, "Perhaps you may have some sort of inkling, idea of what they may be concerned with?" She slightly squirmed because of the grammatically incorrect sentence structure she was struggling into articulation.

Another shake of the head.

"Some of your behaviours, particularly in the dormitory, are making other girls feel uncomfortable."

Alice was careful to extract any adverbs or adjectives that might, ever so slightly, imply a bias or prejudice in favour of one party or the other, and she didn't trust the younger tutor by her side to take them out should she ever so slightly slip up. Perhaps she thought, rather too late, she should have consulted one of her superiors before she had this conversation. Finding the words was difficult. Clearly 'wanking' was out, as was 'jacking off' but was 'masturbation' or 'self-satisfaction' fine? Perhaps, just 'pleasing yourself' was less confronting. Alice wasn't one to think too much about other people, she just wanted to avoid being in the dock with a brilliant opposing barrister.

She persisted with a slight clearing of the throat, "I'll just put it out there, and this is not intended to be awkward. They are saying that you are masturbating in the dormitory."

A silence while the dust settled on this suggestion. Alice inwardly panicked for a nano second as her brain scanned through thirty years' worth of awkward moments, moments where words and intentions had been misinterpreted, moments when a student, or more likely a parent, or another ambitious teacher, had just been waiting for a wrong turn, when words had purposely been misquoted. Thoughts arose of suspension for the accusation, reports to unions, court cases, comments on the internet, the whole gambit that teachers navigate as they try to care for students. She had let the cat out of the bag with this one and she couldn't now put it back in. The tutor's tap tapping became increasingly intense as the climax of the issue had been reached and the clear record of it had been saved.

"Oh yes."

Jessica's eyes became plates of deep brown innocence and the young tutor's tapping relaxed and stopped.

Jessica nodded, her fingers squirmed a tad and she just shook her head. "They're wrong."

"Thank you for considering this matter. Wrong? Can you tell me why from your perspective they might think this?"

"They're just wrong."

"Why do you think they may say something like

this? Let's be clear, it is unusual."

"Maybe they hate me."

"That's a strong word to use. Why may they dislike you?"

The tap tapping restarted at a gentler intensity. "Jealous?"

Jessica withdrew one of her hands from between her thighs and gesticulated in some Oscar Wilde fashion towards the door. For what reason, Alice couldn't fathom and ignored the act.

"Jealous?"

"'Cos I've got a boyfriend."

"Ah!" There was a bit of a pause as Alice tried to link the three matters: masturbation, teenage girls and boyfriends. The links just weren't that strong in her older, jaded adult mind. The pause was just a bit too long and the young tutor came through with the goods.

"So, you are saying that you masturbate because the other girls are jealous that you have a boyfriend?" A pause while she caught up with herself on the keyboard, "Sort of like, this is what I do with him?"

"What?" Jessica looked confused.

Alice raised her eyebrows to cover another smirk, "So you masturbate in the dormitory?"

"No."

Confusion set in. Alice thought that they had better rewind and clarify.

"Let's take this back."

"Do you know what it means to masturbate."

"My English teacher is always telling me to stop masturbating in class."

"Really..."

Both Alice and the tutor looked rather taken

aback.

"And what are you doing in class when your English teacher says this?"

"Chewing gum. She says I look like an old cow in a field and tells me to spit it in the bin. Rude, I think."

"Aaaaaah," Alice could barely suppress a laugh. And the moment seemed to lighten and gave her the entry she needed.

"Do you know what wanking means?"

"Of course. I don't do that in class." Jessica was very certain of this.

"I don't suspect you do. But, perhaps, you do this under the blankets in the dormitory."

"Not always; sometimes I don't have the blankets over me."

The turnaround was complete and now it seemed like it would be a mere gentle caress towards a resolution. Alice wished Patricia could have been there for this watershed of comedy and the moment of release. The humour that had to been contained within her was tempered by the seriousness of the ambitions of the young tutor and the thought of having to have a rather awkward discussion with Jessica's parents to explain future plans.

"Right," Alice started, somewhat gingerly. "Riiight ..." and she slowed her words and lowered her tone and felt rather like Piers. "Do you understand why other girls might find this all a bit uncomfortable?"

Jessica shook her head.

Alice was searching for words and expression, "Do you see other girls acting like this?"

More head shaking.

"Okay. Riiiight. Well of course, they probably do, but in private. There is absolutely nothing wrong with doing it, but we really don't want you to do it in public. It is a most private affaire, something that you do between yourself and you."

She paused, realising the idiocy of that last comment but then wondered if Jessica had even heard it. She wondered about what was going on inside the head of this girl sitting opposite, twiddling her fingers between her legs who was apparently jerking herself off in this most private of moments 28 times a day. She thought this fact could perhaps come later, if at all.

"But we do in Cardiff."

"What?"

"We do in Cardiff. All my friends do it."

"Are you saying that the Welsh wank freely?"

"Oh yes."

There was little else to respond to this than, "Well the English don't. And that's that." Short and to the point. "Can I ask you not to do this when you are in England?"

Everyone shifted ever so slightly, and Alice thought that she might be on culturally sticky ground and wondered how she had got herself to yet another ridiculous comment. She may have to address this again later and she came back to the present.

"Now then, you realise that I will need to talk to your mother about this matter?"

Jessica was an only child and her mother was on her own. On Jessica's arrival at the school, an arrival, as we know that was fairly circumspect considering it was in the middle of the year, her mother had told Patricia all the intimate details of her failed marriage and her husband's predilection for younger models. It was a story that both Patricia and Alice had heard over and over before. A spurned wife left holding the child whilst watching the spoils of marriage descend on the trophy wife and the teenage daughter. She had left London and found a job in Cardiff where she could find time to breathe before re-introducing herself to the London lot and presumably finding another husband. Wounds take time to lick and heal and much easier to do this without the burden of a teenage daughter who would clearly be far happier in a boarding school closer to London. The thought of having to add to this burden Alice felt was an unpleasant necessity. Jessica nodded and uncrossed her legs. Withdrawing the only hand left on her thighs, she rose, thanked the teachers and left.

If Patricia had been there, one of them would have immediately jumped up, shut the door and they would have both started laughing fairly uncontrollably at the idiosyncrasy of the whole occasion. They would have ended up in Patricia's kitchen drinking gins, aperol spritz or sangrias while girding Patricia's loins for the talk with the masturbator's mother.

This evening, however, the earnest tutor tapped out the last sentence, saved the document and sent a copy to Alice which was duly signed and sent back and re-saved. Alice sighed, looked at the phone and wondered where the joy in the job had gone.

Always best to get in before the daughter. She found the mother's details on the database and started to dial. It was half past four. Not quite the right time of day but not as bad as the evening when any mother was sure to have had a couple of drinks, waiting for a husband to return and in need of a talk. Mornings were always a good time to call mothers; they were either eagerly getting themselves off to pilates, or yoga, or were in the middle of a coffee and so 'couldn't talk'. Alice always kept that mental note when communicating with mothers. Easy to pass on information in the mornings. Evenings are not good. Afternoons, you were hedging your bets a bit. She wondered what people in Cardiff did around half past four and thought that they probably weren't publicly masturbating.

"Can you hang around and record this conversation too? I'll put it on speaker, but don't say anything."

The tutor was already late for a date with her boyfriend but was only too eager. She could see how this was going to look on her CV.

Someone picked up.

"Ah, good evening, is that Georgie?"

There was a tentative affirmative.

"Good evening. This is Alice Elliot. I'm the Acting Head of House, standing in for Patricia while she attends to some personal affairs. Let me put your mind at rest. Jessica is absolutely fine but I do need to talk to you about some matters that involve her. Is this a good time?'

"Is she okay? I can come right now."

"As I said, she is absolutely fine. But is this a good time to talk?"

"Yes. Yes. How can I help? I only just spoke to her after lunch today."

"As I said, she is absolutely fine." The third reassurance meant that Alice heard a tangible sigh of relief. Usual pattern. "But I have been chatting to her though, as there's a little bit of an issue in her dormitory. I must tell you that I have another tutor with me and you are on speaker phone."

This heightened the seriousness of the situation and usually put a parent on guard.

114

"Is this okay with you if we carry on with our conversation?"

"Yes. Yes. What is the matter? She has been saying that girls have been bullying her. But y'know, girls will be girls. Y'know how girls can be. I wasn't goin' to saying anything quite yet."

"Ah. It's not quite that. It's just that some girls came to me to tell me that... and look we encourage the girls to look after each other, and I applaud those girls who have come forward with their concerns. I suppose there is no easy way to say this but the girls told me that Jessica has been masturbating, really quite publicly in the dormitory."

Alice paused for a reaction. There was nothing except some heavyish breathing the other end of the line and the resumption of some heavyish tap tapping of the tutor taking copious notes.

She continued, "I'm sure that you will agree that this is a slightly awkward scenario and it has made some of the other girls quite uncomfortable."

She paused again; she certainly was not going to tell this mother that her daughter had become a school joke.

There was a heavy intake of breath from somewhere in Wales as Jessica's mother almost groaned, "She wouldn't do that."

Alice thought again and went the direct route. "Georgie, I have to be honest and clear. Jessica has admitted to doing this."

"Oh."

"And this is also a little odd but she has also suggested that it is normal for Welsh people to do this. I mean Welsh people in public. Actually, this isn't coming out very well."

More heavy breathing and the thoughts were almost tangible in the phone.

"She knows better than that. She shouldn't say such horrible things about the Welsh. They have been very good to us while we've had to be here."

"Can we refocus this on how other girls are feeling because of her actions?"

A silence.

"We have asked Jessica to be more English. To be reserved and contained and to act in a more restrained manner in public. We are wondering whether you could endorse this and have a chat with her along similar lines?"

The long and the short of it was that twenty minutes later Jessica was excitedly packing her bags and three hours later, Georgie had collected her daughter for an early holiday and was winging her way back towards the Welsh border and that was the end of the Welsh wanking saga – apologies to Welsh women or men everywhere – remember we are just playing with alliteration here.

The debrief with the tutor had been more sangfroid than sangria. Process had to be followed, more notes printed off, signed, returned and saved, a report written for her superiors and Alice was ready for a drink and a toke.

The Bridge posse beckoned and provided a stark diversion for Alice as the group wanted to know more as they questioned and wondered, digging and diving into what had or what could have happened on the fateful night of Piers' murder and Henry's horrible end. Alice certainly seemed to have been the last person to have seen Piers alive, except of course, the person who wielded that heavy candlestick.

"How do we know it was a candlestick?"

"She told us in the meeting this morning."

"Who?"

"Goth."

"Oh."

"So you didn't say anything else to him or see anyone else?"

Alice remembered that she had said something like he was lucky to have a meal cooked for him and wished that she had added he was lucky to have a house and a job at his age, but hadn't.

She mentioned to the police that she had passed the odd student on the way home. There was the girl yelling at someone, presumably her mother, on her mobile, "I hate you," and "You bitch, you always take her side," followed by a sob-accompanied, "You never understand me." There was a boy kicking the curb, clearly waiting for someone around the squash courts: a notorious place for a bit of nooky. A teacher exuding buoyancy and well-being ran towards a boarding house, clearly late for evening duty. The teachers' running group puffed past her, a melange of forty-something men hellbent on maintaining their virility. The Headmistress, out on her evening walk. Another couple of girls giggling their way from behind the cricket pavilion probably smelling of cigarettes. The boy and girl coming out of a bush behind the Deputy Principal's house probably smelling of sex. None of these had seemed worthy of comment or notice even though the police said everything was important. It had been an entirely run-of-the-mill walk home armed with a soggy slice of warm congealed lasagne.

Karin tried to move the group forward, towards the Bridge table. They had to pass her collection of roadkill. An eclectic gathering. In her younger years, Karin had been enamoured of skulls and at every opportunity had stopped the car to collect whatever had been silly enough to venture too far into the realms of humanity's tarmac. She had found that mornings were good, and oftentimes ventured out for the sole purpose of finding the early offerings, more often than not a rabbit, more excitingly a hare or pheasant, sometimes a fox and once or twice a wombok – no that's a Chinese lettuce – a muntjac, which must have caused the other party an awful lot of damage. When she found them, mostly flattened into the road, she would take out a butcher's knife and decapitate them. Once home, she would bury the head in the garden for six months until the flesh had faded and fallen back into where it had come from, and she was left with the greyish bone. The skull was then marinated in hydrogen peroxide, bleach or whatever else was handy in the lab at the time, until a time when she could fish out the whitened art and stick it on the shelf alongside the others. Since coming to the school, she had added skulls of seagulls, terns, a swan and a seal.

Alice was both intrigued and repulsed by the ever-growing collection, and every time she passed the growing dead menagerie, a vague electric current meandered across her shoulder blades and there was always that nagging question in the back of her mind.

Adrienne pushed past and found a seat. Karin had put out two decks of cards and a scoring sheet and suggested that she and Alice play together opposite Peter and Adrienne. This left Robert and Stephanie to chat. Someone cut, someone shuffled, someone dealt and no one kept quiet. The gossip was just too good.

"No bid."

"No bid."

"One spade."

"No bid."

"Are we playing five card major?"

"Think so."

"Right. Two diamonds."

"No bid."

"Two spades."

"No bid."

"No bid."

"Three hearts."

"Damn you, Alice. You always do that!"

Alice grinned; always good to put a spanner in the works.

"Three spades."

"No bid."

"No bid."

"No bid."

"Three no bids so we're in three spades. Whose spades are they?"

The bidding was repeated and it was rediscovered that they were Adrienne's spades and so Peter was dummy.

"Whose lead?"

"Me." Alice threw out the three of hearts and the play began.

In the background Stephanie and Robert were dipping into the crisps and chilli enhanced hummus as they probed into the watery woman on the boat.

Robert worked on and off, for the local newspaper, having retired from English teaching at the school a few years earlier. He submitted the odd article now and again, usually commenting on the arrival of a lesser spotted migratory feathered friend from the steppes of Russia or the plains of Canada. Sometimes he reviewed a new local restaurant; at others, he would comment on the local walking club that had just raised more money for charity. Every now and again he would produce a feature on an oddity of Australian culture which he found endlessly and fascinatingly humorous: the meaning and uses of the meat pie, the difference between a Queenslander and a Tasmanian or the longest golf course in the world. This particular evening his work at the local rag meant that he was able to share the name of the charred woman's husband. A one Sebastian Ford.

"And his wife's name?"

"Joanne."

"Jo and Seb."

There was an echo from the Bridge table as they had more than half an ear to the conversation.

"Jo and Seb Ford."

"Play a card."

"Righto."

"Remember that time when a student reduced a study of *Antony and Cleopatra* to *Cleo and Tone* in an article for the school magazine? Clever. So clever. Sounds a bit like that."

Peter collected the cards. The hand was being played quite quickly because no-one was particularly interested in it.

"Who are they?"

"Were…"

"Some locals?"

"Hold on! Were? He's still alive isn't he? This Sebastian chap."

"Yes, he's alive. We saw him. Wasn't that him?"

"Not sure if they were locals. I don't think so," Robert was remembering overhearing a conversation between a couple of the reporters.

"They think they came from Plymouth or somewhere. Or was it Portsmouth? Somewhere near the sea. Either way they seem to have got around a bit. The boat that is. Seems to have been moored in many harbours and estuaries. Apparently, there's an app where you can map where every boat in the world has been."

"Fascinating."

"Every?"

"Apparently."

"So what happened?"

"Not sure."

"Accident?"

"Police aren't saying."

"Autopsy?"

"Think that was yesterday. Probably waiting for the report."

"All too close to home for my liking."

"Bit suss you reckon?"

"No smoke without fire."

"And there was certainly both."

All chortled.

"What I meant was, so many dead, all in a very close circle."

"Whose turn to play?"

"Karin, think it's you."

"No, I think its Adrienne from the table."

"Yup, won it with the queen over there."

"Ah sorry."

"Bit suss, I agree."

"So wha'd'y reckon? Henry killed the girl, Piers

killed Henry and..."

"Come on, Piers was a pain but he couldn't kill anyone."

"Not now he can't."

"That's a bit sick. No. But he wouldn't have had the stomach for it and frankly not the backbone."

"Bet he could."

"He was weak."

"And neither could Henry kill anyone."

"I suppose we could say that of quite a lot of murderers."

"Whose turn to play? Last trick. One more to win."

"Arh – ha – you made it. Well done!"

"Whose deal? Whose shuffle?"

"Perhaps it was 'un crim passional'."

"Is that Italian or French?"

"What? Piers killed the girl because he wanted to bonk Henry? Really? I think not. Henry bonking the girl?"

"Too disrespectful, too disrespectful."

"Have another glass."

"I'm confused."

"Just deal."

And so the evening went on. Alice and Adrienne stepped away from the table and Stephanie and Robert took their places. Quietly they went out to the courtyard and that brick wall and the dope, leaving the Bridge and the gossip.

"Are you going to the funeral?"

"Which one?"

"Oh, I suppose both. But I rather thought Henry's was much more of a private affair. I was really thinking about Piers."

"Has it been announced yet?" Alice drew on the toke and let the breath weave itself through her body and into her mind. This was better than running a boarding house.

"Yes!" Karin had one ear open to the goss in the courtyard and was wondering how to join the two outside.

The Headmistress, had, apparently just written an email announcing that the funeral for the legend would be on the following Monday and that all necessary pomp and circumstance was being arranged. She had expected that all would be going and so all classes were to be cancelled from mid-morning until lunchtime. All staff were expected to attend – Alice and Stephanie rolled their eyes – and around about 4000 were expected. Stephanie gaffawed at the figure and Peter rather agreed, saying that he was surprised that there would be so few.

"Why would you kill him?"

"Probably knew something."

"He knew masses."

"Everything."

"At a cynical best, it could just be a money raising exercise."

"Oh come on now. That is low."

Everyone looked into their wine glasses and had a giggle. Adrienne and Alice were smiling by the door. Karin and Peter stood up, attacked the camembert and the Bridge resumed.

There was still confusion about whether their own convention known as the Bangladeshi Vibe really had legs if you had seven in one suit, and the normal chortle emanated when it was decided that if One No Trump was the most difficult contract to play, then it was only kind and entirely logical to put your partner into Two No Trumps.

Adrienne ended up with an extra card at the end of one hand, making the whole play null and void and entitling everyone to an extra swig of wine while they searched for the errant card under the table.

At the end of the evening, the score was declared a draw as it seemed that many hands hadn't been recorded due to the slightly sozzled concoction of death, dope and murder. Some were working out whether they could attend funerals and how many, and really there was just too much gossip and discombobulation to keep score.

"I wonder if his murderer will be at the funeral?"

"They usually are in *Midsomer*."

It was with this thought that the murderer was in their midst that lulled some to sleep that night. How close was he? Was it, indeed a he? How safe were they all? Most on the school grounds, and others off, checked twice that their doors were locked and their curtains drawn. Murder made many just ever so slightly squeamish.

5. FOUR NO TRUMPS

The morning of Piers' funeral dawned and all within the school grounds seemed suspended in some mystifying mist of mythical madness. A number of marquees had been erected over the previous days. One particularly ornate stretch of embellished canvas stood adjacent to the mock-Jacobean chapel in readiness for the overload from a chapel built for 400, trying to accommodate 600 and anticipating, on this auspicious day, 4000.

Announcements had been made at meetings, assemblies, by email, by snail mail and on the website about catering, music, seating and flowers. Students had been called out of classes, sports practices and prefect meetings for choral rehearsals, usher and acolyte run-throughs and orchestra practice. Staff and students were all expected to attend the ceremony. Students were excited to have a morning off class, staff were exasperated at the loss of more precious class time, particularly when their 'A' Level statistics were on the line and their students still didn't know how to question, librarians were intrigued, gardeners and kitchen-hands exhausted and the games teacher confused. Few of them were to be welcomed into the chapel and a gigantic screen, surrounded by speakers and super woofers was to be set up in the gym where all the very unimportant people, students and staff, would gather.

Only those able to demonstrate a very close kinship with Piers were allowed within a pigeon's fart of the chapel. Huge heaters were imported and seats painstakingly placed in precise rows on almost-worn vaguely mauve carpet. Flowers in red and yellow and white cascaded over the ends of pews and fluttered in flurries around the choir stalls and altar. Bemused bunting, sporting the heraldic crests of dubious descent, dripped around the supporting marquees, dangerously close to the 'just-in-case' outdoor heaters posing as elegant daleks. Funereal men in dark suits, a mixture of Dickensian dourness and Blues Brothers humour, floated with anticipation, tiptoeing with egregious readiness, semi-bowed heads, fairly limp wrists and perpetual half-smiles.

Cars started to arrive at nine for the eleven o'clock ceremony. Parking was at a premium. The rowing club had run a raffle to raise funds for a new boat. Thirty successful winners were granted the honour of being able to park in the minute chapel carpark. Losers had to stop at the rugby pitches where they were directed, by parking attendants clad in those rather natty high viz vests of lime green, lemon yellow or plain orange, to just another spot in the lines of assorted cars. From there, women, picked their way on high heels across the sods of dew-damp grass, stabbing their way through the shortest route to solid ground.

The early arrivals tended to be the ones who had not seen the school since that heady day when they had given it the bird on their departure after their last exam. A kind of perverted interest brought them back and posses of exclamations echoed throughout the school as they marvelled at the changes that had happened over the intervening years: new boarding houses, ice machines and girls' changing rooms. They wandered into and out of the Dining Hall, the quadrangles, the boarding houses and thought it was their right to visit the dorm, and even lie on the bed, that had been theirs, thirty years earlier. Little had changed, and much was new.

As the sun rose higher over the school, the air seemed to suspend in some expectant stasis ready to watch over the hordes of cars that were rolling in and pouring out their contents into the walls of future influence.

Piers' closest relatives – a couple of nephews, an accompanying wife and three bemused great nephews and nieces who were just pleased to miss a day of school but were fractious from the long early morning drive from the mud of a pig farm - had reluctantly driven from Norfolk. Another branch of the Van Whatever family tree had driven down from the Cheshire bakery the night before and had stayed, uncomfortably on a couple of zbeds, with those who had ventured to live in London many moons before. This family conglomerate nodded quizzical passing-acquaintance looks at each other as they took the very front pews and provided the vanguard of dark glasses and floppy black hats.

Behind them, it was difficult to fathom how the ushers had been instructed to administer a seating hierarchy. It could have been kinship, money or marketing potential. Piers' old students, of whom there were gaggles, jostled for positions as their memories worked in romantic overtime to mythologise a man who had stood for morality, geniality and name-dropping. Then there were his friends; those whom he had known, those of whom he knew, and those who thought that they'd better know him. Boundaries quickly blurred into the agreeable amalgam of family, friends and presumably foe.

There were the Darby-Buckleys and their cousins, the Estrus-Hortons, arriving in Thursday's roller having driven down from Scotland the night before and stayed at some third cousin's castle on the Downs. They were joined by The Honorable Candida Rey-Sparks all dressed in black velvet and recently separated from her husband. Her dark glasses suggested a dissatisfaction unrelated to the present funeral. Almost like a sleight of hand, Lord Virgo inveigled himself into the pew next to her and unleashed upon her his total attention despite the fawning and bleating of others all wanting to make his acquaintance; after all, he had been known to mix with the footballers and the soap stars. Tommy Blitherington with his tombstone teeth, who had once been a circus acrobat, grunted and snorted his way to a pew but was turned about by a conscientious and astute usher as someone who may not be quite as well connected as he should. He was guided gently, genially and purposefully to a most comfortable and appropriate position, behind a dalek on the mauve carpet under canvas. Dear old Mr Vane-Stagg accompanied by his stiff bent chauffeur pushed a walking frame painstakingly precisely down the aisle and plonked himself down with a snort which might have been a fart. His erstwhile wife had met a very Scottish end, the head gamekeeper finding her face down in a clump of heather with a rather large staff through her heart. In the end, it was seen as an unfortunate accident and Vane-Stagg had subsequently enjoyed a merry litany of beautiful young things who were up for a good rutting.

In flowed the Freestone-Ferrules who lived a little further south on the Scottish Border. The journey from Coldstream had been haphazardly negotiated in a cavalcade of black, shiny Range Rovers, which was designed to look like the arrival of royalty. Their daughter, Venetia, had horrifically married one of the ghillies from the nearby beat on the Tweed. The couple had snuck off in the middle of the night and returned beaming and pregnant two months later. Difficult to sack the father of your grandchild and so Ted Badcock (wouldn't you change your name?) had been welcomed, with open arms and closed minds, into the burgeoning family. The four of them slipped in beside Eddy Arbor-Know and his squeeze of the year. Eddy was the Earl of one of those many castles along the border which could chameleon-like be either Scottish or English in heritage, dependent on the situation, and Eddy lay claim to both Flodden and Culloden ancestry which could sometimes complicate but more often illuminate. He kept the castle going through tourism with a just a little bit of male escorting on the side; after all, what respectable American lady wouldn't want to say she'd danced the night away with a real live Scottish Earl? And to go one better, who wouldn't want to be able to say that she had slept with him?

The Trenchers followed en masse. Ferdi Trencher had married a catholic, "Bless me father", and there seemed no end to the children, perhaps nine or ten. The boys all got names of Apostles but when the girls came along, Ferdi's wife got stuck after Mary and settled on Octavia who had followed Septima. The Trencher tribe would take up a pew and a half. Thomas, the youngest, was still snivelling behind the rest as he still wasn't allowed to sit in the front seat and he doubted he'd ever be allowed. Peter had denied him three times and James and John had spent the journey squeezing him from both sides on the back seat. The ushers looked a tad queasy at the sudden influx but gathered themselves in the knowledge that Ferdi was donating large sums of money to the building of the Table Tennis Centre, funds that he might have been creaming off his interests in the Cayman Islands. The Trenchers were found pride of pew.

Then came the Babblers, the Spinners and the Stalkers, all with vaguely similar wives whose children bore a remarkable similarity to men who were sitting in nearby pews. All these had attended the school and so had their fathers, grandfathers, right back to their great, great grandfathers. All had been taught by, tutored by or had just been at the school roughly at the same time as Piers and of course, all of them were his friends. It was difficult to imagine that amongst this mix of genteel English society must lurk the more unseemly, the murderous, the criminal.

A lull in the proceedings meant that conversations could be had, old acquaintances remade, old acquaintances purposely avoided and much head cocking and eye catching, angling for new acquaintances. It was reminiscent of days gone by when, as students, all would ogle at the new students as they came into the Dining Hall for the first time or

when a newly hitched couple would share their first
meal together, an almighty cheer would arise above
those sticky tables, to celebrate the recent copulation.
But short-lived gossip and interest was quickly
forgotten when the next scandal or spectacle arrived.
This tradition had served the students well and much
had been learnt about how to size up sex appeal and
wallet size on the benches of the Dining Hall.

Alongside all this activity, the next charge
arrived, Henry Hornblower and his new young wife,
Felicity, who looked most smug dressed in pink with her
chin slightly raised and her eyes surreptitiously
supercilious. Her stilettos were firmly pricked onto the
stone and concrete beneath and there was a slight
foxiness to her as she held onto the tweed clad arm of
her new old husband with that aura of ownership
towards the audience and subservience to her husband.
Hornblower had been in Piers' English class for every
one of his five years at the school and Piers' reports had
continually waxed lyrical in the most illustrious terms of
Henry's industrious attempts to understand the
abstract workings of metaphors and similes.

It was generally thought the Bullard-Sterms had
gone to ground but to the surprise of some and the
horror of others, they arrived at the entrance, surveyed
the scene and trotted down the aisle as though they
had never been headline news, had never been to jail
and had never been found with five kilos of pretty pure
heroin under the floorboards of a horse float Mr
Bullard-Stern had borrowed to transport a new hunter
from what had been Prussia.

The Arthbutnotts came in side by side. Angela
was carrying a bag and Anthony was still using a stick,
having fallen into a ditch during the New Year shoot in

Rutland (apparently the county with the most eligible bachelors). A stint in hospital stymied his shooting season and being fairly disgruntled by this, he had refused to wear anything but his shooting tweeds and plus fours to the funeral.

A brace of young chaps hung behind them. They had just left the school and had a jauntiness of proprietorship. Their Saville Row suits looked a little large and out of place – just a bit too dapper and perhaps a little reminiscent of those school blazers bought by mothers to grow into – and the ushers softly, gently and surely turned them about towards the marquee.

Patsy Beaumont looked rather sure of herself as she beat down the aisle, consciously carelessly bashing at pews and bouquets with her oversized designer handbag. She was always on the lookout for the next catch, the hawk of the occasion all ready to set up the prey, hovering and swooping on any eligible and more often ineligible gentlemen whose wives, whatever their opinions of each other, would close ranks, herding and packing together whenever she came into their sights. Hair dyed the colour of ebony and skin as white as snow made her look a tad like a badger but she certainly got the attention of those gathered.

Sir Bertrand Bissett, who once told a dinner-party that he was the most boring man in Derbyshire, smiled through his red face and bulbous nose and lead his diminutive wife up the aisle, guiding her into a pew where she sat upright, eyes front and immobile for the entirety of the service.

A litany from the Home Counties followed: Jackie and John Polkinghorne whose parents actually admitted to paying for their grandchildren's education,

Michael and Emma Round-Ramsay whose parents had lost all their money in the Lloyds debacle and heavily relied on family handouts to stock their cellar, provide Mediterranean holidays and put their three children through the school; Stephen and Jane Herbert who might have been descended from the poet but were making a fair quid now in all things organic and felt a little out of place. Here there was a miasma of dark glasses, slickish suits, Gucci and Chanel copies, high heels and patent pumps. Perhaps some had even hired a beamer for the day.

The diplomatic set was headed by Dusty and Dirty Tollemache who had spent much of their working life in minor ambassadorial posts such as the Gilbert and Ellis Islands and colonies such as Australia. People like Ian and Mary Grant who could always find the right words to say and who did all the proper things at the right time, dressed in precisely the right outfits for the occasion and who were often sent far afield to smooth over another diplomatic gaff by another undercooked ambitious government official in some lesser known colony were followed by Thomas Bond and his umbrella who may have worked in MI6 but who could say?

Gary and Wendy Endicott looked a bit out of place and were directed to the marquee, Wendy sporting heavy bling on gold stilettos and a dress just that much too short for her time in life. Gary wore a chunky gold necklace which dangled mischievously behind his white open-necked linen shirt. Their four children had been put through the school courtesy of Shell Nigeria but had ended up trading cocaine through the East End of London and Port Campbell in Australia, which now gets another mention.

Mrs Frost, who had been born Lady Anstruther-

Philips, the daughter of the Earl of Norwich and who had gone through two fairly weighty marriages, waddled through the door. She had been heard, during one of her marriages, saying, "Anyone who arrived in England after 1066 was frightfully nouveau." Her previous two husbands had died in hunting accidents, the first bouncing from saddle to five-bar gate to ground and breaking his back, the second diving into the ice-hardened ground and breaking his neck. Her third husband was plain old Mr Frost and he didn't like horses.

Those who came from London seemed to come later, leaving at the last minute, trusting that the M25 would be clear and that the roads down to the school would flow. They arrived with an arrogance of ownership and spent much of the time checking their apps for stock prices, contract notes and court hearings.

Teddy Hambleton peeled out of his Lamborghini, forgetting that he had picked up his current shag from her Acton flat that morning. He strode towards the chapel remotely locking the car, troubled by the morning's magnificent tumble on the Bitcoin market. She was left panting inside the locked car.

Sean Hopper, Charlie Chase and Kevin Kelloggs arrived in one car. They had all shared the same dorm for many years and had contributed to the school's new shooting range many years ago. Having already stopped for a quick snifter at the Red Lion in Little Sleeping, they were definitely quite chipper.

Countess Eloise de Chanson was accompanied by two young hangers on and they looked remarkably similar to the two that she had had at the Fortune-Geary wedding outside Palermo last year.

Lord Bissett-Haggard, a distant relative of the most boring man in Derbyshire, seemed to have forgotten to shave or wash, as his 1980s Land Rover snorted and farted itself onto the rugby field.

And watching all this with wry amusement was Samuel Clemens, one of Piers' closest acquaintances who had positioned himself on the chapel's bookshelves and waited for a particular character to arrive.

Johnny Kemp looked frightfully dapper in his clothes, a fine example of entrepreneurship sprouting from his lineage of shop-keeping and chain stores.

There was the tech mogul, Paddy Paternoster, who had made his fortune between Hong Kong and Taiwan and a myriad of Chinese tecchies in between.

All these, and so many more, came to Piers' funeral. Chatting and nattering, gossiping and nodding, talking and smiling, so much so that the coffin seemed to get lost amongst the grave waves of dubious energy.

It was indeed a grand affair, the coffin that is. An intimidating black shiny box containing a cold, white corpse. Gold embossed handles dazzled against the sides of patent black and atop, an extraordinarily large panoply of out of season flowers. It lay on its bier in the middle of the aisle, perhaps a little closer to the altar than most. Piers had been a religious man, a single man, not quite married to God, but almost, practically married to that promise of immortality. Overhearing all the chattering were the drapes of white, yellow and red flowers adorning the end of each pew; they gave off a slight smell, akin to incense but not quite. The school vicars, politically one woman and one man, just to show that the school was genuinely progressive in its age old traditions, were beetling about with the tech guys to ensure that the mics were working and half a dozen students, all spruced up in their school uniform best – dark grey with a cherry stripe around the edge and atop the pocket, white shirt and cherry tie – were handing out heavily embossed, thick paper programmes that promised a very, very long service.

Indeed, it was no other than a service written by the dead man, the fulfilment of a promise made to himself. A service of mythical proportions that would lead him to eternity.

A bell chimed at the back of the chapel and those who had been students immediately fell silent, as though some beadle with a white wand was just about to strike a blow should they murmur or move. Those who had not been at the school were slower to silence. Moments later, they too, in turn, realised, somewhat awkwardly, that this was the done thing, and mid-sentence stopped. It was at this moment that they really felt they were somehow not quite part of this monolithic tradition and they would never quite be accepted, not understand the intricate wheels in the machinations of thought, expectation and decorum.

The organ struck up with Elgar's *Nimorod* from the *Enigma Variations* followed by Bach's *Blessed Jesu We Are Here.* The two school captains, again politically correctly one boy and one girl, slowly walked a step behind the crossbearer. The candle bearers and the acolytes led the procession, through the lesser nobles of the realm sitting in precise rows in the marquee, up to the chapel doors and through the less-lesser nobles sitting in the pews. Behind them minced the new Headmistress sporting a dashing pink tailored suit, actually - come to think of it - a very bright pink suit, recently bleached almost white blonde hair and heavy layers of white foundation suitably plastered to enable a palette of pink blusher, eye shadow and lipstick which were all, well just, pink. Her sensible heels meant that she minced with an entitled confidence and an air of ownership that was ever so slightly incongruent against the panoply of pink. For a few moments she tried a demure, eyes-lowered pose that could be apt for the occasion, but that proclivity for the dramatic could not be suppressed and very quickly she sported that wide square smile and wide-eyed stare which we have come to expect, as though she wanted to embrace all and sundry because they were, of course, her closest acquaintances. It was just so exciting for this protégé of Bury to be so close to people who knew people. By the time she was passing the coffin, she was practically dancing to *How Great Thou Art* and it took all of her energy to calm that emaciated body in the pink suit so that it could be enveloped by centuries of tradition within the arms of the Headmaster's, now Headmistress's seat, a heavy carved oak chair that sat next to the choir stalls at just a height to put the incumbent in sight of the congregation but to give her an opportunity of quiet contemplation if required. It had come from the monastery in the Home Counties at the time of dissolution and had cossetted and comforted many in time of trouble. She had, days earlier, ordered a sturdy cushion that would increase her height and now she sat, pert and perky, looking rather smug, just slightly above the shiny coffin, at the centre of the occasion.

Confronted by this sight, it would be difficult for anyone sitting in that congregation to imagine that there could be a real, live murderer in their midst.

As the hymn ended, there was a slight rustle

in the congregation as everyone settled, all perhaps a little nervous that they may, indeed, be sitting next to the cause of this occasion. They had found out who could sing, who couldn't and who wouldn't. They were settling into their territory and making ready for the long haul.

The male chaplain climbed slowly and painfully – he had a terrible hip – up the short steps to the pulpit. Purposefully surveying the mixed pack and in that long breathy way, where pauses are made at odd moments in sentences, and are sometimes so long that you think that maybe the orator has died and a defibrillator would be useless, or at best he's forgotten the point of the sentence because it has become so long and unwieldy that everyone has forgotten the beginning and certainly has lost the point, he welcomed the congregation and admired everyone's long and arduous journeys. With the niceties done and through the long white beard and ruddy pock-marked face, he signalled to a fading chap in the front row who approached the microphone in the aisle and gave the first reading from Song of Solomon 2:8-14 which apparently had some relevance to the occasion but few could deduce.

In fact, much of the rest of the ceremony went very much along the same lines, a reading which was fairly obscure then an even more obscure poem followed by Canon Henry Scott-Holland's poem *Death is Nothing At All* to which most breathed a sigh of relief because they understood it but others rather took exception to its main thesis. The odd *The Lord is my Shepherd* and *Guide me O Thou Great Redeemer* meant that most popped up their heads and our pack was starting to settle in. This was well and good because by sermon time it was necessary for everyone to be sitting comfortably. The Headmistress had wisely decided that this momentous delivery should be served by someone of substance, someone of standing, someone who could, perhaps, generate donations, marketing copy, insta-moments, and that someone was her.

And so amongst tradition of tweeds and brogues, of Barbours and Dubarrys, with the smell of gun oil and fish innards and the hint of vast poverty disguised as immense wealth and immense wealth disguised as vast poverty, the pink clad Headmistress mounted the steps to the pulpit. As she was doing this, a couple of tecchies erected an enormous portable screen in front of the rood screen, just above the shiny coffin, and covering the entire sightline into the apse. Another couple of tecchies were erecting a small projector at the other end of the aisle and the whole shenanigans looked like it had been stage managed and practised weeks in advance. Within seconds it was lights, camera, action and the screen was adorned with twirling and curling, flying and sliding pictures of the murdered man splurging from left frame to right frame. From behind the screen, the cherry robed choristers craned their necks to try to see as the activity and visuals on screen enticed the rest of the pack to sit up and pay attention and those who had drifted off were pulled back into the fold. The Headmistress had armed herself with a laser pointer and a remote control which she proceeded to press with precise abandon. Pictures of herself sitting on the edge of Piers' hospital bed just weeks before the candlestick affair, pictures of her and Piers pondering over an old photo of the school, pictures of her and Piers sipping wine, you get the drift. At one point her gaze went from screen to congregation as she walked across the width of the chapel with her chin held in the crook of her forefinger and thumb, a contemplative moment as she shared her selfies. And against this backdrop she began.

"I was such a dear friend of Piers. I shared his intellect, his knowledge and his curiosity." She read the script with a type of cold precision and purpose. "I am honoured to have known this esteemed man. This was the first time that I met Piers," the next photo popped up on the screen, "when he was having just a brief moment in hospital having a gangrenous toe chopped off. I comforted him and took him in a favourite tipple of his, a bottle of Baileys."

She waited for the customary titter amongst the pack and then pressed the remote and there was a photograph of Piers in his twenties when he had just started at the school.

"Piers had a long and honourable career at this school and was loved by many more than just myself, many of whom I know are sitting before me right now. You all have had relationships with him. Like myself. I feel so privileged to have known him so very well and I hold him so dear to my heart. In fact, I can feel my heart thumping as I think of this dear," slight pause, slight moment in the throat, and then onwards, "dear man. And as you can see, I am having trouble holding back the tears at the thought of his passing."

At this point that old hand on the heart gesture was made and there was a slight hint of a sniff. Her eyes wandered, unwantedly, to the Detective Sergeant and his Detective Constable who had, Midsomer-like, just entered the chapel and were having a good old gaze at the congregation.

She didn't miss a beat and continued with the well-orchestrated charade, clicking to the next slide, a picture of her leafing through one of Piers' books, whilst saying, "And so this week has been so very difficult for me and the school and I know for many of you because he meant so very much to all of us and I thought that this would be a fitting tribute to him."

On the screen was a picture of the ancient promotion poster for *The Dambusters* film. And then she signalled to a techie and through the speakers filtered the theme music to the film. The congregation started to shift in their seats, mightily confused and somewhat taken aback. They sat quietly but shiftily and some were surreptitiously grinning at others – there didn't seem a murderer amongst them – as others were praying that this intruder in pink would quickly shut up, sit down and let them get on with the mourning. But not a bit of it.

After the end of this charade, she took the mic and there were another five minutes of obsequious praising of a man who had done really very little except create his own myth, providing an avuncular persona for the marketing department, and get himself murdered. She ended this powerful sermon with another PowerPoint display of a YouTube clip of Bob Geldof's *Live Aid,* and if you hadn't got the *Dambusters* analogy, you certainly weren't going to make head nor tail of starving Africans and she sat down smug as a bug in a rug.

An hour and a half later and many obscure readings and more obscure hymns, family incantations and bidding prayers, the chapel spat out its contents. The mauve carpet buckled under the added weight and it took the wiry haired Deputy Headmaster with a megaphone to direct all towards the Dining Hall where cucumber sandwiches, cupcakes and cups of tea were

141

waiting.

Now with all the palaver of myth and mysticism, we seem to have forgotten the reason for our little story of murder and intrigue. Let's recap: a watery drowning, a plasterboard impalement and a fair old knock on the head by a cheap and nasty reproduction candlestick, the latter being the reason for the present funeral, a murder of a man who had been part of the fabric of the school for nigh on sixty years. He had been well on his way out with a mixture of Parkinsons, perennial prostate and a creeping gangrene which could have started with gout but murder most foul did seem a little harsh.

It was not odd that there were a few plain clothes policemen mingling among the throng where almost everyone knew there must be a killer or two. They were eavesdropping for clues and not one seemed to be willing to rise.

Bridge that night was sure to be rife with speculation.

6. FIVE HEARTS

Gathering at Alice's that evening, Peter rode his bike along the sea wall from his house on the outskirts of the town. Just past a fairly decrepit sluice gate, designed in the nineteenth century to drain the inland grazing land if a king tide broke the bank, but which had now been superseded by an intricate and most modern dam and flow system to the east, he dismounted and decided to walk because the path had become a little too rocky for his thin tyres.

An older couple was sitting on a bench, eating fish and chips out of a cardboard box in front of him and he could hear the insistent, and some thought ugly, squawking of a dozen or more seagulls as they fought over the couple's intermittent offerings. He watched amused, as one or other of the pair threw out a soggy chip and a hoard of screaming gulls descended in a murderous madness upon the innocent chip. A funny sort of joy crept through him as he watched the ensuing fight of nature play out. Preferring crisp chips, cooked in hotter oil, he rather felt that the soggy chip got what it deserved. The husband saw a gull with one leg, it seemed to be holding back, and couldn't get to the jettisoned potatoes fast enough. He singled it out and threw a particularly large chip towards it whilst his wife threw a handful the other way to attract the rest of the flock. It scooped up the charity and quickly flew over the other side of the sea wall but five or six of the diverted flock spotted its flightpath and followed. Who knew whether it enjoyed its meal? Peter laughed. Nature.

He was content. He could always find something fascinating in any situation and as the days were long, the evenings more often than not balmy and the air filling with summer promise, there was something calming about walking and watching. Life in retirement was good; his wife he thought, was happy, his children had all found jobs in London and so really what was left other than to play Bridge, golf, to find unusual places in foreign lands and buy cut-price aeroplane tickets.

Having spent much of his pre-marriage days with a rucksack on his back, he had a litany of extensive and generous offers of free beds in palatial castles and castellated palaces, bed-sits, dives and the odd suburban home. This convenience, combined with his curiosity in farther and farther far-flung places, meant that he was spending a goodly many months every year travelling. When he wasn't travelling, he still made himself available to the Mathematics Department at the school for tutorials where he was known to ensconce himself well into the evening with numerous poor mathematicians helping them to understand the intricacies of calculus and matrices in the hope of raising their grades just an infinitesimal little. It gave him a bit of pocket money to add to the familial coffers so that it did not look like he was living off his really quite wealthy wife. No one quite knew whether this wife, who was a partner in a London solicitors' office, sanctioned his wanderings or cared whether he had an income or not. She remained stalwartly and supportively in the background. The topic was never raised.

The topic that did raise its head both within and without Peter's head was that his overall contentedness was currently clouded by the recent turn of events. As an old boy of the school, he didn't like the idea of it being front page headlines on too many occasions in one year. Here he perhaps was the antithesis of the school's Marketing Department which seemed to hold a similar opinion to Oscar Wilde, that it was worse to not be talked about than talked about, and it appeared to do little to keep things out of the press. Of course, the local rags and on the odd occasion those national tabloids, liked to get hold of the odd story of this very famous school, clinging to the edge of a fairly famous country. Sometimes, the stories celebrated the school's latest charity drive or a past student's achievement but too often it seemed that they revelled in some catastrophe or new-found skeletal remains in a cupboard.

This week the school had made it twice to the front page and both for rather similar unsavoury things. There was the Piers' incident, and there was yet again a story about the new old-chestnut, buggery in the boarding houses: another ancient master unmasked for his actions thirty odd years previously.

Both stories niggled Peter. They both hit a weeping sore that he would have preferred remained deep in his psyche. He was after all, an old boy, and he had been immensely fond of Piers and even fonder of the values he imbued. It was that feeling that so many boys had of their masters in the good old-fashioned *Biggles* and *Dambuster* value system, that nostalgic reverence where perhaps school masters did take the position of physically and emotionally absent parents. A time when the odd master forgot boundaries. After all, men were men and boys were boys and love for each other was left unstated and praise for one another knew no bounds.

The modern day trend to blast open a past emotion did not sit as easily with Peter as he thought it should. It niggled and wriggled with his conscience that someone somewhere may be about to blow the lid off centuries of traditions and old boys' networks. Most of these networks were solid and stable, built on a structure of well woven webs, most were good. He wondered which grubby little journalist would do the deed, uncovering an horrific misdemeanour, and thus tarring the whole with the same grubby little brush. One sort of bastardization would become synonymous with another, he thought. He wondered who would blow the cover and wondered what they would drag up. Not one of his acquaintances would break that bond that bound the brothers, bastard or not.

As he pushed his bike past the couple of the bench and the gaggle of gulls, he thought about the funeral and the wake. Again some niggle in him nudged him into assuming that the murderer had been among them and a shiver accompanied the discordant sound of the gulls and travelled through his body at the thought that he may have been standing shoulder to shoulder, eating cucumber sandwiches with their crusts off and butterfly cakes, with a killer.

As an old boy of the establishment, he did get a seat in the marquee and a ticket to the wake in the Dining Hall. He had chatted and gossiped to many with whom he had shared a dorm, a desk or a clandestine cigarette. Sometimes there were vague or subliminal references to incidents such as when Fergusen Minor had been found, stark naked, in the broom cupboard tied to the duster peg or when Satullius Ponsonby had been made to clean the urinals with a toothbrush because he had red hair. But generally tales were told with much laughter and over the years they became taller and taller with the telling, such as the time they sneaked into the chapel and drank the left over communion wine or the time that they left three dead mice in the wellington boots of the housemaster and when this group of grown men remembered Borthwaite's hilarious prank of running three bras up the flagpole, they were right back as fourteen year olds again.

Much nostalgia was mixed with a real sense of foreboding as Peter wandered along the sea wall towards Bridge. Amongst the afternoon's chatter, over those cucumber sandwiches and Earl Grey tea, they had wondered who would kill such a harmless chap. They wondered whether it was an internal job. They wondered what he knew. Someone had links to the Detective Chief Somebodyorother at New Scotland Yard, but that lead had fallen dead in the water. They wondered who knew stuff, who knew the stuff they knew.

Anyone who had been at the school over twenty years ago knew stuff but they didn't know what stuff was relevant. Was the fact that Biggy Minor had been buggered regularly in the end shower by the balding bearded Chemistry teacher called Pinter? Or was it Pointer? Either way his nickname was Panter. Was the fact that Dasher Deakin was doing dope deals on the sea wall every Sunday afternoon – buying from some dude who trained it from London and selling it on to the Fourth Form for inflated prices? Or was the fact that Jensen kid had actually killed himself rather than return to the school knowing what would happen to him in the back room of the Library? This latter fact was mere supposition by those who didn't know him that well.

Most of the time when these old boys got together they sat in worn leather chairs in some London club, drank brandy, smoked cigars and were rich together. They talked nostalgically of their time at the school and more often than not as they shared their tales any sense of impropriety ran off their egos as rain off their Burburries. Awkward moments were quicky truncated as they were able to turn the horrific into humour, making the grotesque bearable.
Conversations at the wake had taken on a sort of clandestine secrecy. All were unnerved and wondered what might come to light, things that they had suppressed for so long. After all, they were all privy to a kind of secret that few knew.

Peter watched another chip being jettisoned towards the marauding seagulls and remembered that evening in Port-au-Prince where he had watched the seagulls dive onto a handful of rice being tossed by a kitchenhand from the back of the Kinam Hotel. Nature doesn't change he thought.

Karin too, was making her way around to Alice's. She had armed herself with a heavy shiraz and a plate of very fine brie, deciding that she needed more than a few drinks after the week's entertainment. The marauding police, the gossip in the Common Room, the rehearsals, the announcements, the funeral itself, the performing principal and the orgiastic fineries were just a bit much.

Coming from a state school in flat old Lincolnshire, the pomp, the circumstance and the plain facades and veneers of such gatherings made her feel just a tad irksome. Unlike many who regarded such rigmarole and regalia with warm affection, others smiled in that ever so slightly patronizing manner and the rest got drunk. Karin just got drunk. She was the shining success of her school, a school where many girls were pregnant by fifteen and onto their third child, all by different fathers, by the time they were eighteen. There was a creche at the school which suggested that it may have been progressive but equally meant that it was encouraging students to produce hordes of offspring ready to replicate a similar world.

For Karin, watching for any length of time the mounting opportunities and unconscious privilege was superficially amusing but ultimately disturbing. Here were the leaders and perhaps future leaders of society and yet they revealed themselves, to her, in all their frail and fragile states in a way of which only they could be ignorant. She thought of her youth and the fading opportunities and mounting debt of her childhood friends.

Karin had been raised by a single mother and she had not seen her father since she was eight. He had left one night and she could only recall the loud voices and slammed doors as she and her younger sister lay still and frightened in the double bed they shared upstairs. From then on, there seemed to be more food in the cupboard and fewer bruises on her mother. There were more cuddles and her grandmother came around more often and baked brownies and spread raspberry jam on toasted crumpets. She remembered overhearing a discussion on how to share the heating bill and the rent and the next day her grandmother had collected her from school, taken her back to her house and shown her to a bed of her own and allowed her to make her own toast at any time. Seamlessly they had moved into her grandparent's house. Her mother took on a job working full time stacking shelves in Sainsburys and when Lidl came along, she was able to secure a job on the checkout. Life was improving. Her grandmother kept making brownies and crumpets until it felt like they were brownied out but then her mother came up with recipes for flapjacks and waffles and it began to feel like home was safe and secure.

It was with a bit of surprise that both women surveyed the letter that told Karin she had attained four Bs, two As and three A*s for her GCSEs; neither of them had sat an exam in their lives. Her mother had been using her contacts to enquire about stacking positions at local supermarkets. Their mouths fell open when Karin quietly but pointedly told them that she would be staying at school to study three A Levels. This concept of the near future went over the top of the heads of the two significant adults in her life. There was an extended and heated discussion about how she was going to pay for this now that she was sixteen and should be working. Their voices must have resonated out of the kitchen and into the sitting room and drowned out the dulcet tones of an excitable commentator of yet another football match. To remedy this irritating impingement on his normal routine, her grandfather, rather uncharacteristically did something. He spoke.

"Let the lassie do wha sh wans. We'll fin th' money."

That seemed to right the problem. Silence in the kitchen. The dulcet tones could be heard again from the telly.

August faded into September and Karin returned to school. There was a sort of sticky, icky avoidance of any discussion around this momentous decision and her younger sister stayed in her room to study. Not a word of dissent. Not a word. The new age had arrived and a new role model sat before her. The scenario sat awkwardly with her mother and grandmother each evening as they ate their well-earned tea. One day Karin's mother suggested that they were a little short staffed at the supermarket as one of the young shelf stackers had gone down with the chickenpox – how this happened in these days of vaccinations she did not know – but, a few days later and seamlessly, Karin was stacking shelves a couple of times a week, studying for her A Levels and adding to the household coffers. The status quo had changed and remained the same and all were content again.

But there was no doubt in the young Karin's mind that she would go to university and her A Level Chemistry teacher thought this too. For him, in this flat town of grey stone amidst flat fields of drained land with only the Stump to see from miles around, here was a project. Not often did a student of Karin's potential, desire and imagination sit before him. His A Level class that year totalled four and three of these were destined for Ds. In previous lifetimes of his teaching career, a deputy principal had asked him why he had such low grades. His response was that "You can bring a horse to water..." He always remembered the vicious vice's response, "How have you salted the oats?" He had felt like punching him on that place on the top of the nose, just behind the tortoise-shell glasses, but had refrained just thinking that this prick should get back in the classroom and try it himself.

But here was a student who needed no salting of the oats. Her energy and desire to move beyond what Lincolnshire offered, even if she didn't know quite what that beyond looked like, meant that she seemed to move effortlessly, except for the odd financial discussion about shelf stacking, to Hull University and a degree in Biology. Her shelf stacking skills moved as effortlessly with her and were easily transferred to a supermarket on the outskirts of Hull, three streets down from her dingy share flat above a curry house. In the winter mornings she would place her coffee on a bathroom shelf while she had a shower. By the time she had showered, the coffee would, more often than not, have a thin film of cumin flavoured ice forming on the top. The rest of the winter day would be spent in three jumpers and a couple of pairs of socks trying to control the shivering as she hunched over biological tomes. She looked forward to her shifts at the supermarket as she knew she would be warm.

Towards the end of her three years, she wondered what she would do; shelf stacking was beginning to pall, especially in the warm summer term. Perhaps because her own journey towards university had not all been plain sailing, perhaps because she still held an academic affection for that chemistry teacher at school, perhaps because it meant that she could stay at university for an extra year and not be expected to go home and follow her mother's career, she applied and was accepted into a postgraduate course in teaching.

The long and short of this decision saw her working around schools that needed her in Yorkshire and Lancashire, a long stint in a school in Northern Thailand, where she also did a mahout course and supported the elephant polo fraternity and on to a rural school in Nigeria.

It was here that she met a teacher who had taken a year's leave from a prestigious English school perched on the southern coast next to an increasingly dilapidated marina, which is the scene of our little tale. The deal was good: a free house in exchange for doing extra hours looking after teenage boys in a boarding house. This meant that she was able to buy her own apartment in Skegness, lease it out and get ahead on the housing rung. Her values were not directly aligned with those at the school but she did, like many teachers, keep quiet and toe the party line. She nodded and applauded at the right moments and watched the incredible flippancy that sometimes can go with having so much money and prestige. Those expectations and entitlements that go with position and privilege both with the student, parent and sometimes staff bodies, were studies in how not to behave and she vowed ever more strongly that eventually her path in teaching would lead her back to where she was needed in the north.

The day's funeral and wake antics had only deepened her resolve and consolidated her determination. The shenanigans which went with the murder of a questionably esteemed myth were worth watching but only from a distance.

By the time Karin had walked back from her

office, through the quad, past the chapel skirting the language rooms towards her and Alice's block of flats, Adrienne was already well ensconced in Alice's living room armed with wine and unlit toke.

Adrienne had, after all, retired from teaching at this school of our tale, only a couple of years earlier. This had meant that she and her family had moved into a rather old and vaguely dishevelled farmhouse in a village just along the sea wall. The plan was to renovate, the money was going to come from somewhere. They had seen it as a project but other things kept coming up. Old pipes and drafty rooms – which they never used anyway – were less important than the electrics of the greenhouses and the acquisition of solar panels. Her husband, Ed, a retired History teacher from the school, was pursuing a career in plant propagation, and hydroponics and ultra-violet lamps were his current interests. Adrienne remained more invested in the school than her husband and liked to attend as many social occasions as was politely possible. This meant that she needed to find places to stay when she couldn't drive home and had become, unwittingly, the innocent campus tart, finding a bed wherever she could on Bridge night or any other social occasion that meant that she would not be able to find her way home safely. She had, of course, attended the funeral and stayed around the Library afterwards, exchanging gossip with the head librarian, not reading books, before wending her way towards Alice's and settling herself comfortably into her kitchen.

By the time Stephanie arrived, she was battering around the cupboards and drawers making her legendary guacamole dip. The avocado was a bit hard, the tomatoes a tad soft and she knew there would be usual debate of whether to add chilli or not. She was not in favour. Alice loved the heat. Stephanie was diplomatic.

By the time Karin arrived, they had drunk a glass of wine each and were well on the way to solving the chilli debate and the multiple murders. Nebulous and nefarious facts miraculously seemed to coalesce into a vague resolution.

"He must've known something."

"Who? Henry?"

"No, Piers." Adrienne stirred the guacamole and Alice found the bottle of chilli sauce in the larder and put it, silently, beside the mixing bowl. "What? You think Henry knew something too?"

"Well, Peter would know who they both hung out with. Actually Karin's been here a long time too."

"So have you and Ed." Stephanie had managed to fill a glass and join in the sleuthing.

"Yeah, but I'm not tuned into those sorts of things. You're not if you're married." She dipped her finger into the dip and screwed up her face. More salt? She wondered. "I didn't think that they all knew each other. I mean, that well." She thought further, definitely more salt. "In fact, I'm sure they didn't".

"Well, what did they have in common? What did they have access to? What did they both know? What did either of them know actually?" A barrage of questions from Alice was countered by a gulp of wine by Adrienne.

"Did you see the number of police hanging around today?"

"Difficult to tell, not all in uniform methinks."

"All those shifty looking ones."

"What, you mean hiding behind a newspaper,

taking time to tie a shoelace or tapping the side of their ear?"

Laughter.

"Most just trying to eavesdrop, I reckon."

"Don't be so melodramatic. Do you really think they'd do that?"

"Wouldn't you? You've got a veritable *Who's Who* of a certain section of the country's upper echelons and there's been a murder or two. You'd think there'd be a lot of hush hush money going around." Adrienne looked at the chilli bottle, "And they'd be able to pick up a few juicy bits of hot goss."

"And the good ones could probably get away with being an old student."

"Dead right."

"You got it."

"Goss. Like what?"

"That Piers was writing a book."

"About what?"

"The school."

"So what?"

"… and its past."

"So?"

"Well he knew a lot and the old students know a lot. And that lot may not want the modern day Board and Adminstration to know about what they know."

"I'm lost."

"Are you talking cover up?" Adrienne succumbed and added a bit of chilli to the dip. "D'reckon it could be someone on the Board?"

"It could be that Piers was about to reveal that someone had been up to no good and the school was covering it up."

Another tablespoon of chilli fell from the bottle

and Alice was grinning.

"There was that thing in the paper earlier in the week."

"Oh come on – another bugger ..."

"For God's sake, you've got to be politically correct."

"I know, I know, but such old hat."

"New old news."

"Not for the victim."

"That won't be part of it."

"Won't it?"

"Really."

"Well who knows?"

"I bet Peter knows. He knows everyone."

"So he'll know something?"

At that moment Peter arrived in the hallway, dropped the packet of crisps he was carrying, fumbled about on the floorboards and waved from the hallway runner. The normal entry scuffle ensued, the greetings, the sound of crisp packets and the exchange of wine bottles but above it all floated the rub of the evening which could float only for so long before Alice pulled it from the rafters and dropped it on Peter.

"Who killed Piers and Henry?"

Peter shook his head, a mixture of shame and just damn despair that his school, the school that he loved so very much, that he admired, could suffer such base disrepute. Karin shook her head to hide a wry smile in response to the fleeting thought of, well, really, let's be honest, everyone's shit stinks. Adrienne scooped the guacamole into a bowl, placed the bowl on a larger plate and surrounded it with a selection of biscuits from that pretentious deli in the High Street, 'Retiring Tarts', or something of that twee ilk. Alice dipped a biscuit in twice. Peter emptied some Walkers cheese and onion crisps into another, much larger bowl, another of Karin's Zambian or was that Zimbabwean acquisitions, and Karin delicately and precisely arranged some slices of carrots and celery around an elaborate hummus dip that she had whipped up from Sainsbury's and elegantly topped with hot chilli sauce. They were all ready for a big night which would perhaps see them playing a few hands of Bridge.

Alice couldn't wait for the fripperies of polite banter, "What d'reckon Piers knew, Peter?" Direct and forthright, if not a tad feisty.

Peter shrugged between guacamole and shiraz, "That's what we were trying to work out at the funeral today."

"Who's we?"

"Oh you know ..."

"No."

"What?"

"What he knew."

"And presumably, who knew he knew."

"Knew what?"

"Who knows?"

"I reckon it's got something to do with what he found in those files," Stephanie could hear just enough to be able to contribute.

"What files?"

"He had files?"

"Loads of them," a pause from Peter. "Perhaps all of them."

"What files?"

"Who knew?"

"I thought everyone knew."

"I didn't."

"What files?"

"I didn't."

"Why did he have files?"

"What files?" Alice began to sound like a parrot.

"He was writing a book."

"On what?"

"A history of the school."

Stephanie had only caught a bit of the interchange, "Do you remember he wrote a play years ago about the history of the school."

"Did he?"

"When?"

"Oh, you know, in the sixties or something, when these things were... Well..."

"What?"

"You're kidding."

"Nup. Hilarious. It was all about how the school attracted students from the colonies, the expat type of family. He tried to make a comment on the invasion of, I don't know, some place in Africa. Moral comment. It came out so wrong. He had natives all running around half naked, and their only lines were 'ugga bugga'".

"For real?"

"Bad."

"No. Really?"

"And the school performed it?"

"Sure did."

"You're pulling our leg."

"She's right," Peter supported Stephanie. "The set was actually quite good. They had the embarking ship bound for the colonies taking off from the shoreline the other side of the cricket pitch. Ingenious really."

"Well, come on."

"Yeah, but it was of its time."

"And culture."

"And context."

"Can say that again. Awful."

"He was a man of his time."

"Sure was."

They'd got off the direction of the conversation and all had images of tawdry social comment exploding in their minds which required generous gulps of wine, as they processed past proceedings.

"So, what is he writing now?" Alice wanted to refocus onto what was relevant.

"Was."

"A history of the school," Peter continued. "So he had access to all the archives which included every student's file. It was a global and personal history of the school dating back to 1673."

"Files that old?"

"Well, he was starting there and then bringing it into a more modern age. I suppose it became more factual, perhaps more intimate as soon as there was a filing system. Don't know when that started. Interesting though." Peter always looked at possibilities.

"So he'd know things."

"Knew."

"Probably knew things before the press got hold of anything."

"So, do you think someone saw someone fucking a goat?" Alice just went straight for the throat.

"He did need to get all the past students' agreement."

"Most would be dead?"

"Everyone loves him."

"Loved."

"Well..."

"But are you saying," and Adrienne was a tad diffident here, "that he had access to all the students' files, and that includes the compromising ones too?"

"Precisely. And the staff files."

"Staff files?"

"There are files on staff."

"Of course there are."

"Me too?

"All of us."

"I want to see mine."

"Confidential."

"Except for Piers."

"Precisely."

"Goat fucking going on here, I reckon."

"What did he know?"

"Who did he find?"

"That I suppose," Peter sighed, "is the rub. Corbett and Reeves had dinner with him, only last month, and apparently he told them that he was up to the sixties."

"Sure to be something there."

"A number."

"That the school would like to deny, cover up, hide?"

"Get rid of."

"Certainly keep out of the press. No news is good news here."

"They can't do that..." Adrienne was generally always surprised when it came to these big ideas of moral ambiguity.

"They can, and they especially can if Piers was telling them what he had."

"Bribery."

"And corruption."

"The plot thickens."

"Maybe..."

There was a pause as they all pondered their position in the plot. Wine glasses were topped up, crisps crushed and carrots crunched. Quite a lot of noise in the silence with their thoughts shouting above the rest. Thoughts of hearts, clubs and dummies had been dismissed although Karin was quietly setting out two packs of cards and a scorepad.

"But... maybe he wanted to cover them up because he had known about them and hadn't said anything."

Another shifty silence as some pennies dropped and shillings were picked up. Surely, there must be something about the recent spate of claims against the school from old students who had been buggered during their time at the school. The thought of Piers being implicated, however much he was a tosser, was horrible, and suddenly not out of the question.

Perhaps a misguided old boy, too loyal for his own good, had done the bludgeoning to save Piers from the courts. Thoughts were nascent and jumbled. At best, Piers may have covered up what had gone on; at worst, he was a perpetrator and found the records of his own deeds in the files.

It was really all too awful.

Stephanie found it all frightful. She moved away from the group and started to arrange the elaborate pudding that she had brought for later on in the evening. It was a Tarte Tatin and was Stephanie's piece de resistance, so to speak. The story goes, according to Stephanie, that Nun Tatin was making a tart for the bishop – get the drift – and during its construction she dropped it on the ground, where it landed upside down. Horrified, and needing to impress her potential beau, she had slid it back onto the baking tray and baked it in its prone position, serving it as though it was meant to be. The bishop was suitably impressed and we can only imagine the emergence of the future relationship; after all, he did name a pudding after her. Stephanie produced a Tarte Tatin at least twice a year for this little Bridge group and it was always greeted with an ever embellished tale, the bishop got sleezier and the nun tartier, alongside laughter and cheer.

More wine was poured, more dips and cheeses attacked and more thought was given to what might have happened to the erstwhile Piers.

It didn't take long for Adrienne to pipe up, "We've just assumed that Peter knows it all, but, but, but, Stephanie, you've been here forever too."

"What?"

"Well, you must know who were Piers' acquaintances in the sixties."

Stephanie guffawed, "I'm not that old, darling!"

"Sorry, sorry, I didn't mean that. But you know what I mean," Adrienne cajoled.

Stephanie was more than astute. A fairly non descript demeanour hid a very keen mind. She was dark, round and really looked like she should have been a farmer's wife, in that old style. She sure didn't look quite right in a female professional power suit. If she was truly honest with herself, she would have loved to have lived in a farm kitchen making hot scones, pancakes on Tuesdays, milkshakes after school, brownies by the bucketload and Tarte Tatins for a bit of excitement after milking. She could imagine herself making pots of tea for farm hands by day and calving cows by night. She would have kept the books, stoked the Aga and created a warmth in her kitchen that often became the centrepiece for gossip and resolution for the villagers. But life had not been that kind to her. A series of totally inappropriate boyfriends: the Australian water engineer who ended up in the arms of a Northumbrian Morris dancer; the funambulist who discovered he was afraid of heights, and the nearest she got to a farmer was the careless snake milker who ended up in a cemetery in Ludlow. All had, of course, led to nothing. She had dipped her toes every now and again into that romantic river over the course of her thirty years at the school, but generally, she had withdrawn them quickly and dried them off and put her socks back on. Nothing seemed at all suitable and anyway, there just wasn't enough time to engage in romantic sweet nothings. She had worked loyally, just another woman of her generation who genuinely thought that if you worked long hours, then you would be rewarded. Loved by her students and totally invisible to the careerists, the rest of the staff saw her as a bit of an intellectual chameleon who could always be relied upon to be just there. Perhaps her keen mind meant that she had cut too many people dead. She thought she tried to suffer fools but seeing through the trite drivel meant that she really didn't. Over the years her girth had expanded, her hearing contracted, and in the end it rather felt that she could have been something other than a damn good teacher but she had been unlucky. Not to be defeated, she had an army of nieces and nephews who provided a sort of substitute for her own children. They were a constant source of interest and her love would cascade upon them in the form of scones, tarts, pies and pearls and gold for birthdays and Christmas. She was the sort of aunt who would enlighten, enlargen and enliven her charges' minds, taking them firstly to zoos and Hamleys, and then to theatres and concerts. It is unsurprising then that Stephanie had quietly and systematically worked out the whole of the Pier's debacle days before the funeral began.

"Of course, Piers knew everything." It seemed like Stephanie had just been waiting to tell all. "He was the biggest gossip, don't you know."

We can only imagine her preparing the Tarte Tatin, stirring the flour, cracking the eggs, melting the butter, slicing the peaches, caramelising the sugar and hopping from one foot to another as her mind was cooking up a storm. She could barely contain her thoughts as she waited for the tart to cook and then hurried with it still half hot to our little Bridge club where she could reveal all. All that she knew, all that she thought she knew, and all that she knew she definitely didn't know. "He would have known who did what. He had the files."

Another general, "What files?"

"You know," she puckered her forehead and opened her hands in wonder, "the files."

"What?"

"Tell us about the files." Adrienne made sure that she was facing Stephanie with this question so that Stephanie could lip read what her hearing did not quite pick up.

"The files on the students," she swigged her

first half glass of wine – she was a big drinker – and then seemed to almost melt down into being the centre of the gossip.

"D'you reckon he came across something?"

"Certain to have."

"What?"

"Whatever happened back in the sixties, and someone didn't want to tell anyone."

"D'you reckon he was bribing someone?"

"Riding someone?"

"B...r..iiibing," Adrienne faced Stephanie and overly articulated.

"Goat fucking, more like," murmured Alice.

"Who?"

"Do the police know about these files?"

"Why would they?"

"Someone should tell them."

"The school's surely not going to tell anything."

"You saying 'cover up'?"

"So who killed him?"

Peter was getting tetchy. He grabbed a deck of cards and started shuffling them, "Let's play some Bridge.

"There must be half a dozen people at the funeral who'd know something."

Stephanie guffawed with that deep resonance that seemed to emanate from the base of her windpipe. "Half a dozen? Half the congregation you mean."

"Are you saying that everyone knows about the abuse?"

"I'm not being obtuse."

"Abuse."

"What abuse? Oh abuse. 'Everyone' is the superlative, but most."

"Huge claim, huge claim." In shuffling the cards Peter had dropped the three of diamonds on the rug and bent over to pick it up. Out of the corner of his eye, he saw a tortoise crawling from behind the worn leather sofa. A scaley brownish head was emerging from its shell and the tortoise was meandering ever so slowly across the rug towards a fresh lettuce leaf. He thought little of it and kept shuffling the cards as he asked, "Okay, who's in? Let's play."

Karin, who had remained largely silent and was never one to get greatly involved in matters of intrigue, gossip or innuendo, quickly took one spot and Peter sat down opposite. North and South were set, so Alice and Adrienne took East and West while drinking, eating, talking and occasionally breathing. Peter started to deal. The jumble of ideas continued to spew.

"So, you're saying that it is a huge conspiracy. A bit like a masonic gathering. Very clandestine. Very old boy. Closed ranks."

"Hush, hush."

"I'm not saying anything."

"You are really," Alice said under her breath.

"But you are," Adrienne laughed out loud.

"Just putting things out there."

"I passed our esteemed Headmistress on the way here." Karin tried to change tack, just in case things heated up.

"What was she doing? Where was she going?"

"Not another death?"

"Is there a function on tonight?"

"Probably reflecting on such a successful sermon she delivered today."

A vague hint of a giggle or two could be heard around the room.

"Yeah, what was that all about?"

"Has she got a brain?" Alice, as ever, straight to the rub. "Actually, we know the answer to that. How could the Governors appoint someone with a degree from Essex University?"

"Great Yarmouth, I think."

"Whatever."

"She looked pretty tarted up."

"She does seem to overdo it on that front."

"Matter of choice."

"Trying to impress?"

"Clandestine relationship?"

"Curiouser and curiouser."

They were all laughing and only some felt a little mean but the feeling quickly passed as they chortled away and continued to sort the cards that Peter had just dealt.

He always felt uncomfortable with these conversations and as it was his bid, he moved things along with, "One diamond."

"One heart."

"Pass."

"One spade."

"Pass."

"One no trump."

"Pass."

"Pass."

"Pass."

"Moving and shaking here."

"Hardest contract."

"Should have put her in two then."

The usual guffaw at this absolutely rational false logic was followed by the normal shifting and shuffling after the close out of the contract and the normal

questions: "Who's dummy?" "Whose no trumps?" and
"Okay, Alice is dummy and Peter to lead." Thoughts
were concentrated on the cards for a brief moment.
The first few tricks were played fairly quickly but as
soon as Adrienne stopped to change her plan for the
next few rounds as Peter had an unexpected singleton,
Stephanie sparked up. She was sitting out this round
having been tarting up her Tatin and she had had a tad
more time to think and return to the discussion.

"She must have a man somewhere."

"Who?"

"The goth."

"How do you know?" As Alice was dummy she,
too, could turn her mind elsewhere and she was always
up for some good goss.

"She always looks a bit different each time she
goes out. She's making an effort."

"Must be a man."

"Could be a woman."

"A veritable tryst."

"How intriguing."

"When do you see her?"

"She has to walk right past my window if she's
going to walk into town, or in fact, anywhere else from
her house."

"Does she do that often though?"

"Oh come on," Adrienne was always the one to
try to give a fair hearing. But few listened.

"Two or three times a week."

"Two or three times a week!"

"That I see her."

"So probably more."

"Probably."

"Maybe she's just going shopping. Like we all

do," Adrienne again.

"Maybe not."

"Give her a break."

"Who's she seeing?"

And Stephanie made a circle with her fingers and put it over the end of her nose, "Fuck knows."

There were a few more rounds and then the conversation descended into supposition, gossip, innuendo and anything else that goes with living in a claustrophobic enclosed encased enclave. Things were said that were really quite cruel, probably true, but cruel all the same. Things were intimated that were probably untrue. Things were claimed that were just plainly wrong. Juicy, gory, titillating but wrong. Perhaps completely typical of a fairly cloistered community. Beneath the rice paper thin veneer of connectedness, trust and honour simmered and bubbled a seething hive of distrust, intrigue, lies and stab-you-in-the-back ambition.

A new headmistress does not have to be that bad to become some kind of Medusa. Even a degree from Warwick may not have saved this one. The animated discussion of this new, young and energetic Headmistress's antics grew from thoughts of a fairly innocent relationship with some chap in town, to tales of this too thin gothic woman getting it off with some nobody in town which morphed into a raunchy affaire with someone's husband and that husband just happened to be a very well known personage in the nation. That's what a couple of glasses of wine and some keen imaginations can do. Thoughts of trysts in far flung places where this well known personage could claim business trips and tax breaks and she could claim parent meetings and educational conferences. Thoughts of sex and bondage with the odd threesome thrown into the mix. Thoughts that demonised this poor woman and yet made them all feel a little bit more virtuous. And then, suddenly, just as things were getting interesting and suggestions that she, dressed in a leather g-string, had tied him to the bed, the doorbell rang, and Robert was letting himself into the apartment as Adrienne was wondering whether she had sex on top or underneath because on top would mean that her face would sag downwards so she rather thought that underneath would be better.

Alice just added, "Goat style."

Robert was pretty well always late. If, on the rare occasion, he was on time, it meant that he'd been able to meet up with his friend Rick, a local journalist, in the middle of the day and they had had time to plan Robert's Sunday morning radio slot. He had a weekly slot from 10-12pm and a few years ago had essentially been given open slather to play whatever he felt appropriate by the local radio station. He and Rick could spend hours every Thursday beforehand, assiduously and forensically, planning the progression of music that would lull through the airwaves. None of the rest of the Bridge group had ever listened to the programme: Sunday mornings were taken up by duty in the boarding house or recovering from one of the rare Saturday nights not in the boarding house. They could only imagine who might listen: those returning from a Sunday ritual, the widowed, the sleepless, those who had long run out of things to say to their spouse. It was odd how often Rick forgot this meeting; one could almost set one's watch by it. The problem was, if he forgot, and he usually did, then they would reschedule for later in the afternoon and then they would get lost in the possibility of choice and structure.

The radio programme gig was one of Robert's many 'post-retirement' jobs. Having retired from teaching, he had mooched his way for the last three years around the periphery of local media. Having taught Media Studies, in many of its forms, over the last forty years, he had vicariously played out a career that he had wished he had followed many moons and Sunday roasts before, and had gone into teaching, rather like many teachers of his era, because he hadn't been able to hang out long enough to make a fist of his first choice of career. Arriving in Australia from the States, he had been a part of that tail end of migration which felt a little like an inversion of the potato famine. Australia needed teachers at the time and he had spent ten glorious years in Wodonga, a town on the banks of the Murray which felt almost cosmopolitan even in the seventies. He often spoke of those years as happy years and fondly remembered the older couple with whom he had found lodgings and shared many, many bottles of Northern Victorian red discussing the merits of Richard Wright and James Baldwin. And it was indeed here, in this rather two horse town, where he met an English girl who eventually drew him back to the Northern Hemisphere and a job at this esteemed school on the south coast. They were due to marry within a month of his planned arrival at Heathrow. Arrangements were made and she drove up to meet him. His ecstasy and excitement of that airport meeting was quickly dashed when she rushed up to his weaving baggage trolley, held out the engagement ring in its box and told him that she had met another love of her life and the wedding was off. He was left with two battered suitcases and one battered ego in front of Boots and wondered how to make it to the train that would take him south. A cold apartment greeted him on his arrival at the school where he sat for the first evening alone on one of his suitcases, fondling the engagement ring. Life goes on he supposed. He spent the first term on a mattress and ate in the staff dining room, but once the holidays came he was able to pull himself together, sold the engagement ring and furnished the apartment. The furniture stayed in the same place for thirty years while he taught Media and English and ached for journalism. He had never dipped his toe in that romantic lake again, perhaps he had been too busy, perhaps he had thought that this lacuna in his existence was too risky to fill. He was seen as solid, content and reliable, never making head of department nor head of house, no ambition, just committed to the school and its students. During his thirty years at the school, he had forged strong contacts, if not friendships, with many in local radio and newspaper circles and so emerging from the mud of this educational existence three years ago, he had managed to edge himself more firmly into those circles, getting a gig at the local radio. It was remarkable how often he managed to be in the right place at the right time, sometimes for a photo opportunity or sometimes just to report on something. It meant, that in his latter sixties, he was developing a strengthening relationship with the local rag. Often, he would have the inside knowledge or gossip of local affairs and would confidentially spill the beans the evening before the paper was put to bed.

It was therefore no surprise that the first thing he said, bursting through the door armed with more wine and cheese was, "She was drugged."

There was a moment's pause where crisps were

sort of semi-suspended in the mouth and a wine glass stopped mid raise, a quasi hiatus in the general gossip. Remember they had been wonderfully embellishing the imagined underbelly of their esteemed headmistress and now had to pause these thoughts, substitute them with this new revelation and respond, "Drugged!"

Considering they had just been talking about the sex life of the Headmistress they all had images of her with leather, whips, all sorts of bondage. Now a good old drugging was padding out the picture perfectly.

"Who?" said the previously silent one.

"How are you, Robert? I'll grab a glass."

"We've hardly played two hands yet."

"Been talking about Piers."

"Who's been drugged?"

"The goth?"

"Must've been to have given that sermon."

"Told you some goat fucking has been going on."

Robert busied himself with pouring a glass and taking a bit of guacamole dip, spying the tart in the corner of his eye and smiling, because he liked hot stuff or perhaps because he liked creating a bit of a stir.

"The woman on the boat."

"The watery woman?"

"The lady of the lake, the maid of the marina."

A certain amount of wine had been imbibed and imagination and its articulation was becoming interesting.

"We'd forgotten about her, what with Henry and Piers' problems."

"How do you know?"

"What's the goss?"

Robert had spent the best part of the day with Rick whose desk was close to the editorial office. Robert had also spent the previous day shooting photos for the passing out ceremony for the Guide Dogs in a neighbouring town. There, he had been talking to another journalist who had been reporting on the case and had links, through his girlfriend, to what the police were finding. Robert had a finger in many pies. He had gathered words and phrases, put them into sentences, which translated in fact and figures and had arrived at a supposition.

Jo Ford, wife of Sebastian, was, or perhaps more accurately, had been the watery woman. The couple had been married for years and years and once their children had left the warmth of the home fires, Seb and Jo had bought a yacht and had started to sail the world. First the Channel, which they referred to as La Manche to their friends, then they ventured to the Mediterranean – the Med – for a number of years where they hung around the squares of Ponza and Ventotene sipping Aperol spritz with their antipasto following up with platefuls of ink squid pasta with a jolly good Montalcino and coming home with a few shots of grappa before negotiating the rubber ducky and weaving their way back to their yacht. A harmless argument with the mayor of Ponza saw them set course for the Caribbean. Between big trips, they would always return to some English port or harbour for a number of months where they would invite friends and family to the yacht and plans for the next voyage were hatched.

Five years of apparent bliss with the children completing university and ending up in Munich and Birmingham, oddly enough, two cities which are about as landlocked as you can get in Europe, had seen them demolish dozens of bottles of Louis Roederer – which is the only champagne one uses when one is making Kir Royale – and devour hundreds of kilos of smoked salmon, foie gras and Beluga caviar. The flip side of this indulgence was the emergence of a particularly belligerently increasing waistline for Jo combined with that rather heavy jowly look so common in her kind of middle aged woman. She bought balloonish off the shoulder dresses and increased the cheekbone emphasising blusher to avoid the hideous thought of cutting back on imbibing and ingesting. Perhaps for them both, the veneer of the high life was the real thing but the veneer could suffice only for so long.

Eventually Jo had wanted home and stability. She no longer wanted to feel the water beneath her bed. She wanted the earth to stay still. She wanted to be able to nip down to the shops for a pint of milk in the morning and to the local in the evening for a glass or two of wine with some steady mates. She wanted a normal married life without the mythical attachments of the buccaneer or pirate. In fact, she knew that they needed to pull in the purse strings and to stop consuming quite so much. Those loose fitting shirts, elastic waisted trousers, even if they are Chanel or Versace, were starting to get even tighter and that generous waistline and those droopy jowls were impossible to disguise however expensive the bling or the cut.

And so they had compromised. Buying a large, thatched cottage on the outskirts of this coastal town where Jo could walk on solid ground while continuing to neck champagne and Sebastian could wander down to the marina to tinker on his boat whenever he felt the need for moist magic, seemed to be the solution. The children came for weekends, either down from Brum or Munich, courtesy of the M5 or Ryan Air and sometimes both depending on Ryan Air's fripperies. With them they bought a seemingly inexhaustible herd of friends who thought that parents who owned sizeable thatched cottages, a Porsche and a yacht in a Royal marina, parents who still smoked a bit of dope alongside the Louis Roederer, must have it all. They bragged of their connections and hoped for subsequent invitations and were of an age where they never asked where all the money came from. The Fords were popular and quite the trendy older couple, a couple who had survived the torrid years of parenthood and had approached middle age with a rather refreshing air.

So, to get burnt in your boat when things appeared to be going swimmingly well must have been a bit of a downer. By all accounts Sebastian had been distraught. After all, we did see his initial reaction from our eyrie in Stephanie's flat towards the end of Chapter One.

Robert was getting into his narrative and knew that he had his audience dangling and so continued to describe how the children had arrived almost immediately, a day after the explosion, and had gone down to the marina to survey the empty space where their mother had been. DNA testing had saved them all from the hideous process of identification and so all that remained was for them to inter themselves in the large thatched cottage and await the results of the post mortem. It was only after this that they would be able to cremate the leftover charred and soggy remains of their mother.

The children had tried to keep up their father's

spirits. Cooking healthy meals of sauerkraut and bratwurst, reheating old Macdonald's and frequenting the local fish and chip shop seemed to offer him some comfort. They had raided the cellar for vintage wine that he had laid down just after leaving university and had waited ever since for the suitable moment to open. This, the children thought, was that suitable moment. They had fossicked in cupboards to find old photo albums and then moved onto ipads and Facebook accounts. They were working on celebrating a memory rather than mourning a loss.

But they were still young and even they had difficulties. The daughter would go off for an afternoon and just walk along the sea wall, watching the dipping and diving seagulls while vaguely wondering if there was more to the moment. The son got drunk with his father, wondering whether his man in Munich was really a long term affaire, so that by ten o'clock each evening he would fall into some vaguely soporific morose mood which became more and more introspective about his own life rather than the death of his mother and distress of his father.

Robert was enjoying his drooling audience. His story had formed over the last couple of days as he pieced together snippets from various sources. Some moments were embellished, some just plainly imagined. The Bridge players were lapping up every word and creating their own, other, stories.

Interviews with the police, Robert reported, had come to nothing. Sebastian had said that Jo had gone down to the yacht for the evening.

"No," there hadn't been an argument – they had had all those years before.

"No," she hadn't been depressed – she'd

overcome all that years before.

"No," there had not seemed anything out of the ordinary.

"Yes," they had a happy marriage, or at least one that they both had accepted, "if you call that happiness."

And so the questions went on and got nowhere. Suggestions that she may have been having an affaire were, in Sebastian's view, grossly misguided and seemed to be fired so wide of the mark they were almost comical.

"So what about the post mortem?"

"Ah, now this is where it becomes interesting."

The audience swallowed more wine and dipped a bit more guacamole.

The local paper had, perhaps by nefarious and certainly through shifty ways, obtained a copy of the results. Evidence of vast quantities of alcohol – not a surprise – were combined with significant quantities of Doecyzone – big surprise. Sebastian had been asked if Jo was on this fairly hefty medication. Her GP records were examined. The police searched the large thatched cottage. There was no evidence anywhere that could suggest that she had been prescribed or was taking anything for depression. Sebastian agreed that the 0.12 alcohol reading was not out of character but he could not fathom the Doecyzone.

The audience pondered. Robert enjoyed the stage. They had all forgotten the Bridge game. More celery dipping, crisp crunching and wine imbibement.

For some reason the two deaths on campus were put aside. Perhaps because they felt a very personal connection to the watery woman because they had been there, unknowingly to watch her firstly smoke and then char. Perhaps they felt they had a close and personal connection to the case.

"Do the police reckon it's murder?"

Robert was nodding and chewing, a sort of habit he had acquired where he could look involved and yet not be partisan.

"Oh must be an accident." Of course this was Adrienne's response.

"Do they have leads?"

"Nope," he swallowed rather purposefully, "but there is one piece of information that is particularly interesting..."

There was another hiatus as thoughts hung just beyond their grasp. Yet again, biscuits made it to the lips but didn't pass further, elbows raised glasses but paused before the sip and the rim rested on lips. It bore some resemblance to that moment when they had all been watching *She's the One* just moments before the big bang.

"...Sebastian Ford is an old boy of the school."

Huge intakes of breath as Stephanie exclaimed, "There's the connection. I knew it. Something was going on." Her voice seemed to crescendo as she moved through the phrases.

The rest remained immobile, silent, processing. Thoughts shuffled around their heads as they tried to make sense of this new hand they had been dealt.

Nobody really heard Stephanie's ecstasy and then Karin quietly and logically piped up, "What's that got to do with anything?"

"Goat fucking I reckon."

"Can you fucking shut up about your fucking goat fucking."

Robert had already made sense of much.

"Probably nothing, but it is odd, or at least, a coincidence that even this death, probably murder, is also connected to the school where there have been two other deaths, or perhaps murders."

"Yeah but why would you kill the wife of an old boy?"

"Do we reckon she knew something about him in the files?"

"These bloody files again. What files?"

"One is definitely murder."

"And do we think Henry's is just unlucky?"

"Another coincidence?"

"Too many coincidences."

Peter sat down and his shoulders slumped forward. He was trying to remember a one Sebastian Ford when he was at school. He didn't want to remember someone who was so connected with such a sordid affair and so it was lucky, that try as he might, he couldn't remember the name and wasn't going to lie about it. He got up needing to find more wine. Opening the fridge door he exclaimed, "Fuck."

The others turned around, jolted from their thoughts.

"Fuck! What the hell... oh... shit." And he shut the fridge door.

"Try the other fridge," Alice called out, knowing what had happened and slightly giggling. "Sorry, I forgot to tell you I changed them all over last weekend as I'm starting to wake them up."

Peter had opened the door of the fridge expecting to grab the bottle of sav blanc; instead, he nearly grabbed one of Alice's sixteen tortoises which were all being gently woken up from their hibernation. The beginning of April always saw her move the tortoises from the tortoise fridge in the laundry into the kitchen fridge. There was no particular reason for this except perhaps Alice felt that her family could now join her in the main part of the house. She would then slowly turn up the temperature in the fridge until they started to wake up and she could move them into the fox proof enclosure in the garden from where each could be given outings into the apartment over the summer.

Peter's exclamatory "Fuck" was one of surprise rather than horror; over the winter he had forgotten about Alice's pets. There followed a perfunctory enquiry as to their health and then all was put right with the finding of the wine in the now laundry fridge.

General sleuthing was reignited as the tortoise interlude had provided the others with more thinking time.

"Do you think that she knew that he had been abused?"

"Where's the abuse?"

"Big leap. Need to think about that one."

"Huge leap."

"What?"

"Perhaps some random from the town just decided to drug her wine and burn her boat."

"Too random."

"Sensible."

"We need more drama than that."

"So connect to the school."

"Much more fun."

"It would be very planned if that was the case."

"Too planned?"

"Not sure."

"We've kind of hit a road block on that one.

Have you picked up anything in the town about Piers'
and Henry's deaths?"

Robert shook his head in a vaguely mournful
manner. He'd sort of run out of drama. But then he
remembered something, and cleaning his very clean
glasses said, "No, no, nothing on Henry, but I think the
candlestick was being finger-printed. Actually, I think
the whole room was being finger-printed."

"Of course. So?"

"Three quarters of the staff will be suspects
then."

Alice, Stephanie and Karin all looked at the ends
of their fingers and all vaguely rubbed them in some
vain hope that they might not become suspects.

"The police are beginning to realise that. And
they are also beginning to realize that people shut down
very quickly when it comes to their own."

"Did they find out anything at the funeral?"

"Not sure. Haven't heard anything about that."

"But," said Stephanie, "the librarians have been
in and out of his house with trolleys loaded with files.
Now we can't miss that. There must be something in
those files. There must."

"Must."

The quick-fire questions and instant conclusions
came from Adrienne and Alice.

For most of the conversation Karin had kept
predictably quiet. Silent. Listening. Observing. She
quietly, methodically and scientifically said, "There's got
to be something in those files."

"There's got to be something in those files."

"There's got to be something in those files."

"I'd love to know what is in those files."

Who would know? What was the connection

between them? The charred woman on the boat, the man impaled by his own ceiling and the chap bludgeoned by a candlestick. Rationally, we would need to think that the three deaths were not a coincidence. But how rational are we?

There would be no more Bridge played that evening as the conversation went around and around in circles as wobbly reasoning sprung from wobbly facts and they thought about the possibilities of what could have happened. It was four rather wobbly and fuzzily addled Bridge players who stumbled or cycled home at about one o'clock the following morning.

****

Given the recent happenings, our little Bridge group was clearly not the only group rife with gossip, innuendo and insinuations. Many others were coming to their own conclusions, far-fetched or otherwise. It was therefore of no surprise that all staff were, yet again, summoned to the Common Room before the start of classes the next morning. There seemed to be a run on these summonses and Alice, Karin and Stephanie had to drag themselves across the quad with thumpingly heavy heads, stomachs running on coffee and breaths that smelt like a distillery. If they had been able to take in the appearance of those around them, they would have seen many likenesses. A myriad of parties had emerged out of the funeral, and like with the Bridge group, alcohol and dope had created a goodly number of sleuths and super sleuths whose investigations had settled on suspects whom no one could quite remember in the seediness of the morning. Few looked like they could take on the rigours of teenagers but the few that did were dressed in their usual badly tailored off-the-peg suits and brown shoes, all ready to take the teaching profession and tip it on its head as they hung to their rung on the ladder.

The Headmistress came in with a flourish, sporting a natty blue and while outfit with a slight gingham theme which had a disturbing Alice-down-the-rabbit hole effect. The gothic foundation had been enhanced by traffic light red rouge on the upper cheekbones and scarlet lips. By her side, lapdog-like but trying to look in control, trailed Oliver Steele, the Chair of Governors.

Steele was anything but in appearance: a round, jovial face was supported by a similarly round tummy, suggesting jolly times with wine and Port Salut. He had been through a number of wives and the current trophy sported a disturbingly orange suntan against bottle blonde locks, dripping bling and an inane smile. She's very much a bit part in this tawdry tale, certainly not a suspect, and with the life of the normal trophy, producing the 2.3 children necessary for her position and otherwise pretty uninteresting. Oliver, on the other hand, is an enigma. And that is not to say he's a suspect either. An old boy of the school who had entered his father's insurance brokerage straight from school, he had risen through the ranks despite the most hard-arsed nepotism. His ability to analyse and reason was regularly compromised by his need to be seen and appreciated. He always sported an almost too large, red and mouthy round smile which was instantly appealing to all. His ability to make you feel as though you were the most important person in the world at the time was uncanny, as was his appointment to Chairman of the Board of Governors at his own school. Given that he had not really risen through the ranks to the dizzy heights of his own middling insurance company, it was interesting that he was essentially overseeing the accounts and directions of the school. But he was seen as the face of moderation and morality. Fiercely protective of his old school, his old teachers and his school mates, he was also liked by the staff. Interestingly, it was he who oversaw the appointment of this bewitching Headmistress. Seeing him beside her in the Common Room it did not take much to imagine him in grey shorts, white shirt, striped school tie and long socks from his school days, but instead he sported a Savile Row suit, cufflinks and Churches' brogues. He was one of those who truly believed that his school days were the best days of his life and everything afterwards seem to fall just slightly short of the joy of being House Captain in his final year. He was therefore the very best Chairman of Governors, determined to protect his school at all costs so that generations to come could enjoy what he had enjoyed and present generations could continue to donate benevolently. His perky, almost jovial, appearance by the side of this headmistress was unusual and so, despite many fuzzy heads, most members of the Common Room set aside their copy of the *Daily Mail* on their ipads or looked up from a FaceBook scroll on their phones to tune into the first few sentences, just in case, in the very unlikely event, something intelligent, relevant or amusing was said.

But Oliver did not speak. She spoke.

"Thank you all for coming, and at such short notice." Her startling teeth shone out from behind the scarlet lips and that huge square smile. A touch of red had streaked onto the teeth and she read from the screen of her mobile phone. "I realise that you are, like me, very busy people and I would not have demanded your presence unless I had something serious," she paused, she made her eyes rove the room, "very serious to ask of you."

The ipads and mobiles had been reraised once people realised she, not Oliver, was going to speak but now they descended into laps as her tone descended a strained octave.

"I have asked, as you can see, Oliver Steele to be with me while I address you about this serious," another pause, "very serious matter." Pause. "I'm sure you know he is our well-loved Chairman and I believe that his presence will underline and emphasise the importance of my request."

She continued to read from the small screen of her phone. Alice thought about how she told her students that this was not the way to give a formal speech but it was a mere fleeting thought. Presumably this speech had been penned by the solicitors in the early hours of the morning.

"I have to tell you that anything that I say now is 'in camera'. That means, for you, and," a barely muffled titter, "if you are like me, as I didn't know what this term meant before last night, 'in camera' means that what I am saying must remain within these four walls. Anything I say cannot be relayed outside. If you do repeat anything, the terms of all of your contracts will subject you to disciplinary action," another forced eye rove, "including dismissal."

Another mammoth pause, as though a lightning bolt had been ordered by the Tech Department but had slightly missed its cue. Nothing happened, except a few shuffles could be heard as some were returning to their screens sensing a déjà vu. Oliver beamed broadly and standing just slightly behind her left shoulder gave a jolly wave to one of his school mates who was now teaching in the German Department. In return, the German teacher raised his eyebrows and smiled coyly.

The Headmistress continued with her square smile, the foundation seemed to have set and the smile was concreted on. "I have to tell you that events over the last few days have been shocking," another pause, general scan, intake of breath, and the repetition, "shocking. The police seem to think that a number of documents have disappeared from the school." Another, almost accusatory cast of the eyes around the room, a movement of a hand to a breast – a tiny bosom – and a look that was presumably supposed to condemn the culpable in the room, one of those stares that makes you feel guilty, even when you know you're not.

But the teachers remained nonchalant, unmoved, becoming increasingly immune to the acting shenanigans of their shiny square-mouthed headmistress.

She continued, "If anyone knows of these documents, which contain vital police information, then you need to come forward. Now. I think you know who you are. You need to give up these documents, whatever they are." At this point she looked like she'd lost her place in the solicitor's script. "And I, for one, don't know what they are exactly. And I honestly don't. But I do know that if I saw them, I would know what they are." And back on script, "You need to give them to me." Another pause. "If this is too difficult to do personally or if you know of someone or something that would reveal the whereabouts of these documents, then you can, anonymously share that information with the police on the number that my personal assistant will email to you." The hand moved on that tiny bosom, "Let me endorse what I have said, and I cannot say too forcefully, that this is vital police information."

At this point Oliver, who had spotted another mate, stopped waving, appropriated a more demure visage and piped up, "And all this has the support of the Board of Governors."

With that, they both turned on their heels and headed out. A stum silence held for a moment in the air. The poorly suited young ones were completely bemused, the vaguely bored older ones even more so. All had nascent thoughts which could take hours if not days to process and articulate. So, there was not much really to gain from staying and everyone meandered out towards their offices, classrooms, libraries or Science labs with absolutely no intention of thinking, in that particular moment, about said documents.

All that could be heard were slight murmurings along the lines of ,"Well, what was that all about?"

7. FIVE NO TRUMPS

The staff had generally dispersed after the Headmistress's documents distress call and most did nothing more than carry on with their 'oh so ordinary' lives as teachers in a vaguely, but not really, prestigious school on the south coast of some first world country, a first world country tenuously holding onto some connection with the greater community across the water and even more tenuously gripping by the end of its fingernails to some historical period of Empire and that idea of gentlemanly behaviour. However, there were many rumour mongers who could wax lyrical about the contents and whereabouts of these documents, which sometimes became files.

Discussion ensued as to the difference between a document and a file and as to who would have them, and indeed, what they may look like. Blue was generally agreed as the colour, although some adhered to the theory that they would probably take the form of a manila folder containing sheets of paper. After all, it was thought, everything used to be ordered in precise manila before the breakthrough discovery of colour-coding which clearly improved the quality of management within organisations.

Gossip mongers in one coven suggested that perhaps something had been purloined, perhaps one of the files held by Piers, and if Piers had known who had nicked it and what it was, here was a failsafe reason as to why he was killed. An opposing coven was sure that the documents made connections between recorded instances of abusive behaviour in years gone by. Piers would have known who did what to whom and someone did not want their name dragged through the mud; victim nor perpetrator.

Someone must be covering up something for someone. Everyone and no one seemed to be implicated in the close community of people connected only by contract. As the excitement of possibilities crescendoed, names were bandied about willy-nilly with no thoughts of consequences, slander, libel or accountability. Connections from the past were remembered, discussed, reimagined and fabricated. There were suppositions of someone being paid off, suggestions that Oliver Steele was a part of an elaborate intrigue of misdemeanours and cover ups dating back to the seventies which were akin to the concurrent Cold War machinations. All were libellous and yet none were libellous as there were no actual accusations, no real allegations, just down-to-earth good fun gossip and innuendo where all tried not to take centre stage. The great thing about this gossip, like so much gossip, was to ensure that you were the first person to know and therefore be the first person to pass on the tittle tattle in hushed whispers that could shake the world for twenty minutes.

Gossip was a fun thing and the Common Room had been playing the goss game for the last couple of years. Essentially this game consisted of two teachers deciding what goss they were going to spread: one of the inhouse lawyers had been a model for Versace; the head gardener kept pythons; so-and-so was pregnant; the school was going broke. It was agreed that one of the teachers would start the rumour and then the bet was on and the clock ticking as to how quickly that rumour could get back to them. The record over the last couple of years was one hour and thirty-four minutes.

And so, given how adept the staff were with spreading gossip, it was unsurprising that the name of a former deputy headmaster of the school came up in this context and then, inevitably, the name of this most obvious teacher.

Before his sacking the previous year, the dangerous Bruce Knight had served the school for nearly twenty-two years. An unusual human being whose penchant was telephone directory collection, he had converted a garage, a shed and a cellar to house his hundreds of directories and boasted inclusions such as Edward Heath, Hitler's mother and John Lennon's third girlfriend. Not once, but many times had he been the subject of a custom's investigation because officers could not let forty odd directories proceed through Customs and Irritations without wondering that something rather more fishy must be in the wings.

Rumour had already ascertained and confirmed that he was writing a 'reveal all' book on the school. He was going to lay bare all the wheels within wheels that kept the place turning, kept it looking like an elegant swan floating effortless on a river, yet paddling like fury against an unremitting current below. A peculiar man who had been educated at Shore in Sydney, he had found his niche at the school where he could wear tweed jackets, with padded elbows and brogues and present as a quasi-Englishman. He had taught Literature badly, not because he was poorly read, but because he didn't think in the abstract. He had, years ago read a critical review that he could follow on *King Lear.* He applied this review to everything that he subsequently taught making his teaching just a tad one dimensional. His eccentricities could sometimes be explained away as character building but his attention to student welfare was, in this modern age, unusual. He ran extracurricula activities for the students such as paper dart making, barbeque cooking and fly tying. The students loved him, the mothers worshipped him, the school hierarchy was wary.

His raison d'etre was to prove that one or other of his conspiracy theories about the school and its fabric was true. Too often staff could be seen rushing away from the Dining Hall having just been caught, like the proverbial rabbit, by another controversial conspiracy theory barrelling at them from the popping eyes of Bruce Knight. Eventually the school had applied considerable pressure, making him accountable for his behaviour, just waiting for him to slip up. He did. One evening, he was ten minutes late to Saturday night boarding duty and was sacked. He was dark. The callous cruelty of the school deserved an equally harsh report into its inner dealings: dealings of cover ups, nepotism, despotism, cronyism and just general bad behaviour. A tell-all book was sure to be on the cards, one that dealt with facts not metaphor.

Everyone knew that Piers had not been happy

to hear about the impending publication. He had made his views well known in the Owen Room on many tedious occasions. And so, it was unsurprising that the front runner for Piers' murder was Knight. The general agreement was that he had murdered Piers out of spite because the old boy would not release to him the final three documents he needed to put the nail in the school's coffin. What these three documents were, and why three quite frankly, and what form they took was anyone's guess.

****

Amidst the suppositions, the wondering and the scandalising, Henry's funeral seemed to get lost. Patricia and her son had not wanted a large affair. They knew that despite the rhetoric, the school was a business not a cosy community, 'a loving family', which the headmistress had, only quite recently, claimed behind that ruby red square smile. In the same caring breath, she had announced that anyone who wanted to go to Henry's funeral would have to apply for leave within the next two hours and only the first four would be relieved of their duties. Patricia had used the rumour mill to let it be known that it was a very private affair and the underground web of concerned members of the Common Room agreed that only her closest four friends would apply for leave.

Alice, Stephanie, Karin and Adrienne were the ones to board the very early London train on the morning of the funeral. Arriving into the acrid smells of Victoria, they dipped down into the underground, jumped onto the Victoria line and hopped off at St Pancras to catch the 7.35 bound for the northern reaches and Lincoln. Weirdly, this flat drained county had produced yet another teacher out of its dykes and Bridges.

Two of our four intrepid travellers were excited by the journey: Stephanie because it was almost like going home, and Karin just liked the thought of another destination. Alice was feeling a bit touchy but hadn't said that they would be passing through Market Harborough, a town she had known well when dating an old boyfriend who had lived in Leicestershire; she knew this train journey like the back of her hand. Adrienne on the other hand always felt that anything north of Hampstead was rather foreign, certainly anything beyond Bedford very much felt like outer space. She was feeling insecure about the day's antics. Lincoln seemed more intimidating to her than Worthing or Brighton and she was pleased when they caught a taxi to the small village church where Henry had spent most of his Sunday mornings of his formative years before heading off to Hertford College to read History.

Their shoes scrunched on the gravel of the weed-framed churchyard path as they passed an array of moss-encrusted gravestones of bygone centuries. Once into the cool portico of the Norman village church, they tried to quietly turn the heavy circular iron door handle of the heavy oak door. Two of them had to push to enable it to swing open and they both almost fell onto the stone flags as the door eventually gave way. There were no ushers, no welcoming handshakes. Inside there was a spattering of dark coloured suits and bowed, hushed heads, presumably a few relatives, a few old friends from Henry's Oxford days, some of their children and one or two grandchildren. Henry and Patricia had been a contained couple, their family favouring privacy and seclusion, keeping themselves to themselves, quite happy in their own and each other's skins.

Our four musketeers surveyed the congregation and hoped they were suitably attired and would be able to blend into the crowd without too much notice.

Patricia wore the customary dark glasses, a demure dark, but not black dress and most suitable shoes for walking on the churchyard path. In Patricia fashion, she seemed most pragmatic about the whole thing. After all, what had happened had happened. Her son was by her side should she need propping up. The church was unadorned except for a large bunch of Easter lilies that lay, vaguely haphazardly, atop the coffin, accompanied by a note inscribed with 'Our Rock'. Barely audible chatter, supportive smiles, the odd touch of the forearm and an undercurrent of murmuring seeped gently through the congregation.

Alice thought that the four of them bolstered the congregation in the pews and was glad that she had set the alarm for five o'clock, fought the desire to hit the insistent buzzing button and go back to sleep, taken two Panadol to combat the hangover headache and joined the others at the school gates to take a taxi to the station. She now felt virtuous, especially as she knew that most had come from Nottingham, Sheffield or Derby and they had made the effort to come from south of London.

The men were mostly in their best Marks and Sparks suits with pre-chosen shirt and tie combo and shoes that needed to see the inside of a cobblers. There were a few farmers who had taken the time to bathe between feeding the cattle, tilling the field or shearing the sheep, and leaving for the funeral. They had donned their smart shabby tweeds and followed their forthright, no nonsense wives into the landrover, driven to the church, swapped roles and led their wives up the scrunchy path. The older women had also shopped at Marks and Sparks, the younger at TK Maxx, although one or two had splashed out at Joules, and they all looked neat, tidy and appropriately demure. Quietly and efficiently they had taken off their aprons, washed the flour from their hands and were rather excited about having an occasion to wear something a little more flattering. The murmurings were warm and soft, the vicar quiet and welcoming, the hymns understated and the organist, who probably needed an extra day to practise the hymns, was quite happy to set her own pace. The readings were short, the prayers pertinent and the sermon brought the whole thing together to honour a quiet, unprepossessing man who had put his family first, and had worked without the need for drum rolls and fanfares. Here was a man who had taken a first in History, had never told anyone, and had followed it with a career as a librarian in some of the great libraries in the nation.

It was apt that no one tried to sing the descant in the final hymn and the service descended into a soft retreat of the coffin down the aisle followed by the close family to the dulcet, caressing tune of *I Vow to Thee my Country*.

The wake was, therefore, an even more sparse occasion in the back bar of the local Crown Inn. At least a dozen of the congregation had had to return to work immediately after the service and so it was a depleted lot who walked across the village green and past the stone trough, the disused stocks and the little girl who was searching for her lost tortoise behind the cobwebby disused red phone box. They had to wait for an hour or so before the family returned from the crematorium and our little group peeled off from the melee and walked around the village, finding remarkable similarities to villages down south.

Both Alice and Stephanie were in dire need of a drink to fend off the increasing after effects of their hangovers and so they decided to sit in the bar of the pub to await the start of the wake. Karin had followed them into a little alcove at one end of the fairly purply-red lounge bar and without communicating, one of them started to deal on the little table between them.

"One no trump."

"Pass."

"Two clubs."

"Pass."

"Two hearts."

"Double."

"Can I up myself?"

"Pardon?"

"Well can I go three hearts?"

"Think of your partner."

"I can see your hand in the mirror."

Adrienne wheeled around and saw a huge pub mirror behind her and clearly everyone in the room could see why she may want to increase her heart bid.

"Oh, we can't do this then."

"Just keep your hand down."

"No, no, I can't do that."

"Don't feel like it anyway."

"Yeah, need a drink."

And so they ordered another round and waited for the party from the crematorium to arrive. Once the doors were open, chicken sandwiches and iced buns accompanied by a cup of Tetleys were the order of the day. Alice and Stephanie stuck to their sav blancs and with Adrienne, snuck out of a side door and started rolling a joint. This left Karin as the only sensible one who thought she'd better be neither drunk nor stoned if they were all going to get back on the train heading south later that afternoon.

While outside a couple of young men joined them. The nephews of Patricia, they were thoroughly impressed to find two *old* women enjoying a joint. Adrienne was immediately transported to her youth. A misspent youth. But fun. The seventh child of eight, Adrienne had been left to bring herself up. An exhausted mother and a father who never really understood why there were so many children, had little time to focus on her needs. Bohemian benevolence permeated the family and the house, and she thrived. She was able to eat what she wanted, when she wanted, wear what she wanted, go where she wanted, no one was particularly interested in her school results and her brothers often let their friends use her for kissing practice. It was perhaps this latter activity that meant, for her, flirtation was the norm and so by the time she went to Sussex University she was well versed in promising all and delivering little. Unwittingly she became a bit of an enigma. Afterall, she was a child of the fifties living her university years in the seventies, dope smoking, rum drinking and wearing peasant skirts. No one quite understood how Ed managed to inveigle his way into her. But he did. Perhaps it was his newly developed hydroponics, perhaps his devil may care attitude, perhaps because he was, in fact, rather brighter than the rest. Together they had finished university, bought a combi, put it on the Dover-Calais ferry and travelled Europe for a year. If that wasn't enough to break a union then nothing would, and here we are forty years and three children later, with Adrienne flirting with two young men in a Lincolnshire pub as if they were those bright young things of the seventies back at Sussex Uni.

She asked questions of them that suggested that they were the most important things in her life at that moment, taking a joint from one or other of their fingers, inhaling deeply and then fixing them with an unblinking stare while asking about their girlfriends, their living arrangements and what they were doing after the wake. It was a scene experienced before by Alice who looked on with amusement, noting what was said so that she could use it the following week. The boys were enamoured and entertained, thoroughly relieved to have a diversion from the rather turgid stuffiness of the deliberations inside the pub. But Adrienne's visit to her misspent youth and to an idyllic past was brought to an abrupt halt when Karin came out to the garden. She had ordered an Uber and they needed to get on that train going south.

There were the usual platitudes to Patricia and her son which hinted at everything that could not be expressed. All understood that 'when this was all over' there would be time enough to share memories and wine. Excruciatingly correct comments, body language and facial expressions were exchanged and Alice sometimes just wanted to laugh out loud and remind Patricia of wanking. But decorum reigned, they got through it all and were soon hugging Patricia, wishing her well and looking forward to seeing her back at work before jumping into an Uber bound for the station and the journey back down south.

Alice felt a little light-headed, Stephanie a bit more so, Adrienne was pretty stoned and Karin wondered how she was going to get them all back safely. Spewing out of the Uber, Alice and Stephanie spotted the off-licence next to the train station. Karin followed and Adrienne lagged giggling four paces behind. With mere minutes to go before the train left for southern climes, they managed to cobble together a box of Bacardi and cokes, gin and tonics, a packet of cheese and onion crisps and a bottle of nuts. A fair picnic for the journey south was the general consensus.

Finding a quiet end of a middle carriage, where mobiles were allowed and therefore they were less likely to be berated for talking, they set up their very own private mini bar. The worn faux velvet blue and grey seat covers had seen their best; most were threadbare with signs of old, desiccated chewing gum stuck in dubiously contorted places, a nostalgic remnant of British Rail. The whole carriage rattled and trundled down the line, stopping for brief and seemingly pointless moments at a litany of country stations that dotted their way down the line.

Our four musketeers realised they had caught the slow train and settled in for the journey with Stephanie pulling out the cards and readying herself to deal. Karin had taken out some wet wipes and swiped and scrubbed the sticky table while Adrienne and Alice busied themselves with booze and nibbles production. Dealing done, they all dramatically swept up their cards in a flurry of purposeful action, sorted them into suits and then took gulps of wine and crisps.

Adrienne giggled and checked behind her for a mirror.

Stephanie called first, "Noooo bid."

"One club."

"Are we playing a strong one club?"

There was much munching and shaking of the head.

"Pass."

"Two spades."

"Oooo a jump shit."

More munching and nodding.

"Bugger, no bid."

"Four spades."

"Whooha, here we go. Already."

"Okay. Stephanie to lead, Adrienne's playing it and Alice is dummy." Karin was sort of taking control and wondering how on earth Adrienne and Alice could really play.

The train pulled sluggishly out of Newark Castle and was heading towards Leicester.

As she lay down her cards, Alice felt the carriage lurch towards a field of lambs and then instantaneously and miraculously, it righted itself and the cards remained in their place on the table. Stephanie had led with the two of hearts and Alice had put down a very weak hand which contained the ace of clubs and two jacks. Adrienne uttered, from somewhere, the obligatory "Thank you" and to all intents and purposes, it looked as if they were set in for a good ninety minutes of fairly intense Bridge even if Stephanie was a tad tipsy, Alice getting there and Adrienne was giggling.

As dummy, Alice could quietly sip her Bacardi and coke and stare out at that English countryside rushing past the window. The trees in copses on the edge of hedged fields, like the hedges themselves, had budded and bloomed with the promises of the riches of a late spring. While, for some, April may be the cruellest month, May tended to mock. The countryside seemed to have heaved itself out of the grey, overcast skies and permanent drizzle; laneways once smudged with smears of tractor tyres were almost clean and trees had substituted their skeletal brownness with the swathes of green life which transformed dark into light, cold into a vague warmth. Hope was in the air; long days and more than a sight of a patch of blue promised much. England had exchanged her winter blanket and replaced it with a spring coverlet of colour which had crept over the hills, through the fields and ended up running down the hedgerows and into the woods. First the bluebells had burst from the ground and heralded the arrival of the canola crops which wrapped up the hills in a bright warm yellow and once they were in full bloom and not to be outdone, the red poppies would soon take over to shout against the backdrop of green and more green. But how often have we English thought that summer was on the way, when May has mocked, and the warm days have transformed into crisp, cold rain and we're back to rivulets of mud running down the lanes, and we get out our jumpers and coats and wonder why we were fooled again?

Alice was not concentrating on the game; instead her thoughts were mingling with the magic of the countryside, her mind moving from brown mud to green crop and yellow harvest and wondering 'Who's next?' There seemed to have been too many deaths in and around the school. After all, you had to include that woman at the marina; it was so close, it was difficult not to, now that they knew that she was related to an old boy of the school.

The others were continuing to collect, or not, tricks, unaware of Alice's brooding. For Alice, her thoughts seemed to be shouting through her skull and eventually she could no longer contain them, "No mention of how he was killed."

The comment came naturally from Alice but abruptly for the others. Although they had all individually thought of this, none had articulated it and at that particular moment they were concentrating on counting trumps. Once the idea was open, however, they did all want to talk about it.

"The vicar did mention something like 'tragically killed'". Karin was, unusually, the first to get involved.

Stephanie was unable to distinguish between the softer consonants, "Magically filled?"

"TTTragically kkkilled," the other three echoed in emphasised unison, loudly enough that the other five travellers in the carriage turned around with furrowed brows and the odd 'pooh pooh'. They winked at each other and remembered that they had to face Stephanie but somehow being a bit tipsy and the noise of the train meant they did not articulate so decisively and Stephanie's mind did not interpret quite so precisely. A long trip ahead Alice thought.

"A falling ceiling. Pierced by a piece of plaster. Is that tragic or just unlucky?"

"Plucky?"

"UUUUnlucky?" And so it went on.

"It's tragic."

"Not in the Aristotelian sense of tragedy."

"You're a pompous git, Alice."

"*King Lear* is tragic. Ceiling piercings are not."

"You're a tosser, too intellectual. It's tragic if you're his family."

"Not really, just bloody awful." Alice did happen to be a bit of a stickler when it came to the use of language. "I mean, you know when the TV reports say something like 'young girl tragically killed at level crossing', well that's not the same as the cathartic pity and fear of finding out you've killed your father and married your mother."

"And your brothers and sisters are also your sons and daughters."

"Is it?"

"Sure."

The others had tuned out. Used to Alice's preponderance for literary accuracy, they dug into the jar of nuts and rustled the crisp packet.

Alice was unmoved, "The press now has nowhere to go because they've used up all the superlative language. When something massive does happen, they've already used up any language that might have been useful to distinguish a massive disaster from a miniscule mishap or whatever."

"Whatever."

Sensing that the others, as usual, were totally disinterested in a linguistic discussion, but needing to just make sure that the point was made, she swigged her drink and muttered into the can, "There's nowhere for them to go."

Karin took a sip, Adrienne smiled at something that had occurred in some far-off country, Stephanie took a crunch and they all looked out at the countryside, which, like them, seemed to want to rush onto another conversation – that conversation about Henry.

"Either way he's dead," Stephanie resumed. "Linguistically," she continued facetiously, "we could look at it from a passive point of view that he's dead, or from the active perspective that he was killed." They all started to giggle. "The point, if we go along the active route is, whether he was killed by a falling piece of plaster, or whether he was killed by someone activating the plaster. Is an inanimate object passive or active in this case? To be active, does it have to have a person actioning the plaster?"

"Is actioning a word?"

"Oh shut up!"

"It's one of those wanky words, that people use to sound like they are either thinking or doing something incredible. You know those words – actioning, state of the art, segue, ethicality."

"Substantiation."

"Authenticity."

"Functionality."

"Financial fortification."

"Professional buoyancy."

"Transfuckingparency."

They all had a reflectively sad chortle, thinking of all the modern buzz words of the administration which were so impressive and gave them such credibility through their vacuous nothingness. Words that could be put into shapes and flown onto a PowerPoint screen, perched on pictures of pillars of pedagogy, presented by some wandering, chin couching between thumb and fore finger guru, claiming to be a strategy that would revolutionize teaching. Hot air and vacuums that would later be sent to the burgeoning email inbox of teachers who were just trying to keep their heads above the administrivia bog.

More eating, drinking and reflecting on the murderous state of the school while being gently massaged by East Midlands Trains was had.

"What do you think?" Alice broke their silence.

"About what?"

"Henry."

"His death?"

"Murder."

"Statement or question?"

"Statement."

"No question."

"Well?"

"Not that many police around his place."

"All relative."

"True."

They began to revisit Alice's earlier account of how the police had been through the house the day after the ceiling collapse. Patricia had accompanied her husband's body up north and Alice had been left to look after the boarding house and their house.

The police had cordoned off the house and garden and that plastic yellow and black ribbon had flapped gorgeously nonchalantly around the scene, suggesting intrigue and possibility. The house had been full of people in white plastic suits, masks, goggles, gloves and floppy shoes. The garden, too, seemed to have been sifted to within an inch of its earth for evidence that someone had been there on or before the hours of Henry's demise. The forensics had borrowed ladders from the Maintenance Department and climbed, albeit gingerly, into the roof and examined the fallen evidence from above, below and from within.

Between class and sport on the first day, two girls managed to inveigle their way through the flapping ribbon and into the house claiming that they were hoping to pursue a career in forensic science. They were quickly and summarily dealt with and ten minutes later were dragging their hockey sticks towards summer training. Two others were very quick to spy a particularly young dapper and completely green policeman who was in charge of the yellow and black cordon. Before he knew it, he was having selfies taken with the girls and ended up in his sergeant's office being severely ticked off for being distracted on the job.

Despite the hormonal interruptions, the police were able to take swabs of coffee cups, dog bowls, doorknobs, garden spades and window latches. Photographs of garden beds, garden paths and garden gates were added to the visual evidence provided by hours of video footage of all the working security cameras on the school grounds and the security guards were praised for their assiduous work in collecting such dubiously worthy evidence.

Unfortunately, three of the cameras hadn't been operating on the evening of the death because three boys had disabled them so they could sneak out and catch a taxi to London for the evening, a common occurrence which the school was addressing.

Eventually, after three days of nothing in particular, the men in plastic suits talked to the good looking policeman and his superiors and it was decided that there was nothing else to examine and the Maintenance Department collected their ladders and started to clear up the mess and repair the ceiling.

"So," piped up Karin, ever the scientist, needing facts, "Did they find anything?"

Alice shrugged, "Got no idea, but no one else from the school came to see." She thought for a moment, "Actually. I lie. The Deputy Headmaster did come and have a chat for about ten minutes one day. But that was that."

"What was that about?"

"No idea," Alice shrugged again, "perhaps he had some information to give to them."

"Perhaps he just needed to know when he would be able to get Maintenance in there." Of course, Adrienne saw the good.

"Perhaps he was trying to find out what they had discovered."

"Probably just wanted to say that he had been in on the action."

"You know what he's like."

"Ego driven git."

"Better than a goat?"

The train slowed, the countryside stopped rushing and the backs of terrace houses with handkerchief gardens, washing lines and ramshackled greenhouses gave nonchalant glances at the passing train. They bumped into the magnificent Victoriana of Leicester Station, where outward pomp truly reflected inner substance. Red brick with white framing arches heralded an era far gone when train travel opened up a world rather than just a journey, an era when it felt like values might have been different. The platforms had, long ago, been updated and modernized with buzz and pizzazz which suggested a better service, streamlined efficiency and cleanliness. The original building had been cleaned from the smoky grime of its past and now echoed of a city that had made its money in shoes and now boasted a harmony of cultures.

Karin was safely drinking a second gin and tonic, confident that they would all find home safely and was happy to proffer, "They've been sniffing around the Library as well. They cordoned off his desk and were going through everything there."

"Did they find anything?"

Karin shrugged, "They were boxing it all up."

"Who is they?"

"Are."

"Fuck knows."

"That nebulous they."

"When was that?"

"Dunno, coupla days ago." They narrowed their eyes and pondered the middle distance. "No, it wasn't. Same day the boss told us to look out for documents."

"Files."

"Documents."

"Whatever."

"She was there not long after."

"Who?"

"Where?"

"I'm lost."

"The boss," Karin looked at them as though it was obvious, "in the library."

"Why?"

"Sounds like a Cluedo game."

"Talking to the police."

"The Headmistress, in the library, with a dewey code."

"Shut up Alice, we're being serious here."

"About what, Karin?"

"Didn't hear."

Lots of shrugs. The train jolted, there was the hissing of the brakes, the hissing of a gin and tonic being opened, the creak of a coupling, more thinking, and slowly the platform moved away from the window. The train gathered speed and there was a sudden attack of the crisps packets. Their thoughts were tumbling and racing and somehow ideas got linked to myths, suppositions and assumptions that morphed into theories which were being formed from dubious facts that could or could not be true and moments that might or might not have happened. None of them pulled the same ideas together into the same theory.

Stephanie reckoned that it was a big conspiracy and the boss was sniffing around to find the documents and had accidently come across the police sniffing around as well. Perhaps, she had thought that she could get there before the police and stop them finding out something about her paragon, Piers. Perhaps, she was protecting Piers. Perhaps, Stephanie suggested, the boss knew that Piers was covering up something and she did not want to besmirch a man whom she had placed, with such precision, upon such a precarious pedestal. They discussed whether this would, in fact, be a virtuous and noble act and half-way through the discussion, you would have almost been convinced that Stephanie's theory was flawless.

"Could be worth a quid."

"Or not."

Karin's thoughts took them in another direction when she revealed that she had seen the Headmistress and Joshua, a junior librarian, talking together in the Common Room, on what, they all thought, must have been the same day as the Library visit. Karin had seen them having warmish but not quite heated words in the corner just beside the coffee urn. Could that have had something to do with the documents? In articulating this to the others, she agreed that except for the fact that Henry had worked in the school Library, she could not reconcile the piece of descending plaster to the pieces that she had not pieced together about the documents and took another swig of gin to try to better formulate the pieces. This got Stephanie further thinking about how to connect descending ceiling with her theory.

It was the timing of the Head's visit to the Library that confused Alice. As Headmistress, it was incumbent upon her to be abreast of whatever was going on, but none of those sitting vaguely stoned or a bit pissed around that makeshift Bridge table in a former British Rail train carriage hurtling itself towards London, could quite remember her ever having had an interest in the library or a librarian before. Certainly, none of them could remember ever having spotted her within its erudite and learned walls. Her new found interest in all things bookish was worthy of note but still no one could connect dots or pieces that would form a coherent plot.

Actually, by now, Karin had finished her second gin and tonic and her mind was moving quite freely. The movement of the carriage massaged her meanderings and she managed to formulate further thoughts which came out as a list of assertions rather than suggestions. "Henry wasn't murdered. Piers wouldn't have killed Henry. It was just a tragic accident. Patricia should sue the school for millions. Can't see how she wouldn't." Her thoughts were being weirdly articulated, partly to herself and partly to the others.

Adrienne was just happy but jolly hungry. She didn't think that any of it really mattered, that everyone was lovely and that no one could possibly have killed anyone. It was all just a frightful accidental mess and the matter of the bludgeoning candlestick was a mere blip in the world of joy. She relished her perfect world as she poured a packet of pistachios into her mouth.

The train slowed again and came to a stop at Market Harborough where the train was far too long for the platform and their carriage ended up on a bridge lurching at an alarming angle away from the horizontal and the passengers all felt that, with a mere slight nudge, the carriage could quite easily hurtle down the embankment and into Older's second hand car yard. All the shiny Audis, Minis, Fords and Renaults with glowing red 'For Sale' signs on their windscreens would have been squashed beneath the tangled metal of the carriage and years of a family run business would have been swatted away like Gloucester's flies.

They all clung to their seats; their ruminations had come to a full stop and any theories seemed to have too much of a slant to them. They had got nowhere. Henry was dead and buried, or more specifically incinerated in the Lincoln crematorium. Piers was dead and his body, having been venerated and revered by thousands of hangers on, had been transported back to his home in a village near Fakenham, noted last year as the most boring town in the country, where he was to be interred in the village graveyard, and the Headmistress was hunting for some dubious documents. There was very little to show for an awful lot of deaths and no one seemed to know anything.

Indeed, our little Bridge group had forgotten about the watery death of Jo Ford, a spectacular sight in the shabby marina; they had forgotten that this little murder mystery had started here. So too, had this little semi-sozzled group forgotten that Sebastian Ford was an old boy of the school. There was only the sound of nibbling on nuts, the crush of crisps and subsequent hissing of opening cans as they hung over the car yard.

As the train pulled away from the station, they felt much more on an even keel, but enough had tilted them off the security of their ponderous theories that little was said as the rolling stock sped through the countryside around Kettering, Bedford and Luton. Indeed, nothing was said until the tunnel, where Stephanie could remember her mother once jumping up to close the windows in case the smoke from the coal-fired engine spewed through the carriage windows, before remembering that the engines now ran on diesel. The intrigue of the countryside with greening fields full of grown up lambs and the odd horse was mesmeric until it all went black and looking through the windows, all they could see was their own reflections in the glass against the black walls of the tunnel. This brief moment of darkness was enough to jolt them out of their own muddled ponderings and as the train shot out of the other end of the tunnel, like a bullet out of a barrel, into the freshness of the southern Midlands, no amount of stale weed or gin could stymie their thoughts.

Was it a sense of fear of who would be next? Was it a need to enliven their ever so slightly dull lives, the need to inject drama into the routine? Was it a need to be ahead of the gossip game? Or was it genuine concern?

That Deputy Headmaster, that bean pole of a man, with a small bald head, who looked a little like an irritating knitting needle could indeed have an oar in the water somewhere. His clear lack of decorum meant that he must be about to let the cat out of the bag if he knew the whereabouts of either the cat or the bag. After all, he did seem to have arrived at the school out of nowhere only a year earlier. He seemed, they thought, because they knew nothing about him, to have a shady past, coming from an international school in

Madrid. He had been fossicking around Henry and Patricia's house; he must be involved.

Or perhaps it was the wiry haired, hot-wired diminutive other Deputy, the one who continually looked like he was plugged in, who had been at the school for thirty odd years; he must know a thing or two. After all, they all knew that he was just a bundle of contrived emotion who's will-of-the-wisp whims could turn full circle on the flip of a sixpence.

"It's that awful, not quite right scouse accent," Alice commented.

"Doesn't make him a murderer."

"True, but you do know that he's not quite what he seems."

Or there was the Director of Academics, mutton dressed as lamb, with long flowing, greying locks and always looking as though she was on the way to the beach. Rumour has it that she had, many moons before, had an affaire with Piers, but following his rejection had battoned down in her flat above the dishwashing room and quietly imbibed seven bottles of wine a week until she was, for no apparent reason, elevated to the dizzy heights of Director of Academics. Photographs of her hammer throwing at the Commonwealth Games adorned her hallway and was a sheer sign that she could do something physical if push came to shove.

More names were dragged up through the murky mud of the school's recent history, and more theories and suppositions, idiotic and not so idiotic, were spouted. The more they discussed, the more blurry the theories became and the journey from St Pancras back to Victoria saw four slightly befuddled oldish women trying to negotiate the escalators, the platforms and the tube whilst posing increasingly ridiculous stories.

The truth, of which there was very little, was buried deep within the psyche of their own insecure frailties where, even at the best of times, they would have found it difficult to differentiate dubious opinion from murky memory or frivolous fantasy from foul fact. The Bacardi on the train out of Victoria did not help.

By the time they reached the slightly kitsch southern station of their hometown where the station master was dressed in a costume akin to the start of the railway era and the station buildings were painted in white with a blue trim to entice holiday makers and Americans down from their dour north, the effects of the couple of drinks on the train were wearing off and discussion and ideas of murder and mayhem was pretty well exhausted, leaving them fairly flat and the poor Uber driver couldn't get a word out of any of them apart from the address of the school gates.

There was little that the funeral-going Bridge players could do that evening except find their own beds and attempt to sleep off the rigours of the day before classes the next morning.

Adrienne stayed with Alice and together they opened a bottle of wine and sat outside for a final joint. It seemed like a good idea at the time. Ed had left a stash of joints in a little wooden box next to the wine glasses and it all seemed too tempting, particularly as their minds were in turmoil. They'd had enough of talking about death; after all, it comes too soon for all, let alone those who are murdered. The two women sat outside in the cool May evening and let the smoke from the toke wrap around them in some comforting embrace that operated far more in their imaginations than in reality. They talked of the merits of existential poetry with such lyricism that anyone sitting on the other side of the fence may have been tempted to believe that they knew something about it. It was all a mask to hide their feelings that truly something was not quite right in the state of Denmark. A creeping eeriness just behind the nape of their necks told them that a Claudius was lurking in their midst.

Alice had read an email from the Headmistress which suggested that no documents, not one, had been found. She was appealing to those who knew about their whereabouts to come forward. Another appeal. Falling on deaf ears? The smoke screened their view of the end of the tiny garden and they both squinted through the dark and the smoke trying to see beyond the haze. She had also had a long talk on the phone with a colleague who had related the day's talk both within and without the Common Room. There were remarkable similarities with their talk on the train they thought. Addled and befuddled, they took themselves to bed and wondered in the morning what on earth they had talked about, as neither one of them could remember a thing since feeling off kilter at Market Harborough station.

8. SIX DIAMONDS

One would have thought that after so many dastardly deaths, intrigues and just plain gossip that the tittle-tattle of the Common Room would run dry. But none of it. After all, the life of a teacher is a little predictable. Students will come and go. September to June followed the same pattern and teachers tended to leap from holiday to half-term to holiday as the years counted down to the next post or retirement. Students were stimulated by some, bored by others or plainly bemused by most. Most students did not share either their teachers' or their parents' desire for success: boys thought about sex, food, sport and sex; girls about love, desire, fashion and friends. Teachers just thought about getting through the term without getting too many complaints. Therefore, the diversion of the odd death, murder or gruesome goth added much to the mix in the melting pot of possibility.

Tittle-tattle, indeed, was well and truly running

over the rocks and through the whirlpools of this river of surging white water. Ideas came from nowhere and went nowhere, arising and disappearing from the miasma of foam and nothingness that formed the basis of the uncertainties and insecurities of many on staff. The best of them thought they were floating buoyantly above the raging waves; the worst thought, for no reason at all, that they could be next.

An already discombobulated staff was therefore completely thrown when five days later our young assistant librarian, Joshua, was found heavily squashed between the compactus in the generally deserted storeroom at the back of the school Library.

Weirdly, and really thankfully, it wasn't one of the librarians who found the body. Librarians are a wonderfully odd bunch who generally react unconventionally to unconventional situations. Much better for two young, emotionally immature lads to find a flattened corpse, less subsequent mess.

The two lads in question were the youthful, recently appointed Head of English and his trusty, even more youthful and recently appointed Assistant Head of English: Tom and Dick. Tom had rather risen to his elevation to the Head of Department of this prestigious school clinging to the southern slopes of a fading empire. As an old boy of the school, he had ventured from the sixth form to the adjacent county and the University of Kent where he had managed to achieve a third class degree. A post grad in teaching somewhere in Sussex saw him step out and apply to his old school for a job teaching the younger year levels where he had donned a tweed jacket, cheap brogues, a cross between tortoise shell and superman glasses, adopted the pose of an elder statesman and waited for the incumbent of the post to pass on. One always felt that here was a young man who just couldn't wait to be middle aged. His vast wealth of experience built over years of teaching combined with his interest in tying flies meant that he was clearly a shoe-in for the job.

It had taken five years, and at the ripe old age of 28, he had ascended to the dizzy heights. From here, he rather felt that his experience, his breadth of wisdom, his depths of emotion would carry the department and hence the school into the realms of exceptional education. His first appointee would have to be someone who could learn everything from him. After all, who better to teach adolescents than youth itself? Who better to teach Literature and the idea of hope against that vast miasma of tragedy that years of life had already thrown at them? Surely young naive, barely read youth were better than those who had lived, loved, lost and got back up on the horse.

Dick, his steady right hand man was after all a keen rugby player who made it more often to Twickenham than to the theatre, to the Hove Cricket Ground more often than the school Library and certainly to the local brothel before his girlfriend's bed. He had a teaching degree from somewhere around Gloucestershire and spoke as if he had a first class degree from Durham. He, too, assumed the pose and at twenty-three had donned the tweed jacket with patched elbows, brogues and braces. The two, dare we say it, looked slightly like a trimmed down Tweedledee and Tweedledum as they made their way through to the back storeroom of the Library that fateful morning, five days after Henry's funeral.

Now one would have thought that these two leaders of world education in all things literary might be talking about the merits of Dickens over Austen, of Eliot over Pound, of Beckett rather than Ibsen. At the very least one would hope to hear of the merits of something like *Casablanca* and the ironies of a film essentially written on the run – a bit like this novel – how clever, they should have been discussing, was the construction, how tightly knitted was the plot, how apt the metaphor, how problematic the ending, all sorts of ideas that leave teachers of other subjects often a bit stum. But how wrong we would be; they would surely, this generation of teacher, be talking about lesson plans, computer generated homework tasks, Excel marksheets, drop down menus, PowerPoints, flow charts and career moves, all those things that enable a student to think more deeply. Again, how wrong we would be; instead, they were talking about whether the 'rather a bit of an all right girlfriend' of one of the local cricket players was really playing up on him with another team mate, and was this the reason why the Sussex team looked set for failure this year. Tom wished he could talk about his side-by-side, but knew that even this was beyond Dick, and dreamed instead about how he might dare to venture to another country and try his new toy in Scotland.

As they were chatting about nothing important at all, they were heaving the heavy heat-controlled door of the storeroom. It swung moodily, slowly, reluctant to reveal the contents of the shelves behind.

"Now what are we looking for?"

"A DVD of *Casablanca.*"

"Not sure why, could just get it off YouTube."

"Apparently, there is a bit about the construction of it, that could be useful."

"Oh," Dick couldn't really fathom this last

thought.

"Do you know how to use this place?"

"Never been here before."

"Ah," and Tom was not going to admit that he hadn't been in this place before either.

They did some heavy head scratching and looked at the letters on laminated A4 sheets stuck to the end of each large grey shelf.

"Hey look, there are wheels."

"Give it a turn."

Dick heaved the wheel on the end of the shelf to the right and the whole grey, heavy metal shelf sped, fairly fast towards another. He got the giggles and thought this was a good game, twirling others and jumping from one wheel to another, cahooting as each rolled and hurtled, crashed and smashed into another. With a flick of the wrist he could move centuries of knowledge, unknowingly crashing one whole movement of thought into another.

"Now then. I have a dewey code."

"A what?"

"Actually, not sure it is a dewey code. But it's a code." Tom looked at the notes on his phone, "Okay, need CAS 33".

Each young man surveyed the end of each case and quickly made his way up the room from the Zs, past the Ms and onto the Cs. Dick was still entranced by bookshelves that ran on tracks, but both young men stopped for a moment when the hurtling crash they expected gave up only a solid soft bump. Rather a disappointment Dick thought, until he saw what he thought was the life-size dummy that the school used for marketing. For big occasions they would dress up the dummy in a school uniform and place it around the school doing things like reading a book, examining a test tube through those safety glasses, playing a flute or counting on an abacus. It was an eerie doll, one you wouldn't want to encounter at the end of a corridor on a dark night for fear that it would come alive and bop you on the head, dead. Apparently it had a different effect on present and prospective parents.

Joshua, of the heated discussion with the boss in the Common Room a few days earlier, had not been a big man. Dick's initial assumption that this heap, sprawled indecorously between two walls of moving DVDs, with one leg under the bottom shelf, two arms wrapped around the head as though ducking a bombing raid, and the other leg perched backwards on top of a BBC production of *All's Well that Ends Well,* was a sophisticated rag doll, is well with the bounds of possibility. This possibility faded a little as Dick screwed up his forehead, narrowed his eyes and pondered a little more deeply the pool of, what looked like blood he thought, around the ears of the rag doll. Tom looked at Dick, who giggled, and walked towards the cold still seeping mass. A moment of realisation crossed their brows at roughly the same time, perhaps Tom's a nano-second before Dick's. One of them let out a sharp intake of breath behind his right hand which had already covered his mouth and the Head of English squeaked.

Little in the brief lives of these two young men had prepared them for the sight of a body squashed between two compactus shelves. Cosy middle class lives and middle class education generally confined to the Home Counties in safe families and secure schools had prepared them for nothing out of the ordinary. Generally sanitised thoughts of blood and guts, gleaned from Netflix and worse *Coriolanus,* did little to crystallize the reality of the brains of some Kiwi spread on the storeroom floor. They were caught, frozen in the moment.

Joshua had been a diminutive chap who had one afternoon packed a backpack in his hometown of Christchurch in New Zealand and decided, with this Auckland Librarianship Degree, with a major in Archivism, in hand, to travel the world. Australia did not keep his attention for long. Big pineapples, large rocks and the odd giant merino did little to stir his cultural imagination. German beer festivals and Finnish sea fortresses held him only for a moment.

The allure of all things English had some magnetic appeal that had started on his grandmother's knee when she would read him the *Tales of Beatrix Potter*. His mother had taken over and read Harry Potter to him until he took control of his own learning and moved to Conan Doyle, Chesterton and P.D. James. The flight from Helsinki to Heathrow felt like he was coming home and he quickly fell in with a group of Kiwis who knew people who knew someone who was leaving a pub job just north of Oxford Street. Not quite an archivist but it would tide him over. The same people also knew, a few months later, people who knew people who knew a prestigious school on the south coast who needed, at short notice, a librarian.

The northern hillsides of Peter Rabbit, Mrs Tiggy-Winkle and Benjamin Bunny were easily transposed to the southern downs in Joshua's mind; again his backpack was packed one afternoon and he found himself sitting on that same train hurtling towards the twee blue and white station. In a matter of days, he had bought himself a couple of tweed suits and suitable shoes. The shoes were shiny and the suits just a little big, as though he thought he might grow into them. Perhaps he thought that he could put on a bit of weight, a bit of muscle; after all, he intended to make a mark on this world. His muscular ambition did not diminish his librarianship abilities which quickly saw him promoted to Head of Archives and from there he lived in constant hope that when his visa did eventually expire, he would have made himself so invaluable to the school that they would sponsor him to remain. He scurried around, helpful, useful, present, polite and always purposeful.

He was never known to take a sick day, it was never known where he went on his holidays. Indeed, no one knew where he lived and what he did at weekends. He did not come into the Common Room, preferring to drink a black coffee and eat a Nice biscuit every lunch and tea break in the kitchenette next to the Library desk. He did not join the other librarians and the rest of the staff at the bar on Friday evenings, nor did he join various parties in various pubs that were not infrequently arranged in the town. He did not join social outings to the bowling club, the theatre in the West End or the football and he did not play Bridge. No one actually knew what Josh did except file old things. But he appeared happy, keeping himself to himself and perhaps fantasising about potters and priests. It was, therefore, surprising to find a rather nice chap, who didn't seem to do anyone any harm, who had nothing to do with anyone, who was really only interested in preserving old things, squashed like an overripe tomato between a set of BBC Shakespeares and some Oscar winning schmut.

Our two young lads were certainly ill-equipped.

Wondering how to react, one was grinning and one
squeaking. Neither had been to La Tomatina in Bunol
and neither had seen a real life dead body. Body
squashing, rather like compactus control had not been
part of their teacher training. Neither felt queasy nor
even wobbly, although Tom did admit to a police officer
later on, that he had gone to the Library loos and
thrown up when he thought no one was listening.
While he was doing this, Dick took another look at the
mangled body and took control. Perhaps injuries on the
rugby field had prepared him a little for the contorted
cadaver in front of him, perhaps he had a strong
stomach. Either way, he did know that the scene
needed to be contained and that it was probably better
to bypass the librarian on the desk and go straight to
the office of the Head Librarian where he could make a
direct call to Maintenance and the police. Joshua's
librarian colleagues were sitting in front of screens at
the main desk tap tapping on databases and
spreadsheets, blissfully unaware that their colleague
was cold and dead out the back. Dick kept it that way,
relieving them of the hideous possibility and hence
recurring images of seeing Joshua in the aftermath of
his final throes.

****

And so our old friends the security guards were
yet again disturbed but it was not the actual ones who
had come to Henry, to Piers or had had a peak at the
watery woman as those were the night shift blokes.
They were not the coffee drinking, doughnut dunking
gentlemen of the night but the tea drinking, biscuit
eating blokes of the day who had no need to carry big

heavy torches from a wide leather belt, but did anyway. They stirred from the creaky chairs and security screens that we know so well and grunted ever so slightly as they waddled towards the door and made their way to the Library.

Of course, there was soon and very soon much bustle and hustle. The Head Librarian, actually all the librarians, who weren't having a day off, were soon having the most dramatic day of their professional careers. The police arrived, the ambulance arrived, the school doctor arrived. You know the drill; oddly, it seems to have happened rather too often in this saga. There were white cordons, black and orange bunting, walkie-talkies and a plethora of students who suddenly had had an epiphany and needed to do some research in the Library. All classes in the building were cancelled and the younger students looked most peeved as they wandered, very slowly, back through the quad to their normal classroom where, they knew, they would be highly supervised and made to work. They were missing their most enjoyable lesson of the week – Library.

The event of the death of someone whom everyone knows nothing about poses problems because no one really knew where and how to start the gossip machine. There is nothing in particular to pin any sort of fact onto and so the rumours are so far-fetched that they become believable.

Some said that knowing Joshua was such a solitary soul that he must have managed to rig up a device that slammed the compactus together so forcefully that he had been able to commit suicide. After all, these folk reiterated, he was clearly a very lonely individual and that in itself was grounds enough to top himself. Despite Tom and Dick denying the existence of such an elaborate suicide machine, this scenario gathered legs and was running apace by lunchtime. Those who joined this race jumped onto the idea that it had been discovered that he did in fact have no qualifications in Archivism – or whatever you get if you're an archivist – and to save face he'd taken the easy way out. There was no evidence for this at all, so others felt that this rumour was just plain nasty.

Others thought that perhaps an ex-boyfriend had come over from New Zealand and found him in the arms of a woman and had acted accordingly. This thought hung around until morning tea but was superseded by the far more thrilling belief that he was really an M15 spy who was secretly going through documents and some big wig in the city had heard he had discovered something revealing and was blackmailing certain members of the school community to keep said documents hidden. Not sure how that linked back to our poor Joshua, but someone somehow knitted it all together. Everything did seem to get back to documents.

Those wretched documents.

Still nobody actually knew what these wretched documents looked like, let alone what they might contain but they had certainly made Joshua look pretty wretched.

****

Too much death makes one blasé. And there was a certain air of inevitability around the school. Whether this was because people were becoming immune to the deaths or because no one really knew Joshua, it was difficult to say but either way the general staff, having rumour and gossip-mongered, just got on with things, and the myriad of services that came onto the campus poked around a bit and left. Leaving the place fairly cold. It was almost as though they were gossiped out and there was little left to say or imagine. A couple of weeks had passed since the incident in the marina and death was no longer headline news.

There were other things to talk about, such as the state of the shepherd's pie the previous evening as it tasted rather as though too much Worcestershire sauce had been added, or the new initiative which was to have a school trip to the Antarctic which was to cost each student a mere £14,564. One bright spark of a teacher commented that when he was at his prep school in Yorkshire, the school trip had consisted of a journey to Whitby on a charabanc. For weeks before, all the little boys talked about the trip, with exciting thoughts of eating greasy droopy congealing fish and chips sitting on a cold grey stone wall. They thought of being in a different place, of riding on a bus, of sitting next to a best friend on the bus, of being given just enough money to buy an ice-cream from the ice-cream lorry next to the fish and chip shop. There had been so much to talk about, so much to imagine, so much to anticipate. And really, this bright spark of a teacher reflected nostalgically, they weren't disappointed. He recalled the happy memory of those fish and chips; he could still almost taste and feel the grease lining the roof of his mouth, while watching the gulls swarming around the incoming boats to duck and dive at the fish entrails being tossed overboard as the crew cleaned the catch.

Another bright spark of a teacher suggested that they would be the first school to send a trip to the moon. No longer would school trips abroad be the thing, they would be quite passé; instead, the schools would compete on their glossy websites for time in space.

But we're digressing from the murders at hand, and I bet you, like me, would love to know who dunnit. Are you wondering if those files in any colour but probably manilla have anything to do with it? Is Henry's death a mere digression? And what is it with the candlestick in the Dining Room?

The gossip turned to who was banging whom, either staff or students, and a new source of dope was rumoured to be coming in from the sea wall side of the grounds. The San's nurse was in a tizz because ten of the fifteen spare Epipens had not been returned after Saturday afternoon sport, the Deputy Headmaster was prancing his way around the grounds with that shock of wire wool hair greeting everyone with ecstatic enthusiasm that fell just short of complete madness and the Head of Drama was back promoting all the productions and his own achievements using every superlative possible in quite the most galling fashion. All was back to normal and yet nothing was normal.

Against this whole backdrop roamed those who kept the school running: the cooks, the secretaries – or should we call them personal assistants, as though they manicure their bosses' finger and toe nails, or brush their hair - the plumbers, the carpenters, the gardeners and most of all the cleaners. They were imperative to the running of the school but seemed more like a secretive, almost scurrilous underclass. Believe you me though, the cleaners knew more about the school than any. Actually, Peregrine the plumber probably knew the most. He was in and out of people's houses like a groom with his new bride. He knew people's business and he knew who was coming and going. He knew what was within and without. Perhaps he had seen something going on... but that's not the point... here the writer is taking part in rumour and supposition... not the point at all. Back to the cleaners.

The cleaners were allocated to various areas of the school and they arrived at 5.30am to do their job and were all finished by 7.30am when the school started to wake with little energy, akin to adolescents in the morning. Once the students had opened their sleepy eyes, dragged themselves to the Dining Hall for a watery porridge, a hard-boiled egg or a jam pancake, dragged themselves, with shoes a'scuffing, back to the boarding house and shuffled themselves to their first class, the cleaners would enter the boarding houses and clean them. Some housemistresses and housemasters would expect little of the cleaners and more of the students and others understood that the students and their mothers considered the boarding house rather like a hotel and expected the cleaners to do everything. Everything included scrubbing down the kitchenettes which had been left crawling in grease and crumbs of raisin bread from the night before. Everything included putting used sanitary towels in the bins provided because the 'little darling' couldn't quite manage it herself. Everything sometimes meant covering for a student when they should have been somewhere and weren't.

Most of the cleaners finished their job by midday and if one entered the school at ten past midday, one would see a trail of the underclass, all dressed in orange uniform, traipsing off towards the car park to go home. But not all went home, some had been resourceful enough to nab private jobs on the campus and some would wander towards private residences of teachers where they would let themselves in and clean.

Little Jill had been working at the school for over forty years. She knew every nook and cranny where dirt could collect and she had seen a litany of younger, stronger cleaners bite the dust. Her diminutive stature masked a giant sense of humour and pragmatism and Jill was loved by anyone who made the time to get to know the underclass of the school. If a window needed cleaning, if a floor needed just another mop, if you had spilled a coffee on a carpet, the person to call, who would not tell tales, was Jill. She was discreet to the point of secrecy and respectful to the point of cleverness rather than sanctimonious obsequiousness.

She was known by few of the more itinerant fly-by-night teaching staff as she could easily pass herself off to this class of staff as insignificant, immaterial and thick. For those longer serving staff, she was considered part of the greater team and certainly a wealth of knowledge, a woman who loved reading and films but could never afford to go to the theatre or opera. She would talk to previous Heads of English about the latest Booker Prize winner or about this year's Marsh Prize biography but to the current Head of English she found that he was not interested in the types of literature she was and despite a couple of efforts to engage him at some sort of intellectual level, she had eventually given up. She could be cutting in her criticism and generous in her praise. Her forty years had been spent cleaning in the morning and educating herself in the evening. Ever since she was fifteen and had left school to go to work to support her eleven younger brothers and sisters, she had almost drooled at the thought of sixth form, A levels and university but marriage and children meant that this had always remained a dream.

Now in her late fifties and widowed with her own brood of six children, she kept her nose above water and her bank account out of the red by sweeping, polishing and dusting. The walls of her council house on the outskirts of the town were lined with bookshelves stacked from floor to ceiling and was the cause of much bemusement to the odd council worker who would come to check on the condition of the place every few years. Perhaps her position at the school had almost given her what she had missed in her youth, perhaps being this close to the possibility of education somehow provided her with some sort of satisfaction. While her colleagues would go to their own staff room to gossip, complain and reflect on the weariness of their lives during their tea breaks, she tended to head to the Library, where she could often be found head down in some book on one or other subject that she had listened to on Radio 4 or read about in *The Guardian*. Or you could hear her excited interaction with one or other of the librarians on another subject that she was in the midst of researching. Rarely would she be heard gossiping; instead she would be adding to her history and knowledge of the life of the school and the people within.

While her cleaning colleagues legged it as soon as they could after midday, Jill not only stayed, but was given a lunchbreak and time to eat a free lunch before she meandered meaningfully down to whichever Headmaster or Headmistress was in residence, as she had the dubious honour of cleaning his or her house. A bit like in Tudor times when the chap who helped the king to shit had the title Master of the Stool which was deemed a high honour, Jill was Cleaner of the Head's House and she was privy to this and that which perhaps she shouldn't.

Over her time, she had cleaned for six or seven headmasters. Her favourite had been a confirmed bachelor who had had a series of the most entertaining boyfriends who were discreetly admitted and spitted. She would clear up the most amusing of the previous night's antics from leather whips, silk cuffs, creams, metal balls, pointy things, soft dildos and a veritable array of gadgets that she knew were for something but she didn't know what. By day, this chap had been the quintessential hunting, shooting, fishing gentleman with slightly loud tweed suits and yellow waistcoats which made him look a little like Mr Toad, and two black Labradors which accompanied him everywhere. By night, he discreetly and wonderously transformed into some incredibly imaginative pink and leather clad gay and seemed to have a much more entertaining time of it than a school of exceptional nature, dangling on the edge of Empire, could offer him by day.

The saddest headmaster was that short-lived Australian, the one who arrived with the tree-hugging wife, the two sets of twins and a litany of past relationships. In himself and his family they were all thoroughly lovely people but put them together and it was a disaster. Each cleaning day Jill would dread the complete and utter chaos that was sure to present to her. Clothes akimbo, furniture overturned, a chicken roasting in the fridge, a child stuck on top of a cupboard, bowls and plates smeared with dried on food stacked in the shower recess and a wife in tears wondering where she had picked up the last bout of syphilis.

The worst was the pompous git and his awful wife. In fact, Jill reflected, he wasn't so bad but she thought that her shit didn't stink and treated Jill like some infected underclass and her apparently retrousse nose would squirm upwards each time she instructed Jill in the tasks for the day. For her, nothing was good enough, clean enough, expensive enough. She had no gratitude, no grace and certainly no friends nor family and Jill was mightily pleased when they left to a poor unsuspecting school in Shanghai.

Like Peregrine the plumber, Jill seemed to see the other side of so many at the school and she sure saw the rawness and fragility of those that presented the veneer of strength and respectability. But her job was to clean, not to gossip, to question or suspect.

She was therefore severely compromised by what she found one Wednesday afternoon a couple of days after Joshua's rather anti-climactic death. She had obviously been chatting in the Library about the spate of deaths and the librarians had their own theories but more and more all were less and less intrigued as the police did not seem to be getting anywhere. Jill had left the Library desk and its contents to their own thoughts and made her way past the Chapel, the rose gardens and the manicured lavender bushes and to the Headmistress's residence. She had the same key that she had had for forty odd years and let herself in.

The house was, of course, pristine and Jill did what Jill generally did on her bi-weekly visit, she stood silently in the hallway for a couple of minutes just wondering what she could do for the two hours that she was supposed to clean a spotless house. It was at this point each time that she had that crystallised thought about the quirky oddities of the school and the traditions that didn't change even though situations did. Her job remained the same although her employers changed. When there was a Headmaster with a young, or even not so young family, and a wife who worked, or didn't but didn't like housework, there were bathrooms to clean, towels to wash, ovens to scrub, baking pans to wash, beds to make, carpets to steam clean, floors to mop and loos to be unblocked and the task seemed never ending. But when there was just a single, rather anorexic Headmistress who was fastidious to the point of lunacy about whether a cup was in the right place, or a plate, that was never used, was exactly stacked upon another, that was never used; when she probably never shat because she hardly ever ate anything; when she would not have entered a shower recess without scrubbing it herself first in case an errant fly in the middle of winter had found refuge on the curtain; when she used a new toothbrush every night and changed her underpants whenever she was near her under pant drawer, then there was really, very, very, very little for Jill to do. In fact the only thing to do was to wash the sheets, towels and tea towels every day and however many underpants depending on how many times the Headmistress had passed her underpant drawer.

Having contemplated how little she had to do, Jill would move from the entrance hall to the bedroom and immediately take the clean sheets off the bed, as was the very clear directive, put them in the washing machine, empty the dirty clothes basket and determine what should be washed and what should be dry cleaned, put the towels in the wash and turn on the machine. She would make up the bed with clean sheets and sit down with a cuppa and read her book while she waited for the wash to finish. More often than not, at this time, she would receive an email with another directive which would require her to clean a picture frame with a qtip or dust the back underside of an occasional table with the other end of the qtip. This was always dutifully performed; after all, it was all money. Then she would heave herself away from her chapter and transfer all to the dryer and sit down and read again. When all was done, she would iron and fold and replace everything with sergeant-majorly precision exactly how her boss had instructed her. It was only then that she would vaccuum the pristine carpets and mop the pristine floors and attend to cleaning the already clean kitchen and bathroom.

For some reason that day, she decided to give the bathroom mirror a particularly good wipe and while pressing rather hard on the left hand side, she felt a click and the door of the cabinet drifted open. What stood before her was a panoply of medicines that would have put a pharmacist for the military to shame. In regimental rows were pills and potions. In one row there was Xenical, Belviq, Qsymia, Contrave and Saxenda. To enhance this was Ipecac and to counter that was Kaopectate. Then there was the row full of Zoloft, Prozac, Celxa, Lexapro and Luvox followed by a row of Dalmanem Lunesta, Doecyzone, Restoril and Silenor countered by Modafinil and that was just the three top shelves. The three bottom shelves had elixirs and salves for every conceivable skin complaint, hair retention, lip enhancer, eye brightener and nail mould. Jill had not been peeping, the cupboard door just opened but she could but stare in awe at its contents.

Of course, she didn't know what some of these drugs were for but she had enough of an inkling of most that she could guess the rest, and knew that there was always Google. When she had taken in the sight, she felt her bottom jaw hang down and composed herself to shut the door and continue to wipe the mirror. It wasn't as though it was a secret cache or anything, it was a normal flush bathroom mirror but it did feel a little like she had uncovered something that she shouldn't have.

She continued to clean and the feeling within her was that she was cleaning for a nutter, a nut case, a nut job and she was not entirely sure, even after over forty years and seven Headmasters and Headmistresses whether she really did want to continue. The cabinet described incoherency, inconsistency and just plain madness and Jill had been a mistress of fading into the background and disappearing behind doors and transparent windows. She did not want to harbour this kind of secret. It was a very different secret to whose boxers she had found in whose bed.

Jill gently shut the mirror door and gave it another wipe such that it could never be suspected that it had ever been opened. Keeping her rubber gloves on, she carefully checked out her work in the rest of the house. She wanted to ensure that she had not missed anything that needed straightening, tightening, shining, grooming, brushing, dusting or sweeping. This day was not the day to draw attention to her work. Things needed to be spic and span. She ran a cloth over nearly every surface almost as if she was wiping off every fingerprint that she could have possibly imprinted earlier in the afternoon. Subconsciously she seemed to be treating the whole house as a crime scene and she felt rather self conscious as she thought about the contents of the bathroom cabinet. But she knew why.

She shut the back door, locking it on the inside and then went back through the entrails of the house and out of the front door which she locked behind her. She forgot to take the underwear that she had hung up a few hours earlier off the clothes line; it was only later, when she had shared her thoughts and was climbing into bed content in the knowledge that she had passed the problem up the chain, that she remembered and thought that perhaps she would get the sack from her position of the modern day Master of the Stool for not collecting knickers off the line.

Instinctively, she went back through the guts of the school, subconsciously perhaps hoping to find someone with whom she could share her thoughts. She did not want to go to the police; she rather felt that they knew too much about her extended family to give her much credence. She wandered towards the cleaners' rooms and pretended to be putting away an old broom and a few dusters but she didn't want to talk to any of the cleaners. They would not have read the papers.

She passed so many people but they just weren't right: the chemistry teacher who had been there for a life and a half and was known to throw chalk and then board-markers at the students, he could not throw computers as the tools of the trade had progressed, but he had been known to throw his own computer at a wall in the privacy of his own office; the temporary art teacher with bright red hair and purple nail polish, a living embodiment of her trade with a character that was as red and unpredictable as the colour of her hair. Then there was the bevy of middle-

aged women sitting in the Common Room and mostly
she could just hear laughter and lots of "Nooooo!"
followed by the gossip that can only emanate from a
coven.

"And have you seen the last email? Yet again
she starts with the first person."

"It's all about her..."

"Sure is."

"And then she justifies it with some absurd
reference to the Bible."

"Which is usually a misinterpretation."

"In the loosest possible way."

"An actress."

"Employed to market the school."

"She can certainly market herself."

"It's such nonsensical gibberish, all put together
as though it means something."

"Got a few fooled."

"Not that many."

"Well we're going to have to tolerate her."

"I'm off."

"Perhaps we can duck under this rubbish."

"Good luck."

"She can't last long."

Jill could hear the chatter, the gossip, the
innuendo, the accusations. It wasn't that she didn't
agree; after all, many in the school could see through
the veneer. It was just these weren't the people with
whom it would be wise to share the kind of information
that she thought she had pieced together.

Then there was a techie, still on site after four
o'clock because one of the teacher's overhead
projectors had caught alight in the middle of the lesson
and it really needed to be replaced by the next day; a

secretary tottered out on her high heels and headed towards the carpark; a couple more teachers in close consultation behind raised backs of hands were also wandering across the quad and still there was no one to whom Jill could turn. She certainly wasn't going to tell her immediate boss, the South African young man, a very nice young man but a young man.

She ambled aimlessly towards the Library, thinking that she might get out another book which would take her mind off her racing thoughts that evening. She even thought that perhaps this would give her a better perspective but as she walked around the sliding doors into the Library, there was Peter, just finishing up his last tutorial for the day. Having known and worked with him for nigh over a quarter of a century, she knew that this was the person who needed to be told and this was the person who would know what to do and what to say.

And so if anyone had gone into the Common Room between five and six that evening they would have seen Peter and Jill huddled over a number of cups of coffee, talking in muffled tones. When anyone came in either to fill up on coffee or to wash their mug, or both, Peter and Jill would fall into a rather awkward silence or perhaps talk about what was for dinner that evening until the intruder left. Peter nodded, stretched, pulled his fingers through his hair, cracked his fingers, shook his head and nodded. Jill seemed to be making much sense but he did not know what to do with the information. He was playing Bridge that night and he said to Jill that he would consult the Bridge group.

Little did the Bridge group know of the momentous information that was about to be shared with them and the decision that they would have to make which could or may not affect one or two lives.

9. SEVEN HEARTS

After leaving Jill in the Common Room, Peter had wandered back home along the sea wall. He walked, pushing his bike along the bumpy, stony track which was now framed with waist-high weeds enjoying the early summer rain and sunshine. The weeds seemed to be waving at him, perhaps goading him into action. He picked his way around the odd dog shit and remained conflicted. The gulls swooped over the gentle waves in almost the same action as the nodding weeds and he remembered a time when things seemed a lot simpler, when people just seemed to know how to behave. One just knew whom to trust and whom not.

His wife was away at some lawyering conference in the realms of Bristol or Blackpool, he couldn't remember. There would be little to eat in the fridge and even less advice to be given. He had promised Jill that he would do something and now he rather regretted that promise.

Thoughts of some utopian arcadia that he had enjoyed in his youth bounced on top of the arc of the gulls. He was certain that Piers could not have done anything untoward; after all, he was a gentleman of sorts. But then why did he have his come uppance? Thoughts of dear Henry caressed the air above waves. Henry would not, could not have done a bad thing in his life. In Peter's mind both these characters seemed to have been caught in a world that was no longer theirs nor his, a world that he did not understand, a creation of outward appearance and inward... well he couldn't quite pin anything down there. His wife would know what to do. She understood these people and their motivations, ambitions and cut-throat politics. He was just a classroom teacher who wanted to help young people find their way in the world. Ironic, he thought, a world that he now didn't understand. Perhaps this had always been the way. He was too old for this game and thought that he should perhaps give up the tutoring.

And so, slightly depressed and world weary, he called an emergency Bridge game at his place. Things did not sit easily with him. This was his school. These were his friends and there seemed too much at stake. The media he felt had had their field day. But how to keep a lid on what Jill had told him? An awful lot of Bridge had indeed been played over the last two or three weeks but he needed to talk things over, even if it was just to dismiss them.

Adrienne and Robert were easy to arrange but Alice, Karin and Stephanie needed to rearrange a boarding house duty, a tennis practice and a Dining Hall duty. Alice was rather pleased that she would miss a Chapel supervision and almost danced her way along the sea wall to Peter's house.

She let herself through the front door and heard the end of the a sentence, "... in the bathroom cupboard."

She put down a taramasalata dip on the bench, pulled a wine glass from the cupboard and splashed out a lot of sav blanc.

"Yep."

"So?" Adrienne had not cottoned on at all.

"Well, why does someone have so many anti-depressants and sedatives in their cupboard?"

"Perhaps she needs them."

"More like a loony," Alice joined in the conversation. "Who's this?"

"Her."

"Oh the loony. What's up?"

"Someone saw the insides of her bathroom cupboard."

"Noooo," Alice cradled her glass as if it would spontaneously implode. "Who's she fucking?"

"Not very discreet is he?"

"Or she."

"All those walks. I knew it."

"Knew what?"

"She was having a liaison."

"Oh, really!"

"That's only 'cos you can't stand her."

"And now we know why."

"What, because she was fucking someone?"

Peter was uncomfortable, the conversation had completely turned in a direction that he had neither intended nor liked, "Not like that."

"Like what then?"

"Someone else."

"Who?"

"Can't say."

"Who else sees the inside of someone's

bathroom cupboard?"

"Anyway she's got a whole lot of drugs there to knock someone out."

"She wouldn't be the only one."

"You're not thinking."

"I am," Adrienne was stirring and thinking as Karin came through the door. She too had overheard elements of the conversation as she had come up the hallway.

"She drugged her."

"Who?" Adrienne and Alice echoed each other.

"Our new bright shiny Headmistress."

"Nooooo," Alice cried, "I had her fucking only a few seconds ago!"

"How?"

"I bet she had Doecyzone in her cabinet."

"Not following."

"Same drug as was found by the post mortem in Jo Ford."

"Noooo ..."

"Long bow."

"What do you know Peter?" Karin was pretty certain. In the six or seven steps that it had taken her from overhearing the conversation, closing the door and walking up the corridor she had worked it out but she couldn't prove it. She had no evidence. "How do you get there?"

"I don't know yet, let me think. I just feel it."

"We know that the newspapers, or was it Robert, said that they had found Doecyzone in her body. So they know she had either taken that herself or she had been given it."

"Her husband didn't know."

"There was no obvious prescription."

"But what on earth has the goth got to do with Jo Ford?"

They sat around, silent.

Stephanie arrived. A shuffle. A bang. A number of very quick footsteps down the hall before, slightly out of breath and barely able to contain herself she exclaimed, "She drugged her."

"Not another one."

"You too!"

"How do *you* get there?"

"What?"

"That's what Karin thinks."

"Must be true."

They laughed.

"Drugged and burnt her."

"Horrible."

"Foul."

"Are we going to play Bridge?" Peter wanted to divert attention away from what he thought could only go badly.

"Can't concentrate."

"Let's give it a go."

Alice laid out the cards. Adrienne shuffled while Stephanie dealt. Peter decided to sit out, too involved in his own thoughts and pleased that he had been able to keep Jill out of the limelight for the moment.

"One heart."

"Double."

"One spade."

"Two diamonds."

A quiet descended and everyone watched as Stephanie filed through her cards, changed the position of some, took a sip of her wine, dipped a chip and then looked around.

Aware that all were looking at her she exclaimed, "Oh, is it my bid?"

A resounding, "Yes."

"Okay, what have you all said?" And there was much repetition before Stephanie called, "Two spades."

"Three diamonds."

"Bit of a tussle going on here."

"Three spades."

"Double."

"Pass."

"Re-double."

"Pass."

"Pass."

"Pass."

"That was a bit of confidence bidding."

"Sort of tells us where we are."

"Stubborn."

"Belligerent?"

"Just want some answers."

"Caution to the wind."

"Kind of."

It felt all very odd, playing Bridge while there was something rather more pressing going on in all of their minds. Drugging, burning, murdering were all the things of a good crime novel and here they were shuffling and dealing. Where was the gumshoe, that disillusioned, divorced detective of the Chandler ilk? Certainly not here. Karin's and Stephanie's thoughts were certainly elsewhere. Adrienne still thought the best of everyone, Peter was pleased he had altered the course of their thoughts if but for a brief interlude and Alice was just plain bolshy about the thought that the goth had done it, and done it to so many good people.

They had managed to play a whole rubber and

were well into a second when another knock on the door presaged the late arrival of Robert. Of course, he was late. He always was. Another door bang, a distant "Helloooo, just me," a corridor shuffle and a beaming smile crept around the door as he held high a copy of a newspaper article and a bottle of champagne.

"I've got it."

"What?"

"What they were looking for."

"Who?"

"They."

"Who's they?"

"Them. Oh I don't know. But this has got to be it."

"What?"

"Well, you know there is a file on every single student who has been at the school."

"... and staff."

"Well this would have been on file."

"Whose file?"

"What?"

"An article, written in the local rag, about two years ago about Sebastian Ford."

"Could have been. Might've been. Was?"

"Why?"

"Perhaps 'cos he had quite an interesting life. Perhaps 'cos he was a bit of a philanthropist. I don't know. But it's an interesting read."

Robert spread out the A3 photocopy in the middle of the Bridge table and he handed out smaller copies to each of them.

They all looked at the headline and photo, a smiling Sebastian Ford all kitted out in his sailing gear in front of a yacht, floating in the shabby chic marina with a hint of the school's clock tower in the background. He looked decidedly chipper and much younger than that sobbing mess hanging over a sodden wife they had spied in the marina a few weeks earlier. All suspected that the photo had been taken just a few years earlier. The heading proclaimed 'Old boy uses sailing to change the world.'

The well-written articulate article sang his praises.

Successful former student is using his power and influence to change the lives of many.

Sailing is not his only passion.

Sebastian has sailed all his life and is never happier than at the helm.

With the constant support of his wife, Jo.

Sebastian has spent his life, since leaving school, sailing the world and raising money for many charities that support girls' education in the developing world.

Starting small, his first yacht he remembers was a 24 foot, thirty year old 'old girl' which he bought in Lowestoft.

The article explained how he had been able to market his trips and raise money.

From there he had sailed around England often mooring in places on the Yorkshire and Suffolk coasts.

Devoted to his causes.

Devoted to his family.

Always the adventurer.

Mapping new courses.

Moving to a larger 34 foot, streamlined Catalina saw him venture further. Often we would see him back at his home harbour here on the south coast but he reminisces of his favourite haunts on the west coast of Wales, a rugged harbour and grey cliffs that gave him shelter and the time needed away from his charity work.

With Jo always by his side, he has spent most of his life onboard, summers in the Med, short autumns around the UK and long winters in the Caribbean.

Now he and Jo are looking forward to putting their feet on solid ground and staying at home for longer periods of time. Time to spend with their children and perhaps taking more of a directional role of his charities. Jo is looking forward to being part of a stable community.

Another photo, inset into the third column was a more recent snap of Sebastian and Jo standing on the jetty of the marina. They looked relaxed, happy, a tad older, looking to the future.

Adrienne finished reading first. Stephanie was still only at the Welsh harbour bit. Karin had got the gist and moved on, Alice chortled and Peter didn't want to read it at all.

"When was this published?"

"Couple of years ago. When they decided to drop the anchor, so-to-speak." Robert explained that the local rag had got hold of this local philanthropist and thought him worthy of a story.

"And it would have been put in a file at the school?"

"Piers is sure to have cut it out and put it in a file."

"Yep, he did that sort of thing."

"Amazing how he could put a finger on any article in any publication from around the world that featured anybody to do with the school."

"Sure did."

Stephanie had been most quiet. She was wriggling her fingers and drumming quietly on the

table. Thinking. Wondering. She couldn't hear most of
what was said, and perhaps that was good as it meant
that she didn't have to filter the irrelevant, the red
herrings, the rubbish. Her intuition was forming into
rational thought, her focus was clear, and that clarity
was pushing through to reasoned conclusions. While
the others were talking files, newspaper cuttings and
good blokes who raised money for charity, Stephanie
stood up, looked around at the bookcase and brushed
her hand over the pile of old school magazines that
Peter had stacked topsy-turvily and almost uncaringly
on the bottom shelf. There were many of them; after
all, Peter had been at the school for a very long time
and there were certain areas of his life into which his
wife just didn't venture.

"What are you looking for?" someone called
out.

Stephanie didn't hear. She was lifting one
year's magazine from the pile, sifting through. She
knew what she was looking for.

"Found it."

"What?"

"The magazine for this year. You would have
thought that it would be on top. But no. Honestly,
Peter, your organization!"

"What are we looking at?" Adrienne, of course,
was bemused and was half-looking to go outside and
have one of the joints that she had brought with her.
Alice was not playing game though, far more interested
in the sleuthing going on around the bookshelf.
Adrienne would have to wait.

Stephanie had the latest school magazine open.
She flicked through to the introduction of the new
headmistress and started to read. The others hovered

over her. Waiting. Sharp intakes of breath. Revelations. Thoughts. Wonderment. Bemusement. Until Stephanie exclaimed yet again, "Got it."

"What?"

"Right. Someone sit down with that newspaper article and let's go through this. Is Lowestoft named?"

Robert had the newspaper article, "Yep."

"Is this town in Yorkshire named?"

"Yep."

"Wales?"

"Yep."

"This particular fishing harbour?"

Rob ran his eyes over the article, just to be sure, "Yep."

"And our town, here?"

"Of course!"

"Okay, pattern established."

"What?"

"Don't you see?" Stephanie resorted to the time honoured murder mystery revelatory language, "Don't you see?"

They waited with baited breath.

"They were in the same places at the same time."

"Who?"

"Sebastian and our headmistress."

"Come on."

"Really."

"So?"

"Well, they knew each other, and they seem to have known each other for a very long time."

"Years."

"Looks like twenty odd years."

"Doesn't prove anything."

"Certainly doesn't, but how far do you take coincidences?"

Alice went to the fridge to dig out more wine. She was thinking beyond the 'jolly glad that a piece of shit was getting her come-uppance,' knowing that they could be onto something here.

"So, they knew each other."

"For a long time."

"And kept bumping into each other."

"In all these different harbours."

"So he was sailing his yachts and harbouring at places near schools where she was."

"And she never took a position at a school that wasn't on the coast."

"Beginning to look suss."

"Sure is."

"So what do you reckon. They're related?"

"Having an affaire?"

"Yep, having an affaire."

"For that long?"

"D'ye reckon the wife knew?"

"All wives know."

"Shouldn't it be the wife who kills the mistress, not the mistress that kills the wife?"

"How?"

"How what?"

"How'd she kill her?"

"Why?"

" ...after so long."

They fell silent. Peter's plan to air what he had heard from Jill in the hope that it would all be dismissed had gone googly awry. Ideas, thoughts and some facts gathered moss and rolled down that proverbial hill rather faster than he had anticipated. The contents of the bathroom cabinet and now this article provided the catalyst for nascent thoughts that had been bubbling in many minds for many weeks. There was no going back now and indeed they did seem to have hit on something.

"So, hold on. That's why she wanted the files?"

"She wanted to get that article."

"Why wouldn't she have done that before she killed Jo?"

"Perhaps she didn't know about it."

"And you think Piers knew about it?"

"Of course he would have known about it. He had got up to people like Sebastian Ford."

"Do you think that when he read the school magazine and her history, he would have put it altogether."

"Who knows."

"But he would have when Jo was killed."

"Sure to have started questioning."

"And she would have thought that she was home and hosed as she would not have known about all the files."

"Ignorant tit."

"A beast of her time."

"Come uppance or what?"

"Still no proof."

"Circumstantial evidence is pretty heavy."

They were all rather celebratory and started clinking glasses, refilling and clinking again.

Stephanie and Karin, together with Robert, were the super sleuths. Each of their questions to each other was helping to clarify an otherwise fairly murky mound of investigation.

"At what point do you think Piers approached

her?"

"And where?"

"Over a large G and T at some donors' function?"

They laughed and clinked again, feeling that they were coming out on top and had 'got their woman'.

Peter piped up, "And knowing Piers, he would have done it in such a gentlemanly-like manner. Probably just commenting on how coincidental it was that both she and Sebastian had spent quite a lot of time, at the same time, near or in the same harbours."

"I feel wretched," Adrienne was never one to think badly of anyone.

"Rat shit? How very Australian of you," Stephanie laughed.

"No, wretched," everyone articulated.

"Same thing."

"Piers wouldn't have suspected foul play."

"Well he might have, but he wouldn't have suspected it would come to him."

"Do you think she asked him for the article?"

"But that wouldn't matter because anyone could get this article from anyone else."

"Look how Robert has got it."

"So he was blackmailing her?"

"She was threatening him."

"Top him off is very much the best thing."

"Exactly."

"He wouldn't threaten anyone."

"Oh, you haven't seen him; he could be quite vindictive. Anyone who did not toe his line..."

"She worshipped him."

"Smoke and mirrors. Smoke and mirrors."

"That sermon – oh Christ it all takes on a different light now."

Another hiatus in the thoughts as they all processed this; some reached out for the taramasalata, others filled up their glasses. In the background could be heard the soft crunching of Peter's crisps.

"What about Henry?"

"Um."

"Yep."

"Doesn't seem right."

"Can't work that one into at the moment, except that he worked in the Library."

" … where the files were kept."

"But they weren't there at the time."

"Hold on though."

"What?"

"How did she kill Jo?"

"Drugged her."

"Set the boat alight."

"But how could she have drugged her?"

"And why?"

"Why would Jo be anywhere near her husband's mistress?"

"I think we just have to imagine that."

"Oh really good detective work that. Really hold up in court."

"Yes, your honour, I imagine this is how it went."

"The police can work that out. We just need to give them a theory."

Peter's crunching stopped, "The police?"

They all turned to look at him, "Well, yes."

"Really?"

"Yes."

He looked uncomfortable. Perhaps he thought that he could keep the school out of the media.

"If we think we have lucked on a motive then we have to tell the police."

They all nodded and Peter shrugged a reluctant acceptance.

Each one of them had their own theory as to how and why the two women would have got together. There was a moment when they all remembered the night of the burning boat and it looked like the Headmistress was about to go onto the jetty but had suddenly taken back her hand. Perhaps she had a swipe card for that gate and did not want anyone to know. Perhaps she was used to going onto the jetty. Perhaps Sebastian had at last called off the affaire and she had gone to see Jo for revenge. Perhaps she had got sick of Sebastian promising to leave his wife but never doing so and had gone to Jo and said that she was going to call off the affaire. Perhaps, perhaps. Did it matter?

At any rate, somehow she had got onto the yacht with a bottle or two of wine and managed to slip enough Doecyzone into Jo's Louis Roederer that would put her into a sound enough sleep that meant that the goth could douse the inside of the cabin with enough inflammable material, knock over a candle and leave the slumbering woman to the vagaries of the curling flames.

Adrienne liked to imagine that Jo had invited her onto the yacht, half-pissed but hoping for a resolution. Alice rather thought this unlikely, feeling that the goth would have inveigled herself onboard.

"That's why she was going for walks all the time."

"Meeting him at the yacht."

"Because Jo was enjoying being back on land."

"D'you think she meant to meet her on the yacht?"

"Ah, maybe she was going to meet him."

"That's it."

"He'd called it off."

"She was going to meet him to end it in a dignified manner. But was going to kill him."

"And Jo was there instead."

"So she changed her mind and killed her."

"Thinking that this was how she could 'get him back' so to speak."

"What a warped mind."

"Loony."

"Told you."

"I feel sick." Adrienne got up, picked up one of the joints on the edge of the kitchen sideboard and headed out into the garden. Alice followed her.

The whole of the supposition seemed all too unsavoury. It was gossip. And yet there seemed rather too much substance in it all for it not to be taken seriously. There were a lot of loose ends and a quick joint seemed a good way to settle the nerves and develop a clarity needed to tie them all up neatly.

They lay back on the stone slabs on a little terrace outside Peter's dining room. The stone was still slightly warm from the day's sun. Letting the smoke drift towards the stars they wanted to forget the murders for a moment.

"Plans for the holidays?"

"Might do France again. Cycle along the Loire. Take the tents. You?"

"Think we might walk a bit along the Northumberland coast."

"Nice."

"Good castle up there."

"Bamborough?"

"Something like that."

"Pretty."

"Pretty mess this all is."

"Fucked really."

"Really fucked."

"Do we tell the police?"

"Fuck knows."

By the time they had wandered back into the sitting room, the others had talked around and around possibilities. To all intents and purposes, the mystery was solved but the evidence was sparse.

"So she essentially killed the wrong person?"

"She had the Doecyzone with her. Was going to put it in his champagne?"

"Revenge."

"Embittered."

"But there was Jo. So she pretended that she was coming to see her?"

"To tell her that she was breaking it off?"

"Sounds feasible."

"Jo would have already been half-pissed and fallen for it hook, line and sinker."

"Ha! Ha! Good one."

"Crushed up the Doecyzone. Offered to open another bottle of champers."

"Poured it, slipped in the doecy and Bob's your uncle."

"All seems a breeze."

"And once Jo's passed out, very easy to let a candle tilt over."

"And Sebastian is none the wiser. Until he gets

a call from someone at the marina to say his boat is alight."

More sipping of wine, more thought. More dips in the taramasalata.

"And Joshua?"

"Why?"

"He would have got the files out of Pier's house."

"Told by the police to keep them safe."

"Asked by the goth to give them to her."

"Remember the conversation in the Common Room."

"Hidden them?"

"Certainly under lock and key."

"Poor bugger."

"Just doing the right thing."

"So that's why she was creeping around the campus so often. Common Room and then Library. What about Henry?"

"Still can't get the Henry link."

"Basically, she wouldn't have known about all of this when Henry was killed."

"Maybe she did. Maybe she knew Henry had said something to Piers."

"Or vice versa?"

"So you reckon that Joshua was clearing out the files from Piers' house. She knew that this article was in those files." Alice was pointing to the A3 photocopy that Rob had brought around.

"In Sebastian Ford's file."

"That this could possibly link her to the murder on the boat."

"So she killed Piers."

"And still couldn't get Joshua to release the

files, as he'd been instructed by the police to keep
everything guarded."

"And she squashed him."

"Poor bugger."

"I feel sick," and Adrienne got up, took another
joint from the sideboard and headed outside. Alice
followed her and so did Peter.

"Are you going to tell the police?" Peter
wanted to know.

Both women shook their heads. Neither really
wanted to be involved at that sort of level. It wasn't
really their business. Peter just wanted it all to go away.
Gossip was gossip, but not now. Now it was
incriminating.

"But someone will."

"Someone should."

"Who?"

"I suppose Robert is the one that should. He
can do it through the paper."

"True."

"Nasty business."

"Of a nasty person."

Peter took the toke from Alice as it was passed
between the two women. Both were surprised; neither
said anything. It was only right that the most upright of
the group got as stoned as them. After all, his world
was being rocked. Prestige, manners, right behaviour
had just been thrown out of the window. Here was a
new set of values when the head of such a prestigious
school could perform something so dire. Now he
needed to reassess and a good way to do that was
through what he held between his fingers. He let the
smoke drift with his values. And then everything
seemed all right.

They sat outside for a while, perhaps savouring the moment of the old world which they knew had just been shattered. They knew that as soon as they re-entered the house, they would be re-entering that new world where nothing was certain and the great foundations upon which they had built their careers had exploded beneath them. Any moment they would pick themselves up off the warm, comforting stone slabs and enter this world of ambition, deceit, careers and promotions and leave behind the past.

Feeling now incredibly light-headed, all three headed back into the sitting room where, yet again, heads were down. Karin, Stephanie and Robert were putting the final touches to the tale.

"Still don't know about her motives in the first place."

"Whether she meant to kill Jo or Sebastian."

"Probably come out in the court case."

"Sebastian will front up, you reckon?"

"God he got away with it for a long time."

"Twenty year affaire."

"Good going!"

"Bloody marathon."

"So Robert," Stephanie was thinking, "Are you going to tell the paper and that way it can get to the police?"

Robert nodded.

10. BID AND MADE

Nothing much happened over the next week or so. Our little Bridge group came down off the high of their sleuthing. Thinking that they had half solved the mystery, they could do little else without clear evidence but they were sure that their understanding of human nature was such that 'she' must've done it. Unlike other moments of gossip, when it was fun to spread something and see how soon it could come full circle back to the instigator, all of them knew that this was not the time to gossip. They had decided that night at Peter's to let Robert say something to his friends at the local rag and then see how things took their course.

After all there were other things to think about now, like planning for the summer holidays and thinking about what was to be taught next academic year. To all intents and purposes, the rest of the staff were just getting on with the rhythm of yet another end of year: revision, examinations, report writing, unit planning, and that old chestnut - which house to live in next year. Politics abounded. Murder and death forgotten. Egos stroked. PowerPoints and spreadsheets were abuzzing as a sign of great teaching. Planning on platforms and shared lessons were all the rage. A linear, step-by-step teaching manual of *Othello* got the nod; Socratic questioning was dismissed.

Most were therefore rather surprised when they got an email early one morning summoning them to the Common Room before class. The usual gossip, rumour and supposition abounded. Having almost forgotten about the dramas of earlier in the term most resorted to thoughts of a suicide of a student, the death of a staff member or another revelation of a paedophile conspiracy. Reluctantly, many of them dragged themselves out of their career promotion activities and slouched moodily into the staffroom.

Again the same old routine. Some bright-eyed ladder-climbers feigned intense interest in the proceedings while most, who just wanted to get back to the business of encouraging students to think, sat back with their papers on their iPhones or iPads. Expecting the red lipstick, white foundation and wide eyed flamboyance of their Headmistress to bob up yet again, they were therefore all slightly taken aback when Oliver Steele appeared around the door followed only a few feet away by the two lapdog Deputies. The wiry haired diminutive Deputy, who always looked like he'd been plugged into the mains, was positively electric with excitement while the pinheaded beanpole was clearly in the depths of dismay. All sat up as Oliver spoke.

"Good morning everyone." His round face was as jolly as it had always been and he didn't seem at all perturbed. "I've got some rather perturbing news and I apologise that this seems like a term of such news. But I feel that this situation is now coming to an end.

Yesterday evening the police arrested our Headmistress and she has been charged with the murder of Piers, Joshua and the woman on the boat. I suppose things come in threes," he chortled. "Now we must abide by our legal system and presume innocence before guilt, and I anticipate that you will all give her the space, time and respect that a person in her position deserves."

There was a slight murmur amongst the chairs and then someone started clapping. Others joined in. Some looked awkward, some looked excited, some bemused. Eventually, everyone clapped, and no one was sure if they were clapping for the call of respect or the demise of a tit. It mattered not.

As the applause finished, Oliver smiled, "I will of course keep you all informed as to proceedings and for the moment we have allocated duties to our two Deputies in whom we have faith and trust. If any of you, and I mean any of you, are troubled by this, we have counsellors on hand and the governors do intend to return this school to one of high moral integrity, slight eccentricity and most of all, one of community. Please, we urge you to talk to us. We are here for you."

There was then time for questions and Oliver was able to field as many as he could before the staff really did have to go and teach.

The excitement of the day was not lost on our little Bridge group who had decided to call an extraordinary Bridge night at Stephanie's place. It seemed apt, that where the story had begun, there the story would end, sitting in an eyrie overlooking the marina. Stephanie had felt the need to make another Tarte Tartin, this time with gooseberries. Alice screwed up her nose at the very thought but she said nothing as she poured herself a very large glass of sav blanc and tipped some cashews into a small bowl. Adrienne had arrived early again and was adding extra chilli into the guacamole dip. Peter was on his bicycle and had come through the town rather than along the sea wall, bumping and rattling over the cobblestones where one particular rut almost bounced his bottle of wine out of the basket before he caught it, threw it back in and squashed the two packets of Aldi crisps lying on the bottom. Robert had texted to say that he would be running late and Alice arrived with a shoe box, apparently full of two baby tortoises that had just been born and she did not want to leave them alone in her flat in case the cat got hungry.

Stephanie had set up the table, this time under the window, so that, if something happened in the marina, they could sit back and watch without moving.

Nothing much was happening in the marina. The pen where *She's the One* and her tubby owner had perished now sported a large gin palace, more in keeping with St Tropez or Monaco, and a number of lackeys all dressed in white were scampering around with polishing rags and marine wax to ensure all was shipshape when their owners flew in from nether parts of the world. Otherwise, all seemed as it was only a few weeks earlier. Old fire hydrants were back hanging on rusty pegs, the gate had been locked, boats in their pens gently nosed up against their jetties and the odd incumbent shuffled around looking for someone else to have a quick snifter with before the sun went down.

Stephanie had laid out the green velvet Bridge cloth and set four chairs around the table. She had placed the cards, scorecard and a pencil beside one chair and all looked most shipshape. The rhythm of below was echoed by the rhythm above and to all intents and purposes nothing had happened. Things were back to normal.

The routine of filling wine glasses and laying out was in swing.

"What was all that about?"

"Told you someone was fucking a goat."

"Who was the goat and who was the fucker?"

"I suppose dear old Sebastian."

"But did he do anything wrong?"

"Come on."

"Having an affair?"

"That's all right though."

"Happened for donkeys years."

"Goat years."

"Let's move on to tortoises."

"How do they fuck?

"Keep thinking about Jo though."

"Probably unhappy for years."

"Do you think she knew?"

"All wives who are being cheated on know. It's just a question of whether they want to admit it."

"What about husbands?"

"Where is she going to be tried?"

"Isn't the Old Bailey the place?"

"Is there a Crown Court in Southampton?"

"Can we go and see?"

"Wonder what she'll wear?"

"Is there a bit of schadenfreude going on here?"

"Anyone could see she was a chump. How did the board not see through her?"

"Make-up."

"Flirt."

"Just pulled the wool."

"But she'd had a lot of practice and many had

fallen for it."

They were all milling around, finding seats, shuffling cards and Adrienne decided to deal.

"Oh bugger, I've dropped a card."

"Not again."

All heads descended beneath the table.

"Found it."

Dealing continued.

"Oh bugger, I've misdealt."

"Everyone count their cards."

"I've got fourteen."

Peter splayed out his cards and Adrienne chose one.

Cards were sorted into suits and the bidding began.

"No bid."

"One spade."

"No bid."

"Two spades."

"One, two that'll do."

"No bid."

And the Bridge began. Three or four hands were played and Stephanie and Alice were well on the way to a rubber when Robert again stumbled through the door, late as usual, his arms piled high cradling a stack of newspapers which he managed to tip onto the kitchen bench before shaking out his arms from the weight. Stephanie was collecting the last of the tricks that would give them rubber and Karin reached to get a wine glass to fill for the pretty puffed out Robert. They were wondering about the newspapers, all eleven of them.

"Oh, it's just 'cos we're teachers. Thought you might be interested in the headlines."

They all got up from the table as he started to spread out the papers.

"I usually read this sort of stuff on line."

"You don't get the range that way." And they all looked. "Just thought it was interesting that all but three of them have run her on the front page."

Peter held his head. This notoriety for his old school was not what he wanted. There had been a lot and here was the culmination.

"Perhaps it's okay Pete," unusually Alice was showing some empathy. "Perhaps this will clear the school." She offered him the bowl full of his crushed crisps. "This way, the bad egg will be at fault and now she's gone."

Adrienne was already gasping at some of the headlines.

Murdering Headmistress.

Menage à trois.

Pariah in Prestigious School.

Who can we trust?

Heads Off.

"Well, I think that this one is the best," Stephanie was holding up one of the rather more vulgar tabloids, one that one reads in nine and a half minutes. The headline read, *Well stick that up your punt.*

"Yep, definitely the cleverest."

"Still can't understand why Jo would share a bottle of wine with her."

"I think Sebastian had sort of faced up to it all. He had called it off and had wanted to meet both women on the boat to tell them together that it was off."

"Very upfront."

"Not normal."

"And they've worked out that the goth sent him a message to say that she was going to be late, so he didn't come down when Jo thought he would. This gave the goth time to have a drink with Jo, drug her and set the boat alight.

"All pretty fine timing."

"She needed about half an hour and she had told Sebastian she would be an hour late."

"Amazing that he would face up to both at the same time."

"Naive."

"But after twenty years, perhaps they all deserved it."

"None such queer as folk."

"Wonder if his children will ever speak to him again."

"Oh, they would have known too."

"Would they?"

"Patricia okay?"

"Yeah, taking the rest of the term off."

"Great, the long summer break will do her good."

"Coming back next September but don't think she wants to be Housemistress anymore."

"No one to roll her joints anymore."

"We can take over."

"Poor Henry."

"Coincidence beyond belief."

"Not sure about that."

"Bloody need for proof. I kinda feel it in my bones that she was in on that one too."

"Yep."

"Sometimes you just have to live with it, hey."

"Poor Patricia."

"She'll be fine."

Stephanie had decided that there was too much talk going on for much Bridge to be played and decided to upturn the gooseberry Tarte Tatin onto the play. Lots of oos and ahs were politely expressed and Alice could feel her bowels turn but still uttered an "Oooo".

They talked about the holidays and what they would all be doing. Plans from only days before had been upended and all seemed normal. Karin would be travelling to the Galapagos Islands via Quito where she promised to pick up a panama hat for Peter. Robert was bunkering down at home and hoping to get ahead with some radio planning. Stephanie was going up home to bake for her family while Adrienne and Ed were thinking of popping over to Amsterdam for a couple of weeks before heading up to their holiday house on the North Norfolk coast for a spot of sailing, golf and other things. Alice was heading to Copenhagen for a week before joining Ed and Adrienne in Norfolk.

"A chap I shared a room with in Lower Sixth sister was eaten by a crocodile last week."

"What?" All stared at Peter, just a little open-mouthed.

"Noooo." Adrienne almost spat out a gooseberry.

"Who?"

"Oh just a girl," Peter pushed some cream around his plate. "I dated her twice. Took her to two school dances."

"Where?"

"Oh one of those golf courses in Australia."

"That's horrible."

"Right place, wrong time."

"Depends whether you're the crocodile or the

sister."

They pondered and continued to eat the tarte. Adrienne felt slightly squeamish, Karin rather thrilled and Alice's stomach was churning, all attention turned back to the cards. They could forget the ghoulish, the skeletal, the lies, the deceit and concentrate on what mattered.

Adrienne dealt again and this time deftly and cleanly. She efficiently sorted her cards before calling, "No bid."

"One heart."

"Two hearts"

"A Michael's cuebid. Now that doesn't happen too often."

"No bid."

"Three spades."

"No bid."

"Four spades"

"No bid."

"Four no trumps."

"No bid."

"Five diamonds."

"No bid."

"Five no trumps."

"No bid."

"Six diamonds."

"No bid."

All held their breath.

"Seven spades."

"Whoooooha."

"Our first ever grand slam bid."

Alice had bid it, Adrienne had supported it and Karin was stroking tortoises in a shoebox. Stephanie led a low diamond and Adrienne laid out her cards on the table. They had thirty six points between them with just one queen and two jacks out against them. Alice had it in the bag from the beginning. She took a swig of her large glass of wine and settled in for a very quick demolition of the opposition. They played quickly, the excitement of the cards trumping the excitement of the arrest of the skeletal headmistress.

Five minutes later, and Alice collecting her thirteenth trick, saw them dancing and cheering and filling up glasses with Stephanie going to the fridge and pulling out a very good bottle of Louis Roederer champagne. There was hopping and skipping; high fives and twirling were accompanied by heavy swigs of champagne and laughter and more high fives.

Ten years of Bridge playing and this little Bridge group had never had the confidence to bid to a Grand Slam but when the world was back to normal and pity and terror had purged pity and terror, now anything could clearly happen.

ACKNOWLEDGEMENTS

With greatful thanx to Ann Raybould my long suffering editer without who this novel would be fuller of grammaticle errer, spelling misteaks and those pesky Ocean Grove hyfens.
Thank you Ann for your constructive criticism, constant encouragement and belief that this work will humour many.

BLACKWOOD